Lois Thought About Her Father Upstairs in His Room.

He was like a large one-celled animal with a man's intelligence. What an object of study. What potential for understanding and developing concepts. She might do her greatest paper before she even entered college.

Of course, her mother could be something of an obstacle. If that should happen, she could work around her or perhaps (and this possibility held out even greater potentials) work on her.

"Well, what do you think?" Mother asked.

"Think?"

"About all that I've been saying. I'm going to need your help."

"I'd have to agree with the doctor. Bring Daddy home. Let's try. Let's give him the best care we can."

She got up and left her mother in the shadows. It was better that her mother didn't see the light burning in her daughter's eyes.

Books by Andrew Neiderman

Brainchild
Pin

Published by POCKET BOOKS

Brainchild

Andrew Neiderman

PUBLISHED BY POCKET BOOKS NEW YORK

This novel is a work of fiction. Names, characters, places and incidents are either the product of the author's imagination or are used fictitiously, and any resemblance to actual persons, living or dead, events or locales is entirely coincidental.

Another *Original* publication of POCKET BOOKS

POCKET BOOKS, a Simon & Schuster division of
GULF & WESTERN CORPORATION
1230 Avenue of the Americas, New York, N.Y. 10020

ISBN: 0-671-42830-6

First Pocket Books printing December, 1981

10 9 8 7 6 5 4 3 2 1

POCKET and colophon are trademarks of Simon & Schuster.

Printed in the U.S.A.

For our children, Melissa and Erik—
may they always feel compassion
and know tenderness

ACKNOWLEDGMENTS

Ann Patty, the creative editor in a diminishingly creative world; Anita Diamant and Humphrey Evans III, personal agents in an increasingly impersonal business

Brainchild

Prologue

Billy Wilson squinted as he studied the small white laboratory rat in the glass cage. The cage was really a converted aquarium his sister Lois had brought up from the basement. She had a small piece of plywood over the top of it. The rat sat peaceably and ate from the grains in the petri dish. Billy concentrated on the way the rat's jaw moved. He was intrigued by how it handled the grains with its paws. He was fascinated by its petiteness, taking a special amazement in the way the rat's eyes jerked from side to side as it chewed.

The rat's fur was a dull, almost grayish white. It was not smooth. Tiny clumps of it stood up, making the rat look disheveled, unkempt, and totally unconcerned about itself. Lois said that it was unconcerned because it suffered from a negative self-image. She claimed that she had initiated that negative self-image. With her thick-lensed glasses down on the bridge of her bony nose, she pedantically explained how she had accomplished the feat.

"I prevented the rat from taking an interest in itself. I kept it from getting sufficient sleep. I deliberately created certain vitamin deficiencies. In effect, I changed the chemical balance in its brain. It became lethargic, sloppy, and uninterested in itself and its surroundings."

"Wow!" Billy said, although he wasn't able to understand most of what she said. She ignored his exclamation. She wasn't speaking to him in particular. She was merely verbalizing to put her thoughts in order.

"One can see a clear relationship between the rat as it now exists and slum dwellers in our inner cities. That will be the thesis of my paper," she concluded, closing and then opening her eyes.

"Will I do a paper, too, when I'm in the twelfth grade?" Billy asked.

Lois smirked, bringing the corners of her mouth in and up. She had a long, thin mouth that habitually dipped at the corners, giving her a sour expression most of the time. Dorothy, her mother, had long since given up telling her to smile more. Besides, her gapped upper front teeth made Lois self-conscious when she smiled. Not that she cared very much about her physical appearance. She was hygienic, but unconcerned about cosmetics or new hairdos.

"Hardly. I expect you will be lucky to complete the regular lab workbooks, much less do extra reports. I've seen some of the report cards you've been bringing home."

"What's a lab workbook?" Billy asked. He was rarely intimidated by his sister, since, at the age of seven, he wasn't aware of her innuendos.

"Forget it; just watch the rat. I'm going to shoot electricity through the wire and into its brain."

"Won't that hurt?"

"It'll be too shocking to hurt," she said, quite pleased with her own pun. She came the closest she allowed to a smile, sending the corners of her nostrils out and widening her dull brown eyes. The small freckles along her flat cheeks quivered and her heavy, untrimmed dark brown eyebrows raised slightly. She had a milky, sickly white complexion, despite the fact that she spent so much time outdoors.

Billy turned back to the rat obediently. Lois had inserted an electrode into its head. The thin black wire ran along the glass cage, up the rear, and out to an electric-train transformer. Lois prided herself on her ingenuity when it came to supplies and equipment. She fingered the control while the rat continued to eat.

Suddenly she turned on the current. The rat shuddered, stood on its hind legs, clamped its upper legs together, froze, and fell to the side. Lois turned off the current.

"It'll be catatonic for a short while."

"I don't know what that means," Billy said softly, staring at the animal. He was impressed and somewhat afraid now, although he wasn't sure why.

"It's a lot like what they do to mental patients in the nuthouse. The electric current acts as a depressant. It can turn violent people into meek little kittens."

"Is the rat going to die like the bird?"

"Eventually," Lois said dryly. She made some notations in her notebook and then stood up and stretched.

It was seven thirty on a Saturday morning, and although it was a gray, rainy day, she had gotten up early as usual and gone right to work. Billy had heard her walk by his room, gotten out of bed quickly, and followed her. He was still dressed in his pajamas, and she wore a robe over her faded flannel nightgown, the tattered bottom of which showed under the robe.

Billy watched his sister reach toward the ceiling. She was big to him in many ways. Of course, at five feet eleven, she towered over many boys he knew and even stood four inches taller than their mother. At three feet ten, he looked up to most people, but Lois seemed even taller than their father, who was six feet tall. Perhaps it was the way he stooped since his "slight stroke," a mysterious event that Billy couldn't remember.

In any case, Lois was tougher than he was. He had never seen her cry. There were times when he started to cry and stopped because she was there and would see it. Lately he had been contrasting himself to her more and more. When she got excited, her eyes always grew smaller, while his widened to emphasize their soft blue pupils and long, feminine eyelashes. How often had his mother sat him on her lap to stroke his fluffy red hair and said, "Can I steal your eyelashes?" His dimples flickered in and out in his puffy kissable cheeks whenever she teased him.

Now he often tried to emulate his sister's fast walk, a gait characterized by its self-assurance. He would catch his toe and stumble when he followed her, his short legs with their chubby thighs straining to keep up. He kept his fists clenched and pressed close to his body the way she did.

Lois ran her hand through her short, dark brown hair. It had been cut at the nape of her neck and she took little time to brush it out. She was satisfied with the way the strands fell naturally, as long as she got the top to rest flat and the bangs to stay out of her eyes.

"I'm going for night crawlers this morning," Billy announced. Lois snapped around quickly and dropped her hands to her sides. The robe lay flat against her small, almost indistinct bosom. "I'm gonna get a lot of 'em."

"What for?"

"Sell 'em. You can get a quarter for the real fat ones down at the hardware store. Mr. Raymond gave me nearly seventy cents for a bunch of smaller ones last week. You wanna see the money?"

"If you had any ingenuity, you could create a worm farm."

"What's in . . . jun . . ."

"Imagination, brains."

"You mean, I could grow 'em?"

"In a manner of speaking, yes."

"Wow! Would you show me how to do it?"

"I don't have the time for that," she said, looking around the pantry.

"But we could make lots of money," he protested, standing up quickly.

"I'm not interested in money," she said. She looked at her rat. "Unless I could get enough to have a real laboratory and not have to work in this converted pantry. I need more room, I need . . ." She stopped and looked down at her little brother, who was staring up at her with pleading eyes. "Forget about it. I don't have the time," she added and walked out.

Billy hurried after her. "What are you going to do today, Lois? Huh?"

"If you must know," she said, spinning around so quickly he ran into her, "I plan to read some Skinner, do some laundry, and try to catch a young squirrel. I have a theory about squirrels. . . ." She thought to herself a moment and then continued to her room.

"Can I help you? Can I?"

Without responding, she closed her door. Billy Wilson stood thinking a moment. Then he went back to the doorway of the old walk-in pantry and peered in at the rat again. It was just stirring. He thought about the electricity, rubbed his own head, and hurried to his room. He was eager to get dressed and get out. He expected it would be a good morning for night crawlers.

1

Lois Wilson closed her Physics I textbook and looked at George Hardy, her science teacher. Mr. Hardy was smiling widely as he thumbed through a copy of a year's worth of "B.C." cartoons. Everyone else in the class was still sitting with opened textbooks. Some were pretending to read while they did other things, but most were only about halfway through the assignment. Lois looked up at the big-faced IBM clock, thought for a moment, and then raised her hand. Mr. Hardy didn't notice.

"Mr. Hardy."

He looked up, the smile still across his long, narrow face, bringing his chin out. The kids called him Plastic Man because of his rubbery facial features and active facial expressions. He was always twitching his nose and pulling up the corners of his mouth. He often tugged on his ears. His eyebrows bobbed up and down when he made a major point in class. When he saw it was Lois Wilson who had called him, his smile faded quickly.

"Yes, Lois?"

"You said we'd only have fifteen minutes to read. If we don't start discussing this soon, we'll run out of class time."

There were groans all around her. Someone mumbled, "I don't believe her." Even Mr. Hardy looked unhappy. He scratched his cheek and studied the clock.

"I guess she's right," he said.

"But I didn't finish yet," Marlene Bockman said. There were a number of seconds. "We're not all brains like Lois."

"Even someone on a fourth-grade reading level could have finished this on time," Lois responded, sounding very matter-of-fact. "If she really read and didn't do other things."

"I was reading. Who does she think—"

"All right," Mr. Hardy said, raising his big hand, "let's not have any silly arguments. Lois happens to be right about the time."

"Well, I didn't finish." Marlene sat back in her seat and folded her arms across her chest. When she caught Bobby Baker's expression, she nearly smiled. Her small but firm breasts had ballooned over the top of her bra, revealing an unusually inviting cleavage, exposed because of the three unbuttoned top buttons of her blouse. Even Mr. Hardy paused for a moment's appreciation.

Lois caught the direction of his attention. "There's no point in making assignments if we're not going to go over them," she said quickly.

"You're right, Lois, and I fully intend to go over this assignment today, or at least start it, but"—Hardy leaned forward on his desk and folded his hands—"it looks as if I underestimated the amount of time most students would need. Soooooo," he said, leaning back, "let's just add what's left of this to tonight's assignment."

There was a uniform chorus of groans. Lois smirked and looked at the wall to her right.

"Nice work, Lois," Larry Sanders said. "Had to open your mouth."

"You shouldn't have to open yours," Lois snapped, "considering the stupidity that always comes out of it."

There was some laughter at Larry's expense. Mr. Hardy clapped his hands for silence. All eyes went back to books, but Hardy looked at Lois because she was glaring at him. Finally, she looked at her notebook. He felt relief and shook his head, recalling the conversation he had had with her parents on Parents' Night.

"You rarely see a student as knowledgeable and as consumed by an interest as Lois is," he had told them. "I think she read the entire biology textbook the first week of school." His tone of voice made it a half compliment.

"She reads constantly. Don't you think she reads too much?" Dorothy Wilson asked.

Hardy hesitated, looking first at Gregory Wilson. "Well . . . it's difficult for any teacher to complain about a student reading too much nowadays, Mrs. Wilson. I think maybe you're referring to the fact that Lois's interests are somewhat narrow."

"Yes, that's it. She doesn't care about anything but her projects and books." Hardy laughed nervously. Gregory Wilson remained silent, inscrutable. "And she doesn't have too many friends, does she?" Dorothy pursued.

"I don't really know."

"The other kids just don't like her. She never gets any calls from boys."

"Oh, Dorothy, come on," Gregory said. "Mr. Hardy's not interested in any of that."

"Well, *I* am. Let me ask you this, Mr. Hardy," she said, refusing to give up on him. He slouched lower and lower in his chair. "Would you like your daughter to be like Lois?"

"That's not a fair question, Dorothy, for God's sake."

"Let Mr. Hardy speak for himself, Greg."

"I don't have a daughter," Hardy said. "I have two sons." Dorothy pursed her lips in frustration and sat back. "But let me say that Lois is a brilliant student, brilliant. She does have some problems relating to other students, who naturally resent her academic abilities."

"That's to be expected," Gregory said quickly. "I suffered in a similar way when I was in college."

"But there's something else," the science teacher said quickly and then regretted it immediately when he saw Gregory Wilson's eyes widen and Dorothy Wilson lean toward him, her face filled with interest.

"Something else?"

"I suppose you'll get it from some of the other teachers and even guidance. It's the way most of the students react to her and she to them. This is my first year with Lois, but from what I heard from the other teachers, it's always been like this."

"What?" Dorothy asked impatiently.

"Well, it's not so much that the other students don't like her. I mean, I wouldn't put the whole problem in that perspective," he said, directing himself more to Gregory Wilson than to Dorothy.

"What would you put it in?" Gregory asked. Mr. Hardy recognized the source of Lois's sarcasm in Gregory Wilson's expression and tone.

"It's more like fear, Mr. Wilson. The other students act as though they're afraid of her."

"That's ridiculous," Gregory said.

"It's not ridiculous," Dorothy countered quickly. "I know just what he means. Can't you see how different she is from other kids?"

" 'Different'? What do you mean, 'different'?"

"Honestly, Greg, sometimes you're so oblivious. Look what she did with that pantry."

"What did she do? She has an interest, a hobby. Would you rather she be like some of these other kids? Don't you hear people complaining because their children are doing badly in school or hanging around with the wrong types? I admit she has some shortcomings, just as anyone does, but when you consider some of the flighty and immoral teenage girls nowadays . . . for crying out loud, Dorothy, look what's going on with drugs."

"As usual, you manage to distort what I'm saying. There should be more to life than schoolwork." She turned to Hardy, who felt like leaving them in the classroom and backing quietly out the door. "How could she enjoy working with rats? It gives me the creeps just to think of them crawling over her hands, nibbling out of her palms. It's so . . . so unfeminine, don't you think?" ·

"Well," Hardy said, "I . . ."

"That's a ridiculous thing to say to a science teacher. Don't you think there are female science teachers?"

"But a female science teacher would have other interests. Wouldn't she, Mr. Hardy?"

Fortunately, the bell rang. He slapped his hands together and laughed, grateful for the entrance of other parents. The Wilsons thanked him, but they continued their argument as they left the room.

Dorothy brought the topic home with her, eager to pounce on Lois now that she was armed with the teacher's testimony. She went directly to Lois's room that night and confronted her with Mr. Hardy's statement.

"I have no idea why he said it," Lois responded. She didn't look up from her book, because her eyes began to tear immediately and she didn't want her mother to see that. Why did she have to come home with something negative? Here Lois had achieved all these high marks and great test scores. When would they appreciate her for what she was?

"I'm sure you have some idea," Dorothy said, walking farther into the room.

Lois finally lowered her book. "Hardy's an idiot. He teaches right from the textbook. Sometimes his class consists of him reading out of it word for word. I don't have to attend school for something as simple as that."

"I'm not interested in Mr. Hardy's teaching abilities. I'm interested in your relationships with other students, kids your age." Lois just glared at her. "I'm not going to be intimidated by your expression, Lois. I think this is a serious thing."

"What is it you want me to say?" Lois asked, pronouncing each word deliberately, through clenched teeth.

"It's not what I want you to say. It's what I want you to be aware of."

Lois realized her mother was about to begin one of her favorite lectures. She considered running out of the room and locking herself in the bathroom.

"I don't have to imagine how you treat other kids, Lois. I've seen you in action. You talk down to people. If they don't have the same interests you have, you consider them worthless. It's not a nice trait. You don't make friends that way."

"I'm not running in any popularity contest, Mother."

"Nobody's asking you to be in a popularity contest." Dorothy hesitated a moment and then spoke quickly. "Doesn't it ever bother you that no boys ever call? You're a senior, and you haven't been to one school dance. You're not an ugly girl. You have some very nice features. If you would just do something with your hair," she said, reaching out to rearrange some strands. Lois pulled back instantly. Dorothy let her hand remain in the air.

"How many times do I have to tell you? Those things don't interest me." She felt her throat tighten, but she fought back. She wouldn't get emotional; she wouldn't get upset.

"Well, they should. Those things were always important to me, and I wasn't exactly abnormal."

"We're different people," Lois said in a consciously subdued voice. She was practically whispering.

"It's not a question of being different. Everyone longs for the same things. You'll regret the things you've missed, believe me," Dorothy warned. Lois looked at her, her expression softer, sadder. Dorothy was encouraged and continued in a more mellow tone.

"I never told you, but I cried the night you didn't go to the senior prom."

"What?"

"It used to be such a big thing when I was in high school, especially for a girl."

"Why?"

"Why? It's a memory, a night to press forever in your mind."

"I'm afraid I don't have room for that kind of nonsense in my mind," Lois snapped.

"That's exactly what Mr. Hardy must mean, that kind of attitude. It's not normal, it's—"

"So I'm a freak. Is that what you mean? You're embarrassed because you have a freak living in your house."

"I didn't say that."

"You don't have to. I know what you think."

"It's not just me. Your father is worried about you, too."

"So you both think I'm weird. So what?" She turned away.

"Why must you twist everything? All I want is for you to be happy. You don't relax enough and enjoy your youth. When you get to be my age, you'll wish you had. I was in such a happy daze. High school was a continous roller coaster of emotions. You shouldn't be afraid of it."

"I'm not afraid of it!" Lois shouted. The veins in her neck strained against the skin. Dorothy stepped back. "I don't care about it! I don't care! I don't care! Do you understand? Do you?"

"What is it? What's going on in here?" Gregory Wilson stood in his daughter's doorway and looked in. Dorothy stood with her hands clenched against her bosom, staring at Lois.

"Get out! Get out and leave me alone!" Lois raised her fists in the air and brought them down on her thighs. Dorothy turned quickly and walked out, brushing Gregory aside.

"I think you'd better calm down, young lady. Just calm down. Your mother's only interested in your welfare."

"Is she?" Lois said. She turned away. "Or is she just worried about her own image?" She looked at her father. "Am I as much of an embarrassment to you, Daddy?"

"I never said anything like that, and I'm sure your mother didn't, either."

"She didn't have to. Aren't you at all proud of my work? You used to be so interested in my projects. We'd talk about them all the time. Why don't you ever ask me about my work anymore?"

"Of course I'm proud of you." He offered a short laugh. "You're brilliant, doing brilliant work, I'm sure. In fact, a lot of it is already beyond me. The only point here," he said, taking on a more serious demeanor, "is that you should try to develop some other interests as well. That's all. No big deal. Nothing to get hysterical about."

"I'm not hysterical."

"Good," Gregory said. "We'll talk about these things when we can all be more rational."

The moment he left the doorway, Lois got up and slammed the door closed.

Protected by solitude, she permitted herself to think what she considered more mundane thoughts. Her mother was wrong if she thought Lois never thought about boys. She had even begun to develop some interest in going to the senior prom. She had rationalized that interest by telling herself it was a sociological event. She would go more as an observer than as a participant. There was a boy she felt she could manipulate into taking her: Arthur Kotin. Like her, he was considered a brain and wasn't very popular. But before she could begin to work on him, she had been victimized by a practical joke that had turned her off the prom idea completely.

The sadistic prank was engineered by Marlene Bockman, Berle Brustein, and Bonnie Diller. They coaxed Gerson Tavorowitz into asking her to the prom. Gerson was seventeen but read on a third-grade level. During his early years he had been in a confined classroom, but when he got up into the high school he was mainstreamed. Although he was placed in a nonacademic tract, he was mentally years behind almost everyone else.

Gerson came from what was known as a poor white trash family. His father worked on a chicken farm and his mother was a chambermaid at one of the smaller hotels. He had five brothers and sisters, and the family lived in a shack reminiscent of an Erskine Caldwell novel. He was often the butt of jokes because of his academic retardation and his poor hygienic habits.

As the prom date drew closer, the three girls, all of whom had had dates right from the start, sat around in study hall and giggled while they imagined what Lois Wilson would look like in a prom gown.

"She couldn't wear a strapless because of those bony collarbones of hers," Bonnie said.

"Maybe she'd come in a fancy lab robe," Marlene said. They roared and were nearly sent out for making too much noise.

"It's too bad no one has asked her to the prom," Berle said. I wonder how she would look and act. I've never seen her at the movies or at a dance."

"I saw her once. She went to see *The Hellstrom Chronicle*," Bonnie said. "I think she took notes during the movie."

"Oh, God!"

The girls grew quiet. It was Marlene who first noticed Gerson in the corner, picking his nose. The idea made her turn red with excitement. When she revealed it, the other two quickly agreed it would make a great prank.

"How do we get him to do it?"

"Let's get him to think Lois likes him," Marlene said, "and she's waiting for him to ask her. He'll believe us."

"It's worth a try," Berle said, and they moved to Gerson's table. He looked up with surprise as they surrounded him.

"How you doin', Gerson?" Berle said. He looked from girl to girl and shrugged.

"If you have any trouble with your homework, we know someone who would love to help you," Marlene said.

"You do?"

"Sure. Wouldn't she, girls?"

"Oh, yeah, yeah."

"She talks about you a lot," Bonnie said. "I think she likes you."

"I know she likes him," Marlene added, taking on a very serious expression. "She told me so."

"Who?" Gerson asked. "Who? Who?"

"We thought you knew," Berle said. "Oh, maybe we shouldn't have said anything."

"We shouldn't have," Bonnie said. She looked guilty.

Gerson's eyes widened. "But you already said something, so ya gotta tell me."

"He's right," Marlene said. "It wouldn't be fair to Gerson."

"In that case," Berle said, "it's Lois Wilson."

"Lois Wilson?"

"But don't you dare tell her we told you anything," Marlene said.

"You could sure get good grades with her as a girlfriend," Bonnie pointed out.

"But she's really waiting for you to ask her to the prom," Berle said.

"She said she'd even pay for everything," Marlene added.

"The prom?"

"The prom, the prom. Don't you know about the prom?"

"I know about it," Gerson said indignantly.

"Well, she's not going to go with anyone else,"

Marlene said. "If you don't ask her, she won't go."

"Almost all the girls are going," Bonnie said, looking at Berle. Berle nodded. "It would be too bad if Lois was the only one who didn't."

"I feel sorry for her," Marlene said, letting an intensely serious expression wash over her face. Gerson was impressed.

"Don't you want to go?" Bonnie asked in a very aggressive tone of voice. Gerson started to shrug and stopped.

"It's going to be the absolutely best ever," Berle said.

"I don't have a car," Gerson said quickly.

"Oh, Lois can take care of that. She can get her father's car. Didn't you ever wonder why she's always standing near you in the hall and why she sits not too far from you in the cafeteria?" Marlene said.

"What d'ya say, Gerson?"

"I don't know. I guess I could. . . ."

"Just ask her," Bonnie said. "Just go up to her table today in the cafeteria and ask her. Say, 'Would you like to go with me to the prom?' That's all there is to it, you'll see."

"Couldn't you do it, Gerson?" Marlene said. "We feel so sorry for her."

He thought for a moment and rubbed the side of his head.

"Maybe I will," he said. "Yeah, I will."

"We'll see you at lunch," Marlene said. The girls left the table, muffling their giggles until the period bell rang and they were safely out in the halls. They passed the word quickly, spreading the story from class to class. By the time the senior-high lunch period had arrived, almost everyone in the cafeteria was aware that Gerson Tavorowitz was going to ask Lois Wilson to the prom.

But it looked as though Gerson had forgotten the entire study-hall conversation. He settled at his usual table, one down from Lois's, and began eating quickly. And as usual, Lois opened a book before her and started to read as she ate. The noise in the cafeteria was slightly subdued as the crowd waited in anticipation. Marlene got Larry Sanders to direct Gerson's attention toward the three girls, who made frantic gestures indicating Lois and encouraging him to approach her. He nodded, remembering.

When he stood up, the cafeteria became silent. All conversations ceased; even plates and silverware were held quietly. Lois didn't notice the change. She was oblivious of all surrounding sound. Gerson tapped her table with the knuckles of his left hand, a comical gesture that produced a few giggles. Lois looked up quizzically. When Gerson saw her face, he nearly panicked. He looked back at the three girls, who nodded and tried to look uninterested.

"So, listen," Gerson said, "you know there's a prom here, so why don't you go with me, OK?"

"Huh?"

"He's asking you to the prom," Larry Sanders shouted, and the entire cafeteria broke into hysterics. Gerson stood smiling stupidly.

"Go sit down," Lois commanded. She did it with such authority and vehemence in her eyes that Gerson simply turned away stunned. Lois didn't blush or leave the table, but she saw that Arthur Kotin had watched the entire event. That convinced her not to pursue him, and she wrote off the entire idea.

Now her mother, and even her father, had the audacity to suggest that she was weird because she didn't exhibit interest in such things. What did they know about how she was abused? Nothing; and yet they accused her of abusing others. She bit her lower lip in frustration and anger. The tears that came felt as though they sizzled on her hot red cheeks.

The day would come when they would appreciate her for what and who she was, she vowed. She chastised herself for reacting emotionally. Whenever she was so disturbed, she would turn more enthusiastically to her work. She slammed the door on her emotions as she had slammed the door of her room. Both actions rejuvenated her spirit; and with the enthusiasm of a patriot going to war, she turned back to her scientific inquiries, submerging herself in the data as a way of escaping from a world she was growing to despise. She looked forward to victories her mother, and perhaps even her father, would never understand.

2

Gregory Wilson owned and operated the only pharmacy in Sandburg. The hamlet actually consisted of only two streets: a long Main Street lined with a fruit and vegetable store, a luncheonette, a bar and grill, a fish store, a bakery, and a grocery; and a street called Post Hill Road that joined Main Street at its center to form a T. Post Hill Road contained the post office, a dairy, another luncheonette, Wilson's Pharmacy, a butcher shop, a barber shop, and a hardware store. There used to be a department store, but it had closed down when the owners retired.

For ten months out of the year Sandburg had a rural quality to it, and its stores reflected the simplistic world. The pace was easy, almost nonexistent; but during the summer season, the hamlet became hectic and maddening. All of the stores were cluttered with stock, for it was their owners' main opportunity to make the year's income.

During the past few years the Wilsons had taken in more and more goods, making the pharmacy into something akin to one of the big chain drugstores. The added efforts and responsibilities had increased the already overburdening work load. Dorothy's contribution was minimal. She worked the cosmetics counter and did a little stocking and arranging and some maintenance cleaning; but most of her time in the store was spent conversing with customers. She was more like a hostess.

During the off season it was a marginal operation, but in the summer Gregory had to hire two counterboys. Lois generally resisted working in the drugstore. During the early years she found it more convenient to volunteer to watch over Billy on weekends when he wasn't at day camp. She had always been a precocious child, mature, sensible, trustworthy. Lois's early maturity gave Dorothy Wilson freedom from the house and its responsibilities. Lois could cook, clean, and care for the needs of her younger brother.

So, as time went by, Dorothy didn't object to Lois's reluctance to work in the drugstore. Instead, she took advantage of it. If Lois was more comfortable being a homemaker and a surrogate mother to Billy, so be it. When she did come to the store to help out, she wasn't much good anyway. She disliked waiting on customers, hated small talk, and spent most of her time discussing the relative psychological and emotional side effects of different drugs.

Gregory enjoyed his daughter's inquisitive mind. He found her intelligent questions a welcome relief from the doldrums that accompanied the long, monotonous summer hours he spent trapped in the store. In fact, he saw something of his younger self in Lois's curiosity about things scientific. There had been a time when she revived some of his early interests and he had actually enjoyed sitting with her and discussing her laboratory projects at school or the experiments she developed at home. He saw nothing wrong with her converting the old pantry into a small laboratory.

But he couldn't believe the vivacity with which Lois attacked her readings. He took great pride in her academic achievements, as any parent would, but even he began to find her rate of mental growth more than remarkable. It was frighteningly abnormal, and although he rejected Dorothy's criticisms out of hand, he quietly found more and more validity to them. Since

Lois had begun school, she had been the highest-ranked student in her class. Her cumulative school average was one of the best ever for Garnertown Central Schools, and all of her standardized test scores placed her in the top one percent of the national percentiles.

A year after his stroke, when Lois was just a tenth grader, he had found it more and more difficult to keep up with her scientific discussions. She'd be practically lecturing to him. At first he had blamed his slowness on the stroke, but lately he had come to the conclusion that his daughter was just too far beyond him.

The Wilsons lived in a renovated two-story house built in the latter part of the nineteenth century. The last owner had been the grandson of Dr. Fleur, the original owner. Fleur was a renowned physician who was said to have been called to President McKinley's side after he had been shot. In any case, he was one of the most celebrated local residents, having married the daughter of George Mortimer Pullman, the man who had improved and developed the use of the sleeping car on railroad trains.

The house was set a little more than two hundred yards off a side road just outside the small hamlet of Sandburg in the resort region of the Catskill Mountains. Its secluded location made it nearly impossible to spot until a traveler was right at the property line. On this particular road, Turtle Creek Road, there were no bungalow colonies or hotels. Four miles down the road there was a twenty-five-room tourist house, but that brought little traffic past the old Fleur mansion. The nearest home was a quarter of a mile back toward Sandburg.

Because of the two large weeping willows in the front of the house and the thick woods on both sides of it, the mansion often took on a melancholy and foreboding appearance. The Wilsons had tried to overcome that by replacing the gray wooden shingles with bright white aluminum siding and glossy black window shutters.

However, this modern face-lifting gave the house a kind of freakish look because the architecture placed it clearly in the nineteenth century.

Even on the brightest days, the weeping willows and surrounding maples threw long shadows over the front of the house. There was a rather large porch the full width of the building. Every six feet, a wide hand-sculptured column rose to the roof of the porch. Four concrete steps led up from the walkway to the front entrance. The door was a thick oak with a hand-carved circular design on the front of it. The old knocker had long since broken off, but its hinges still remained. Now there was a buzzer with a tiny light just to the right of the doorknob. Under it was a small rectangular name-plate that read Gregory and Dorothy Wilson.

The large window of the sitting room faced the front. Although the long lace curtains were kept drawn open most of the time, the mixture of shadows and glare turned the glass into a mirror reflecting the gleam of automobiles that passed along Turtle Creek Road. Whenever Dorothy Wilson stood on the road and looked across the front lawn at her home, she was invariably dissatisfied.

"No matter what we do, it always has that deserted look," she complained. "Sometimes, when we come home at night and the house suddenly appears in the darkness, I get the chills."

Gregory listened attentively but offered no new solutions.

Lois tried to get her mother to analyze her feelings. "It's the weeping willows and the slanted roof. You've got these horror images imprinted in your subconscious. What you're doing is called association, the ability to draw inferences from past experiences and relate these past impressions to present situations."

"Huh?"

"Actually, it's a form of conditioned response. Repetition of the stimulus and response binds the two together so that the activity becomes nearly automatic.

In this case, your fear of the house at night is a response to hundreds of stimuli given to you through movies, television, books."

"Greg, what the hell is your daughter talking about? All I said was . . . oh, what's the use?"

When Dorothy gave overall consideration to the house, she agreed that it had been a good buy. It was so very roomy. Above the sitting-room window were the two windows of each upstairs bedroom. There were two bedrooms at the rear of the house on the first floor and three bedrooms upstairs. After entering the front door, one could either go to the right and into the sitting room or go straight and eventually enter the kitchen. The dining room was just off the kitchen. From it one could go into the sitting room as well.

Dr. Fleur had converted a large downstairs bedroom into his main office. Now it served as another study, the shelves filled with old books, collections of Dickens, Cooper, Guy de Maupassant, books inherited with the purchase of the house. Most had yet to be pulled off the shelves.

The stairway rose from the end of the corridor and turned at a thirty-degree angle into the upstairs portion of the house. A dark walnut-stained banister, also hand-carved, ran along the carpeted wooden steps. All of the carpeting in the house was a thin nylon material, much of it worn-looking but weathered with personality. Gregory and Dorothy were considering investing a few thousand dollars to replace all of the downstairs carpeting.

The walls of the house had been painted recently, but the crevices and cracks formed over the years seemed to work their way out through the newer coats of paint. Dim lights revealed them, making them look like the arteries and veins of the building. Lois often sarcastically remarked that the house suffered from varicose veins. Dorothy talked constantly about paneling the place, but Gregory thought that would take away from the house's distinct personality.

Actually, the poor condition of the shelves and walls of the walk-in pantry had been the primary reason that Dorothy didn't resist Lois's desire to turn it into her personal laboratory. Now the worn and chipped wood walls were covered with charts and graphs. Wires ran up and down two sides as part of Lois's method to improve on a lack of light and a lack of outlets. The shelves that remained were filled with her paraphernalia: small cages, wires, transformers, prongs, some chemical compounds, jars filled with pickled fetuses, and a small microscope. In the center of the pantry was a long table that usually held Lois's current experiment. It was a long metal picnic table she had found in the basement. There was only one small chair in the pantry, and it was kept in the far right corner so Lois could move about her experiment table more freely. She despised her cluttered and crowded conditions, but she recognized that her mother would fight her acquisition of any other room in the house. For the time being, she would have to make do. Ever since her father's stroke, it was futile to get into any all-out arguments. Her mother would simply refer to his condition as a reason to end "the tension."

Gregory Wilson had always had a persistent but relatively controlled blood-pressure problem. He was reasonably careful about his diet and up on the best possible medications. Nevertheless, in late May of Lois's sophomore year, he had suffered the worst head pain he had ever known and then gone unconscious.

Dorothy didn't realize what had happened. When she didn't see him standing in the prescription window, she looked out to see if he was talking to someone. It was not like him to leave without first telling her, because someone could come in for a prescription.

He was nowhere in sight. She went back to the rear of the store. He wasn't in the bathroom—the door was wide open.

"Greg?"

She didn't see him until she walked around the

counter. She was so shocked when she confronted his collapsed form that she couldn't speak or utter a sound for a few moments. She didn't bend down to see what was wrong; she ran out of the store and stood on the sidewalk screaming until Patty Morganstein, the town cop, came running up from the restaurant. They got the volunteer ambulance squad in minutes.

Dorothy was going to follow in her car. She went to the phone instinctively to call Lois and tell her. She wanted her to come along. Later, she would sit in the hospital lobby and resent her daughter's rational and calm responses, even if they were the right ones.

"Well, you don't want to leave Billy here alone, Mother, and you certainly don't want him to come along."

"He could wait in the lobby."

"It would probably frighten him to death, and what difference could his presence make anyway? We'll wait here. You go along and call when you learn something specific. It usually takes a while before they'll give you a diagnosis anyway, Mother. He'll be admitted to the emergency room and they'll check his vital signs and—"

"I don't want to hear all that."

"Get a grip on yourself, Mother. The best thing to do is take care of the paperwork while you wait. There's always so much paperwork at a hospital."

Whenever Dorothy Wilson recalled that phone conversation she'd grit her teeth. Her daughter had treated her as though *she* were the child. What hurt so much was that Lois had been right about everything: the paperwork, the waiting, the procedures.

Dr. Bloom, their family physcian, finally came to tell her the diagnosis.

"He's had what we call a CVS, a cardiovascular stroke. Blood didn't get to the brain. Fortunately, this was a pretty minor one, and he's young and strong. It's an early warning."

"What do you mean?"

"He's got to watch himself, even out his temperament, stay on his diet, keep to his medications. Maybe he should take on some help this summer in the prescription department."

"Oh, there's not enough work for two druggists in our store, Doc."

"There is if the druggist has to slow down," he warned.

That first CVS had had a major effect on the Wilson family. Billy was too young to relate to it, of course; but Dorothy developed all sorts of new phobias, and Greg began to baby himself. Lois found it an interesting subject for a new study: the physical ramifications of emotional stress. When she went to visit her father in the hospital and told him about it, her excitement took him by surprise. At first he thought she was excited because of him. Then he realized she was treating him as though he were a specimen.

That made him think about Lois more in the way Dorothy perceived her. He did compare and contrast her to other teenage girls. Sometimes he secretly longed for her to have less intelligence and more attractive physical features. Sometimes he wished she'd be silly and more like a teenager. Once, he came to the conclusion that the one thing he disliked about his daughter was that she had denied herself a youth and therefore denied him and his wife the joys that should have resulted from that youth. They couldn't delight in her growing up, because she was always grown up. When had it happened? Somehow, she had jumped time, skipped an entire period of growth.

Where were the tears for him to wipe away? What had happened to the laughter and the charming confusion of adolescence? He thought about his sister and the way his father had built her into his little princess: the daintiness, the softness, the aroma of roses and lilacs. There was no way he could envision Lois as his little princess. It was easier to imagine her taking and analyzing his blood than taking his love. In fact, the only times he felt any deep bond or strong communication between her and him were the times he took an interest in her projects and work.

"You see," she said to him one day while he was convalescing at home. He had looked in on her in the pantry converted into laboratory. "There are fears that are acquirable. Caution in an animal doesn't necessarily have to be interpreted as fear. When you get too close to a bird and it flies away, that's simply an intelligent act, a logical choice. You don't see one bird trying to act braver than another in order to gain the admiration of the flock, as you see with people." She pronounced *people* as though it designated a lower form of life. It occurred to Gregory that his daughter enjoyed working with animals more than she enjoyed working with people.

He noticed she wasn't even looking at him when she spoke. She projected a certain intellectual arrogance, and that annoyed him.

"People aren't birds. It's not very scientific to compare them."

"Oh, no, Daddy, you miss the point. There are bonds, common paths all living things follow. We branch off according to our sophisticated development, but there are basic patterns. For example, all living things retreat from painful circumstances." She looked away again when she said that, and he considered that she had just given a rationale for her own retreats: she submerged herself in her private world of science to escape painful experiences, whether they were her failure to live up to Dorothy's expectations or her own frustrations in relation to her peers. At that moment, he felt sorry for her.

When she paused, he could almost hear her mind behaving like a typewriter carriage going to another paragraph.

"The simplest form of protoplasm has irritability. Reflexive action is irritability carried to a higher level. Now, putting aside instinctive behavior for the moment, it is possible to come to a better understanding of man's basic behavior by studying the animal world."

"Yes," he said, thinking he had caught her, "but people, at least, will on occasion endure pain to achieve a higher goal."

"Only because of something they've learned or acquired, which takes in emotions as well. If two Homo sapiens develop an intense love relationship, one might endure pain for the other."

"Two Homo sapiens?"

"But listen," she said, moving out of the way so he could see the rat in the cage. "I had a rat here I simply called Eighteen because it was the eighteenth rat I had. I began a project. Whenever I fed it, I gave it an electrical shock. After a few times, it wouldn't go near the food. What I did through conditioned response was create an unnatural fear of food in the rat.

"But when it became very hungry, it began to endure the pain and the fear so it could eat. When I increased the voltage, it stayed away for longer periods until its physiological demands overcame its acquired fears. In fact, it began to build up some resistance, so I had to increase the voltage even more. Eventually, I killed it."

"You killed it?"

"Well, actually it killed itself, in a sense. So, you see," she went on, "it is possible to effect a change or a ramification in a pattern of behavior. Of course, it's more difficult to change instinct. Very little human behavior can be classified as purely instinctive. I don't think we have instinctive fears; we have acquired fears. There is no instinctive fear of the dark, for example. If other people didn't demonstrate that fear to you when you were young and impressionable, you wouldn't have it."

"Very interesting," Gregory said. He was beginning to feel overwhelmed.

"Now, Bergson has an interesting theory," she said, oblivious of her father's loss of interest. "Primitive man, like primitive animals, depended on his instincts

for survival. As man developed and organized socie-
ties, his need for those instincts diminished and the
instincts dulled. Modern man has replaced it with
something known as 'creative intuition.'"

"I think I'd better go back to—"

"Take a puppy dog and place it on the windowsill of a
high building and it will whimper and cower in fear, but
put a human baby on that windowsill and it will giggle
and gurgle right over the edge. That's because its
instinct is dulled and it hasn't developed creative
intuition. Creative intuition is simply the ability to
foresee, and that comes from experience. You learn
that height can be dangerous, you see yourself falling,
you know what can happen, you cower like the dog
when you come to the edge. I bet you think the dog has
a definite advantage, then," she said, changing the tone
of her voice as though she were talking to a fourth
grader. Gregory Wilson could only stare at his daughter in amazement. She seemed unrecognizable. It was
as though she had changed into someone else right
before his eyes.

"I guess you really like this stuff."

"Of course."

"Why?"

"Why?" The question appeared to have thrown her
off for a moment. That pleased him.

"Yeah, why? What do you get from all this?" He
gestured toward the latest rat. It was on its hind legs, its
forelegs against the wall of the glass cage. It sniffed at
the barrier. Lois looked at it for a moment and then
smiled.

"Power, Daddy," she said. "It gives me a sense of
power."

3

Billy Wilson sat on the living-room floor and eyed Barbara Gilbert, who looked as though she were hypnotized by the homemade chocolate chip cookies on the plate set on the small round table by the couch. They were waiting for Lois to bring in the tea. Barbara was the only friend Lois had, if she could be termed a friend. She came over occasionally on weekends. Lois never invited her to sleep over and Lois never slept over at her house.

Barbara, a heavy girl who still suffered from acne, wore a faded blue sweatshirt and jeans that strained at the seams. Her heavy bosom lifted the shirt away from her body so that when she reached across the couch she revealed folds of fat along her waist. Her obesity contributed to what developed as distorted facial features—wide nostrils with a wide bridge, small eyes lost in the soft, pudgy inflated cheeks, large swollen lips that continually pressed against each other, and a protruding forehead. From time to time her tongue would surface and wash along her lower lip—a nervous habit that had encouraged other kids at school to nickname her Snakeface.

Lois didn't seek Barbara's friendship. More often than not, she was annoyed by her presence. But on occasion, she welcomed her because she was a good audience: attentive, idolizing, pliable. In school they seemed to gravitate toward each other naturally because both were alien and obnoxious as far as the general student population was concerned.

Of course Lois was aware that the two of them were the butt of continual jokes. It was a favorite pastime of many students to come up with names for them, names like Batman and Robin, Mutt and Jeff, Starsky and Hutch. It was Marlene Bockman who came up with the most popular: Amoeba and Protozoa.

Barbara's parents, owners of a fuel-oil distribution company, knew only that Barbara was friendly with one of the smartest students in the school. They were happy with such a friend and they didn't give the relationship much thought. The few times that they had met Lois Wilson they thought she was plain, innocuous, unassuming. She was certainly unlike any of those other teenagers who seemed wild and wasteful. Whenever Barbara made reference to Lois, it was always with adulation and admiration, bragging about Lois's academic achievements or verbal wit. Her parents certainly saw no danger in the relationship.

"I'm collecting night crawlers and other fat worms," Billy said. Barbara turned her attention from the cookies. Billy Wilson's cherub face with its rosy cheeks reminded her of the plate of cherry vanilla ice cream she had had for dessert last night.

"Huh?"

"I get these worms and I bring 'em down to the hardware store and I get money for them."

"How gross!"

"I got more'n five dollars already. You know any places where there's a lot of worms?"

"Hardly. I don't keep track of worms," she said, running her tongue over her lips.

"You eat worms often," Lois said as she entered with the tea.

"She does?" Billy said. He looked more directly at Barbara, his eyes widening.

"I do not. Don't listen to her. I don't even like touching them. I hated dissecting them in biology class, and I had that class right before lunch."

"Did you eat them for lunch?" Billy asked. Whatever his sister said was gospel, as far as he was concerned.

"Aaa-ooh," Barbara said, grimacing to show her revulsion.

"You eat worms," Lois insisted calmly. "We all eat worms." She put the tray down gracefully. "We eat fish. Fish eat worms. Thus, we eat worms by eating the fish whose flesh is made from the flesh of worms."

"That's gross."

"Why do you use that stupid word so much?" Lois asked quickly. She sat back and crossed her legs, her eyes small, inquisitive, and intimidating. Barbara looked away.

"I don't know."

"I do. You use it because all the other girls use it and you're trying to be like them. You're hoping they'll accept you because you talk like them. Fundamentally, you want to be like them and you're trying to get other people to think you are like them. You can't stand being an outsider. You're a victim of subversive peer pressure. I've seen it a thousand times," she added, a note of boredom in her voice.

"I'm not trying to be like anybody." Barbara looked at Billy to see if her denial held up, but he was building a community of toy cars, plastic soldiers, and houses constructed from cigar boxes he had taken from the drugstore.

"I'm not accusing you of anything. It's not a judgment; it's a simple diagnosis. Teenagers behave like primitive tribes. They have their mores, their codes, their unwritten rules."

"You're a teenager," Barbara muttered. She could never contradict Lois directly.

"Only in chronological age. Fortunately, I can step aside and analyze. That's all I'm trying to get you to do when I ask you why you use *gross* so much." She leaned forward and took a cookie. Barbara quickly followed suit.

"It's just a habit."

"Habit," Lois said disdainfully. "People use that word as if it will excuse behavior. Don't you know that things which become habits were once conscious acts? By doing them over and over, you allow your brain, nerves, and muscles to work automatically. There was a point when you had control."

"All I meant was—"

"I suppose you would call your overeating a habit too."

"I won't say *gross* anymore, OK?"

"I couldn't care any less about it, believe me. It's just that you should understand why you do these things, that's all. It's the mark of an intelligent person."

Barbara looked away again. Her eyes watered, but she didn't want to show any pain. She knew Lois was critical of people who revealed their emotions. She was certainly not the kind of friend to go to for sympathy. But what Barbara did enjoy about Lois was the way she attacked the others. She was tough, cutting, cruelly sarcastic. The others avoided her and rarely took up the verbal gauntlet if Lois threw it down. When Barbara was with Lois, she felt protected. She would never tell Lois that, though, because Lois would ridicule it.

"Cindy Weiss is having her Sweet Sixteen tonight."

"Christ, what a pagan ritual."

"Pagan?"

"Worshiping an age, acting as though there's something special about reaching sixteen. If girls want to make big deals about a landmark in their lives, they should do it when they get their periods. That would make more sense, because they've reached an important stage in maturity: they can ovulate, conceive."

"What would they call it, Period Parties?" Barbara laughed at her own joke and looked to Billy, but he showed no interest in their conversation. Lois didn't laugh, but she came her closest to it—she smirked and sipped her tea. "So what are you planning to do today?"

"I'm working on a new experiment."

"You want to tell me about it?"

"Not yet."

Barbara was disappointed, but instead of showing it, she reached for another cookie.

"Actually," Lois said, "it has to do with eating."

"Oh?" Barbara held her cookie to her lips, but she didn't open her mouth.

"Yes. Did you know that a starving animal will eat almost anything, even itself?"

"No," Barbara said, her eyes getting as big as they could. "How gro . . . terrible."

" 'Terrible' is a judgmental term, having little or nothing to do with scientific notation. Right and wrong vary from environment to environment. For certain tribes in Africa, cannibalism is both right and proper. I can't see Burger King or McDonald's ever selling People Burgers, can you?"

"Oh, Lois! People Burgers." Barbara looked at the cookie and then put it back on the plate.

"Don't tell me I've spoiled your appetite. Listen," she added, leaning back and taking on an arrogant demeanor, "starving people have been known to eat bark off trees. You know that book Laura Kaplow had, *Alive?*"

"I know, I know. Can't we talk about something else?"

"Of course we can. Shall it be something of great importance, like the latest rock album you bought?"

"I haven't bought a rock album in weeks."

"Amazing." Lois leaned forward and put her cup on the tray. "Have you decided what you're going to do this summer?"

"I'll probably work at Rosenfield's Tourist House again, baby-sitting at night, helping in the kitchen during the day."

"I know you like working in that kitchen. But God, where's the intellectual stimulation, the challenge?"

"Well, it's something to do, and my mother says I can't sit around all summer. I don't want to work with her in the office, that's for sure."

Billy suddenly stood up and kicked his toy soldiers away. One bounced off Barbara's thick ankle.

"Anybody wanna go worm huntin'?"

"Of course not," Barbara said.

"Go yourself. Just don't go away from the yard."

Billy bit down on the inside of his right cheek for a moment and stared at his sister. Then he looked suspiciously at Barbara Gilbert. They both looked eager for him to leave. He remembered a time once when they hadn't thought he was in the house. He had entered the house quietly and heard them talking softly in Lois's bedroom. When he went to the door, he found it locked.

"Go away," Lois had said.

"But I wanna come in."

"I said go away."

He had left, but his curiosity had been aroused by the fact that they were in a locked room and they wouldn't let him enter. He went outside and crawled up by Lois's bedroom window.

When he peeked in, he saw Barbara Gilbert lying on her side on the bed. Lois was at her desk writing something. The scene was extremely disappointing, and he was about to leave to go play in the woods when he noticed that Barbara was looking down at one of the big books Lois had on the top shelf of her room. It was one of the books she would never let him touch.

He angled himself a little better and got some more height by digging his right foot harder against the siding of the house. From that perspective he was able to look over Barbara's big shoulder. What he saw puzzled him.

Barbara was studying two big pictures, each of which showed a naked man and a naked woman twisted and entangled around each other's bodies in what he thought were weird ways. Was it some kind of wrestling match?

Inadvertently he tapped the window with his forehead, and Lois turned around quickly enough to catch sight of him. He ran around to the back of the house, but she was out the back entrance, anticipating his direction. She caught up with him before he got to the woods and dug her fingernails into his shoulder until he fell to his knees.

"What were you doing? What were you doing, Billy?"

"I just wanted to see," he pleaded.

"What did you see?"

"You're hurting me, Lois. I'm gonna tell Mommy."

She released him but knelt down so she could look him right in the face.

"Don't you ever tell anything about me and what I do," she said slowly, pronouncing each word with a cold, knifelike emphasis, "or I'll do to you what I did to the garter snake last year."

He was so frightened he couldn't speak. All he did was shake his head and run off. He wouldn't tell, not ever. Later, Lois was very nice to him and gave him one of the garter-snake skins she had in her glass case under her bed. He put it on his wall with a tack, but whenever he looked at it, he could only think of Lois's fiery eyes. So he took it down and put it in a drawer.

Remembering that incident now, he decided he was better off letting them alone and leaving the house. Anything they would do would be boring to him anyway.

"I'm gonna dig in the backyard," he said. Lois just nodded.

"So tell me," she said after she was sure Billy had moved out of earshot, "are you still having frequent wet dreams?"

"Lois! I'm sorry I ever told you about that."

"Oh, come on, Barbara. By now I'd expect you'd be

mature enough to discuss these things without behaving like a junior-high student."

Her fat friend straightened up and took a deep breath.

"I wasn't going to tell you, but I . . . I had an experience."

"Experience?" Lois read Barbara's expression. "You had sexual intercourse?"

"No, I don't mean that."

"Well, what's an experience? A fantasy?"

"I let Bernie Rosen put his hand under my blouse."

"Jesus, Barbara!"

"It wasn't there long," she said quickly.

"I don't mean that," Lois said and shook her head. "I couldn't care less if he had his hand there for three days and three nights. I don't call that much of an experience."

"It was for me."

Lois studied her for a moment. "You had an orgasm?"

Barbara nodded. A warm, self-satisfied smile formed on her face. Lois sensed an envy growing in her and despised herself for feeling any sort of jealousy, especially of a girl like Barbara.

"Tell me about his reactions," she said, the tone of her voice becoming more formal.

"What d'ya mean? I told you, he put his hand under my blouse."

"Did he get under your bra? Did he touch your nipple? Did he have an orgasm as well?"

"I don't know. He tried to press his thing against my thigh," Barbara said, widening her smile and remembering.

"'Penis,' not 'thing.'"

"I'd rather say 'thing.'"

"Go on."

"I moved away. I could feel it. It was so hard. Like a piece of pipe or something."

"Was he breathing fast? Did his face get flushed?"

"I don't know."

"How can you not know these things?"

"Well, you didn't tell me about those things when you told me about that city boy, Teddy Fishman."

"For God's sake, Barbara, I wasn't more than a day into puberty. The only reason I let him get under my skirt was to see what it would do to my own physiological reactions. You misinterpreted everything I told you about that incident."

"Well, I didn't take Bernie's pulse, and when he tried to get under my bra, I pulled away."

"And that was your whole experience? There are girls in the eighth grade who've been pregnant twice, and that was your experience?"

"Well, I'm not looking to get pregnant. You think I want to be like Shirley Numar just to learn something new about life?" Lois simply stared at her. "Now what are you thinking about? Honestly, Lois, you could scare someone to death looking at them like that."

"I've been thinking about a project involving sex."

"Really? What sort of project?"

"Why, are you interested?"

"I don't know." Barbara was silent a moment. She reached for another cookie instinctively, just to feel something in her mouth. "What do you have in mind?"

"We're not going to play doctor. I can assure you of that. I have something a great deal more sophisticated in mind. Do you think you could get Bernie over here tomorrow afternoon? My parents are taking Billy to the circus in Middletown. I have the house to myself."

"I suppose so. But you've got to tell me more about it," Barbara said, folding her arms under her breasts and sitting back.

"I will. I will."

Lois thought about Bernie Rosen for a moment. He was a light-haired boy with big ears. The other boys in school nicknamed him Alfred E. Neuman after the funny face on *Mad* comics. There was something

stupidly clownish about Bernie's perpetually idiotic
smile. Yet none of that mattered. In fact, his low
intelligence might make him a better subject, she
thought.

"I won't do anything perverted," Barbara said.
Lois's expression of deep thought frightened her.

"There are no perversions. That's a judgmental
term. I've told you that before." Lois's eyes grew
smaller. "Tell me," Lois said, "did it ever occur to you
that we are the only animal that wears clothing? We're
the only one with so-called private parts."

"No, it never occurred to me."

"During man's early existence he was surely as naked
as any other animal. Do you think that meant that there
was continual fucking?"

Barbara winced at Lois's use of profanity. She so
rarely did it. When she referred to the human anatomy,
she always used the proper scientific terms. Other girls,
especially in the locker room, talked about boys' cocks.
Lois never said anything but *penis.* Barbara could count
on her fingers the times she heard Lois use the words
screwed or *laid.* It was always *intercourse* and *foreplay*
and *coitus,* for God's sake.

"I don't know about primitive man's sexual habits.
All I know is I wouldn't want to be naked all the time."

"Why not? Aside from the need to be warm, I mean.
How did we develop this need to be covered? Why
don't primitive tribes in Africa or Australia have this
need to cover the 'private parts'? And note the fact that
even though they aren't covered, they still have social
mores and ethics. Why, there's even less sexual viola-
tion. Did you ever think about that?"

"No. What does this stuff have to do with my getting
Bernie over here?" Barbara asked, tilting her head
slightly.

"Just do it and you'll see," Lois said. There was
something in her voice that gave her words erotic
overtones. Barbara Gilbert felt her heartbeat grow
faster. She was embarrassed by the warmth that trav-

eled up her legs and settled in the moistened pocket of
her pelvis, so she crossed her legs and looked away.
Lois didn't seem to notice anyhow. She was in even
deeper thought now, mechanically gathering the cups
and the remaining cookies. She already knew what the
title of this paper would be. She had written the first
paragraph months ago and left it in her desk drawer
with the others. If either Dorothy or Gregory Wilson
had opened that drawer and read some of their daughter's theories, they might have saved themselves a lot of
grief. But Lois's things were private. In any case, her
papers were far too technical to be of any interest to
anyone but her. At least, that's what Dorothy Wilson
thought the one and only time it ever occurred to her to
read any of them. So she let them be, she left the words
unread, the thoughts ticking away, waiting for their
proper time to come to light.

As Dorothy Wilson sat in the car and waited for
Gregory to lock up the drugstore, she switched on the
little light by the vanity mirror and patted the sides of
her new hairdo gently to get the disobedient strands
back into place. It was only then that the irony struck
her. Here it was Saturday night; she had gone to the
beauty parlor for her weekly appointment; she had
taken advantage of the long lull in the store's business
to redo her makeup, putting on some of the new eye
shadow the Revlon salesman had brought her. In her
closet she had that new pants outfit she'd picked up at
Melissa's Boutique two weeks ago. Yet she was going
nowhere. They hadn't even discussed the possibility of
a night out.
   She heard Gregory close the door and watched him
fumble for the keys to lock it. When he turned toward
the car, he looked tired, older, slumping more than
usual. During the last two hours she had heard him
fidgeting behind the pharmaceutical counter, tinkering
around, organizing. She knew he was doing an inven-

tory and wouldn't want to be bothered by her small talk. But she was restless now and she felt she had worked hard enough all week to deserve a real night out. They hadn't gone out on the town for weeks, it seemed to her. But from the looks of him as he walked across the street toward the car, she didn't expect he'd be all that delighted by the idea.

"What's the matter?" she asked him as soon as he slid in behind the wheel.

"Why?"

"You've got that Monday morning look on Saturday night?"

"Was a lousy week, with the sewer backing up and that order being misplaced."

"You've got to get the business out of your head sometime. You've got to simply relax and forget it."

"Yeah, well, it's easier said than done."

"How about going up to Phil's Holiday tonight? We could have a few drinks and listen to the band."

"I don't know. I've got this headache, and we promised Billy we'd take him to the circus tomorrow."

"Wouldn't have to be late."

"I don't know. We'll see."

She knew that meant no. As they turned down Main Street and headed toward Turtle Creek Road, she looked back at the dark and deserted hamlet. All the stores, save the bar and grill, were shut tight. Only a few dogs and stray cats roamed the streets. The scene depressed her, and she groaned under her breath. What had happened to the excitement, to the music, to the dazzle of lights? When had it all passed from her life, and why hadn't she seen it go? She looked again at Greg. He was so drawn and weary-looking for a man of forty-two. She recalled the energy he used to have, how she was so quickly captured by the light in his eyes, the softness in his voice, the strength in his hands.

Damn, she wasn't going to permit herself to be relegated prematurely to an old-age home. It wasn't right; it wasn't natural. When they pulled into their driveway and she saw how dark the house looked, she thought about her daughter. Most likely she was sitting in her room reading. Billy was probably watching television by himself.

"It's Saturday night," she said when Greg turned the engine off.

"So?"

"People usually go out and have a good time." She slammed her door and began walking to the house.

"That's ridiculous, going out just because it's Saturday night. If we had somewhere special to go . . ."

"We never have anywhere special to go. It's just good to get out sometimes. It helps you relax. The doctor told you to relax more."

"Don't use the doctor."

"Oh, I don't care," she said, and entered the house quickly. She was surprised by the darkness in the living room. "Where is everybody? Billy? Lois?"

"What's the matter?"

"Your children seem to have disappeared."

"What d'ya mean?" He closed the door slowly. Dorothy walked down to the kitchen entrance and then went on to the bedrooms. Gregory put the lights on in the living room.

"Not here."

"Not here?"

"Not in their bedrooms and not here," she said. "Did Lois call and tell you she was going someplace and taking Billy?"

"No. Maybe they're upstairs." He looked at the stairway and then walked up quickly. Dorothy waited a moment. She was about to follow when she heard muffled steps. The only thing that prevented her from screaming when the basement door opened suddenly was the way she sucked in her breath. Billy stumbled out, his hands all black with dirt. Lois followed calmly behind him.

"Not here," Gregory called.

"They're here. What were you doing in that basement?"

"Basement?" Gregory came down the stairs.

"We found a family of bats," Billy said excitedly.

"Bats!"

"I heard them passing down the chimney," Lois said, revealing the flashlight she carried in her right hand. "Since we had the glass doors on the fireplace, they simply traveled on through the ash release into the basement."

"Bats?" Gregory said. "But this isn't the season for them. It's not warm enough yet. Don't they sleep throughout the cold months?"

"Yes," Lois said. "They usually do. That's what makes these bats interesting. For some reason they've aborted their hibernation."

"Bats!" Dorothy stepped back. "And you took Billy down there?"

"I wanted to go," he said, with some pride in his voice.

"They're perfectly harmless, Mother."

"Sometimes they carry rabies," Gregory said.

"There hasn't been a case of rabies in this area for years and years."

"That's not the point."

"Oh, Greg, you've got to kill them. Maybe you should get an exterminator."

"Oh, no," Lois said. "Let them be. I want to study them for a while."

Dorothy Wilson looked at her daughter as though she were a creature from outer space.

"Study them? Are you crazy? Are you totally out of your mind?"

"All right, just relax," Gregory said. "Lois will show me where they are tomorrow and we'll get them out of here."

"But can't they get into the house tonight?"

"No," Gregory said, but he eyed his daughter to see if she would concur. She simply looked disgusted.

"Well, I don't see how I'm going to fall asleep thinking about bats in the house. I can see where this is goin' to be one helluva Saturday night."

"Damn it," Gregory said, "I'll get a broom and go down there now. How many were there?"

"Four," Billy said quickly.

"But two of them flew out through the soot hole," Lois added. "You might as well wait until tomorrow." She shot a quick glance at Billy. He was silent.

"I'm going to need a Valium," Dorothy said. She headed for the stairway.

"Why didn't you say they *all* flew out?" Gregory asked his daughter, in a low voice. "That would have eased her mind, and I could have gone down and blocked up the soot hole after killing the two that are there."

"I keep forgetting that Mother has to be kept in a world of perpetual fantasy," Lois said. Then she turned and walked to her room.

Gregory stood there a moment, his heart beating faster. He looked down at his little boy, who stared up at him quizzically.

"You weren't afraid of the bats, huh, Tiger?" he said, rubbing the top of Billy's head.

"Oh, no, Dad," he said, straightening up his little body. "Not with Lois there."

The smile faded from Gregory Wilson's face. He didn't relish the thought of having to face four bats in a dark cellar. From where did his daughter draw her courage? Was it courage? Or was it something unnatural? His ruminations were broken when Dorothy shouted for him.

"You're going to have to go back to the store," she said, talking from the top of the stairs. "There isn't a single Valium left in the bottle."

"Wow. You've got to take it easy with those things."

"I have. Maybe you've taken more than you think."

"I haven't taken one for weeks."

"Then . . ."

"I saw Lois give one to one of her rats once," Billy said. He regretted saying it the moment the words came out and shut his mouth instantly, almost biting his tongue.

"Oh," Gregory said, and looked toward his daughter's room.

"Don't tell I said it," Billy pleaded. Gregory was surprised by his son's real look of fear.

"That's all right," Gregory said. "I don't like a snitcher, either," he added to put Billy at ease. As he left the house he thought about those pills he couldn't account for at the store. It wasn't many, but . . . he knew he should talk to his daughter about it and made a mental note to do so. And yet he felt strangely reluctant to do so. It was almost as if he were afraid of what he would learn.

He imagined the sound of bats' wings and walked quickly to his car.

4

Despite the one-hundred-fifty-watt bulb he had in the cellar fixture, Gregory couldn't get very much illumination through the basement. The house had only half a cellar because the back of the building was constructed over a shelf of solid rock. The old fieldstone foundation had been reinforced with cement, but here and there the rocks were naked to the view. There had never been anything but a dirt floor, and the Wilsons, having little use for the basement other than for storage and as a place for the hot-water heater and water pump, had done little to modernize it. Now, with only one light to work by, Gregory regretted that he had not done something about the electricity.

He had gotten up early in the morning, collected a flashlight and a broom, and made his way down the creaky, soggy-looking wooden steps. Dorothy was still asleep, having sedated herself into it last night. Just before he reached the cellar door, he met Lois in the hallway. It was as if she had been waiting for him. He said nothing to her, but she followed close behind him.

"Where are they?" he asked when he reached the bottom of the stairway.

"Just to the right of the hot-water heater."

He pointed his flashlight in that direction. The cellar's ceiling was just six feet high, but there were some floor beams that hung a few inches lower, making it necessary for him to crouch. He moved slowly, the flashlight in his left hand, the broom, held like a lance, in his right hand. He stopped when he saw the furry black mounds huddled beside one another on the wall.

"Hold the light on them," he said. Reluctantly, she came up beside him and took the beam. "God, they're ugly."

"I don't see why you say that," she said. "Actually, they're a marvel of nature, with their built-in sonar and their wings. I find them fascinating." She said it with such relish that he hesitated for a few moments. Perhaps it was wrong to kill them, but he had no other way to rid the house of them. He wasn't going to pick them off the wall and throw them out.

"They don't belong in the house." He lifted the broom like a baseball bat.

"I'm sure they didn't know they were entering the Fleur mansion."

He swung a little wildly, catching only the one on the far right. It crumpled to the floor. Lois followed it down with the light and they could see it move its tiny legs. He slapped it again and it stopped all movement. Only one of the other three moved at all, inching a little away from the other two. He hit it with a much straighter and harder stroke than he had the first and it fell crushed to the floor. He was sweating now and he could feel his heart beating so rapidly and pounding so hard he thought it would come crashing out of his chest. He paused to wipe his forehead.

"Thank God they're too stupid to know what's going on."

"It's not in their experience to know what it means to be attacked with a broom while sleeping," Lois said dryly.

"Just keep the light on them."

He lifted the broom, more confident now, and brought it down with a swift stroke, smearing the next-to-last nocturnal creature down the wall. It rolled into a ball and died quickly. When he looked up, Lois had moved the light off the last one.

"Get the light back on it."

"Can't you let me have this one?"

"What?"

"I want to study it. I'll keep it trapped down here. I can do it," she pleaded.

"Are you crazy? That's all your mother has to find out."

"She won't if you don't tell her."

"It's out of the question, Lois. Now get the light back up."

"But—"

"Get it up."

When she moved it to the spot, the last bat was gone.

"Damn," he said. "Give me that light."

He backed up when she handed it to him. Then he ran it up and down the wall and over the ceiling, checking the rafters until he spotted the creature secured between a floor beam and the ceiling. "Now hold this light on it," he commanded, turning the broom around so he could jam the handle into the bat.

"No," Lois said. "I don't want to be part of this vicious cruelty." She turned to the stairs.

"Lois, I told you . . ." She kept walking. "Shit." He held the light in his left hand now and tried to coordinate his stabbing. His first thrust was off the mark. The creature moved farther into the crevice. When it did so, Gregory instinctively stepped back, afraid that it would fly out at him. The tension had brought a sharp pain to his head. He looked back, but Lois was already up the stairway and out of the cellar. Stepping closer, he studied the bat, brought the broom handle up higher, paused, and then jammed it as hard as he could into the crevice. He felt it crush the creature's body, but the animal did not fall out. He had to work its body out. When it fell forward, he jumped back.

He ran the flashlight beam back to the other three bodies to be sure they were still there. Then he looked about for something to put them in. There was a carton filled with some old clothes. He emptied it quickly and swept the dead bats into the box. Before he left the cellar, he ran the light over the beams and walls to be sure there were no more. He didn't want to find any and really made only a perfunctory search.

As he walked up the stairs he thought about Lois's impertinent desertion and grew angry. He took the box of dead bats out to the garbage pail and shoved them, box and all, into the can. After he closed the lid, he paused for a few moments to get his breath and calm his nerves. The morning fog had the house clutched in its cloudy fist, making it look ethereal and dreamlike. Indeed, he felt as though he had just traveled through a nightmare. He was still dressed in his slippers and bathrobe.

When he got back into the house, he went right to Lois's room. She was sitting on her bed, her back against the pillow, thumbing through a copy of *National Geographic*. She didn't even look up when he entered.

"Do you think that was right, to leave me like that?"

"I couldn't stand there and watch that wanton killing."

"Wanton killing? For Christ's sake, they're vermin."

"I hate that word. It's such a stupid word," she said, her eyes small. She looked as though she would cry. He hesitated. Her reactions confused him.

"Look, Lois. If you want to live in a zoo, that's fine when you're on your own. You can move in with rats and spiders and bats, whatever makes you happy; but while you're living here, you'll have to understand that the rest of us don't share your views on animals, OK?"

"It's not OK, but I understand."

"Don't get smart with me, young lady."

"I'm not getting smart. I just wanted to have one to study, that's all."

"That kind of studying belongs in a laboratory, Lois. This is just a house—a house."

"All right."

There was a long pause between them. She turned the page of her magazine.

"And before I forget it, did you take some of your mother's Valium to use on your lab animals?"

"Who said that?"

"Nobody said it. I'm just asking you."

"I was going to do a personality transformation with a drug catalyst," she said quickly. "I read about—"

"Then you did take them. Where do you get off doing that without asking me or your mother first?"

"You can't be serious. Ask Mother?"

"I *am* serious, and you're getting too damn smart. Now, did you take any other drugs from the store?" She stared at him, eye to eye. "Well?"

"No," she said, and looked down at the magazine.

"You're lying." She didn't deny it. "We're going to have to all sit down and have a serious talk about this, your attitudes, your stealing, your experiments."

"What attitudes?"

"I'm going upstairs now. My head feels like a neon light. I don't want your mother to know any of this, and I've got to take your brother to the circus today. I want to get some rest." He turned but stopped in the doorway. "But you and I have to have a long talk, young lady," he added, holding his forefinger up. She shut her magazine and turned away. He looked at her for a moment and left.

She didn't come out for breakfast, using as her excuse stomach cramps brought about by an impending period. Dorothy brought her in some Midol and felt her head to be sure it wasn't a virus. Then the three of them left. Lois waited a good five minutes after she heard the front door slam; then she came out of her room, got the flashlight, and went to the cellar door. She turned on the light and went down the stairs quickly. When she reached the bottom, she went to her left quickly. She turned the flashlight on the upside-down water pail. Kneeling, she carefully lifted it and directed the beam under it. The small bat remained still, frozen by the light. Without the slightest hesitation, she pinched it behind the neck and dropped it into the right-side-up pail.

When she got to her pantry laboratory, she uncovered the old birdcage, put the bat inside, and covered it again. She went back to the cellar door, opened it, and threw the pail down the stairs. Satisfied, she turned from the cellar door, put the flashlight back, and went to make herself a big breakfast. All this morning activity had given her a big appetite, she thought. Besides, she was anxious to eat and then sit down and plan the afternoon's experiment involving Barbara Gilbert and Bernie Rosen. It was going to be a good day.

With a quick and surprisingly graceful motion, Lois lifted her T-shirt over her head, revealing her braless small breasts. They quivered and then became firm with erect nipples, nipples that were rather large for the size of her bosom. Their deep, dark brown hue brought out the milky whiteness of her breasts. Heavy blue veins ran along the surfaces, mapping the flow of her blood as vividly as a medical diagram.

Bernie Rosen was both shocked and excited. His mouth remained open and his eyelids blinked rapidly. He made a quick attempt to smile, but it was as though he felt that the slightest motion would erase the scene being created before him. He practically held his breath. For a moment no one said a thing. The silence became heavy, even oppressive. Then Barbara shook her head and looked at Bernie. His intensity frightened her.

"Lois!" she said, bouncing in her seat. She was undecided whether or not she should place herself in Bernie's view.

"We're all going through certain predictable physiological reactions," Lois said in an amazingly calm tone of voice. In fact, her calmness made Barbara question the reality of what was happening. Lois folded her T-shirt over the back of her vanity-table chair and then sat down to face Bernie, who continued to gape. His Alfred E. Neuman smile melted away and his face became frozen with intensity—eyes small, lips still.

"I don't believe you," Barbara said, holding her arms across her own covered bosom. Somehow Lois's partial nudity made Barbara feel nude as well. "I had no idea she was going to do this," she said, turning to Bernie. He didn't look her way.

"It's all right with me," he said.

"What is the point, Lois?" Barbara was at the edge of her seat.

"What I plan to show you is that patterns of behavior that are reinforced by society can be changed, even totally reversed."

"I believe you, I believe you," Barbara said. "Put your shirt back on."

"I'm not revealing anything that Bernie hasn't seen before," Lois said, looking directly at Bernie. She leaned back in her seat, her left arm over the top of the chair, her right elbow resting on the chair arm. Her posture pulled her breasts tighter, the nipples pressing upward. Bernie leaned forward. His mouth watered. When he licked his lips, Barbara automatically licked hers.

"It still isn't right, Lois."

"And I know exactly what Bernie has between his legs. I know how his penis is pressing against his underwear right now, pushing into an erection."

"Lois! I don't believe this," Barbara said and looked down at the floor. She kept shaking her head.

"But she's right," Bernie said, his smile returning.

"Oh, God!"

"I mean, our bodies are common. Some of us are smaller or bigger, fatter or thinner, but there's nothing unique about any of us. We all are having the same predictable reactions here. I'm sure your nipples are hard and erect, Barbara." Bernie turned to her as though he expected her nipples to be clearly outlined against her blouse. Barbara put her head in her hands and looked down between her legs.

"Oh, Lois."

"Well, aren't they?"

"Sure they are," Bernie said quickly. He wasn't sure what Lois was intending, but he liked the direction of the conversation and he feared that Barbara's hesitation might bring everything to an end.

"You shut up, Bernie Rosen. You don't know anything about me or my body."

"Oh, no?" Bernie said, his voice rising.

"Barbara, for crying out loud! I thought you were going to be adult about this. I thought you were interested," Lois said. She glared at Barbara, who raised her head slowly and faced Lois as though she were coming under a spell. "I mean, if Bernie's willing to be a participant . . ." Lois added, turning to him.

"I am, I am."

"After all, it's just an experiment."

"An experiment?" Bernie said, disappointment clearly in his voice. "How do you mean?"

"An experiment in behavior—physiological, psychological, and sociological. Our social mores are a product of all three."

Bernie smirked. Somehow this girl was making an exciting event seem educational. Despite her nudity, he felt his erection begin to wane. He was beginning to lose interest. And besides, there was nothing really attractive about her. The way her rib cage protruded, that little line of hair running down her chest, the morbid whiteness of her skin with those little blue veins crisscrossing everywhere . . .

"What do we have to do?" Barbara asked. The note of hysteria in her voice was now absent. She swallowed hard.

"Well, first I'd like us all to just get completely naked," Lois said, standing up again and unbuckling her jeans.

"Completely? All of us?" She looked at Bernie, who looked lost now.

"Naked?" he said. This idea revived his excitement. "Well, well, well." He rubbed his hands together and widened his eyes. Barbara bit her lower lip and then sent her tongue out over it.

"If we do it quickly, we won't think so much about it, right, Bernie?"

"What? Yeah, sure," he said. He stood up and took his shirt off roughly, practically tearing the collar. Lois stepped out of her jeans and slipped off her panties. She hung them over the corner of the vanity chair but left the jeans on the floor. Bernie stared at her pocket of pubic hair and then worked frantically at his own belt buckle. Barbara stood up but stepped back as though she were thinking of a retreat.

Bernie slid his pants down and then goose-stepped out of them, while Barbara simply fingered the top two buttons of her blouse. Bernie's erection had created a large bulge in his briefs. For a few moments Barbara could do nothing but stare at it; and when he peeled off his underwear and his penis snapped out from under the descending garment, she was fascinated by the thickness of the stem of his prick.

Lois, on the other hand, was all business. She was seated again, her legs crossed, a pad of paper in her hands. Her posture and position, combined with Barbara's hesitation and failure to take off even a sock, suddenly made Bernie feel stupid. He sat down quickly and crossed his legs to hide his pulsating erection, but the tip of it peeked up and over like a tiny animal, frightened but curious.

"Will you hurry up, Barbara," Lois commanded.

"But what are we going to do?"

"This has to be done step by step," Lois replied in an uncharacteristically patient tone of voice. "If I describe everything at once, it will lose its validity."

"I don't think I want to do this."

"Oh, for God's sake, Barbara! You're not being fair

to either Bernie or me now. We thought you were with us."

"Yeah," Bernie added, still quite unsure what it was he had agreed to do. "It's unfair."

"Well . . ." She undid three blouse buttons and then turned quickly to Bernie. "If you say anything about this to anyone . . ."

"Barbara, we're all adults. Can't you try?"

"What am I going to say?" Bernie asked. He raised his shoulders for emphasis. "I don't even know what's going on." Bernie's sincere innocence encouraged Barbara and she took her blouse off and unzipped her skirt. She stepped out of it and then reached around to unfasten her bra. Her large breasts and heavy shoulders made it difficult.

"Need help?" Bernie asked.

"No, thank you." The bra was finally unclipped. When her breasts fell forward, Bernie's eyes widened. He uncrossed and crossed his legs, but he couldn't give his erection the breathing room it needed. Barbara sat down, pulling her panties over her knees and dropping them to her ankles.

"Now what?" she asked, quickly folding her arms over her enormous bosom.

Lois looked up from her pad. Both Bernie and Barbara stared at her, completely attentive, unable to turn away. Her eyes burned with purpose. Her face, white and still, was as magnetic as death.

"We've got to get used to one another's bodies," she said. "We've got to overcome social and behavioral patterns that cause us to have certain predictable responses."

"I don't understand," Bernie said.

"You will." She was so certain that he believed it. "All right," she said, "we stand and we walk around each other. We look at each other closely, but we don't touch and we don't hide ourselves in any way from one another. Drop your arms to your sides, Barbara," she commanded sharply. Barbara did so immediately. Bernie tried to swallow but found he couldn't. Lois stood up and took a step closer to Bernie. He looked up at her, his gaze moving slowly over her bony knees to her pocket of rather thick pubic hair, onto the thin line of it that traced a route to her belly button. "Stand up," she said.

Bernie did so. His erection was so stiff and thick it began to transmit a slight ache. He wanted to touch it or press it against her, but he was afraid to move an inch closer.

"Get up, Barbara, and keep your hands to your sides." Barbara did so, but she kept her gaze forward. She bit her lower lip and sent her tongue out over it. "All right, everyone look long and hard at everyone else, but keep your distance," Lois warned.

Bernie turned to Barbara, who looked up instead of at him. The rolls of fat on her body had layered along her lower back and over her hip bone. Her backside was flattened by the hanging weight. She appeared to have no waist. For a moment Bernie felt more disgust than sexual arousal. He looked back at Lois, but she, being the other physical extreme, offered hardly more erotic interest.

"This is just like a nudist colony, huh?" Bernie said.

"Yes, Bernie, in a way. Nudists have overcome a social pattern. The point is that nudists get along very well without having continual sexual intercourse. Can you imagine how funny it must seem to them to see people pay so much money to get into topless shows?"

"Yeah, I never thought of that."

"Did you ever wonder why this society has such a need for these sexual perversities?"

"No," Bernie said. He smirked. He couldn't believe it, but when Lois spoke, it was as if neither of them were naked before the other. It was only Barbara's exaggerated breasts that created any sexual excitement at this point. He turned to her again and shook his head in appreciation.

"How long do we have to stand like this?" Barbara asked.

"I think the time has been sufficient. Now, we've got to get used to one another like this."

"When do we experiment?" Bernie asked.

"This is all part of it, but I want to build us to a point where we can turn ourselves on and turn ourselves off."

"Like a faucet, huh?" Bernie said, smiling.

"In a sense. If you both cooperate, I will bring your sex drives and my sex drives under control. I . . . we will be able to manipulate them at will; therefore the expression: 'Turn off and turn on.'"

"That's incredible," Bernie said, but the more Lois talked, the more his interest began to falter.

"It's simply a matter of imprinting."

"I don't know if I want to do that," Barbara said.

"Oh, sure you do. It will make you a stronger person. It will make us all stronger. Now, we'll begin today by doing things we would normally be able to do fully dressed."

"You mean this is going to take more than a day, this experiment?" Bernie asked.

"Of course. We need reinforcement. You'll see. Now we'll sit around and talk, maybe watch a little television, or perhaps play a game of Scrabble."

"Huh?"

"We want to all relax, Bernie," Lois said. "That's most important. Try to block the sexual thoughts from your mind."

"I don't think I'm going to be able to do this."

"Of course you will," Lois said with determination. Her eyes were so gripping and her tone of voice so self-assured that he simply nodded. "Let's all sit down," she said. Everyone did so. "Now, Bernie," she said, her face softening, but her posture remaining stiff, "what are your plans for after graduation?"

For a long moment Bernie Rosen felt disoriented. The two young women with him were totally naked. He could reach out and touch nipples, caress breasts, stroke ass. He could bury his face in pubic hair and nibble at vaginal lips—things he had fantasized often. Just recently he had tried to get at Barbara Gilbert's breasts, and now here she was, naked and beside him, less than an arm's reach away. Yet Lois Wilson's tone of voice and commanding presence changed the effect of it all. Was there something wrong with him? He really didn't understand what was happening, and it was happening so fast.

He was amazed at how his penis had shrunken, retreated into itself. Was he really going to sit naked with two naked girls and act as though they were all dressed? Even though he was disappointed about the immediate rewards, he was fascinated by the event. Lois Wilson opened up whole new possibilities. She was making him question his very sexual being.

"After graduation?" he said. He looked down for a moment, recalling some of the long discussions he had recently had with his father. "I was thinking about going into accounting," he said.

Lois Wilson permitted herself a half smile. It was going well. The first session was going just as she had planned.

5

Martha Gilbert turned off the floor lamp in the living room and gently shook her husband Joe's shoulder. He blinked quickly and sat up on the couch.

"Wake up and go to sleep," she said. He wiped his eyes with his short, stubby-fingered fists and swallowed to rid his mouth of the bitter aftertaste that lingered from the three cups of coffee he had consumed at dinner. His jowls shook. Weighing one hundred ninety pounds at a height of five feet seven, Joe Gilbert was pear-shaped, with soft round shoulders and thin, bony-kneed legs. Ribbons of varicose veins were mapped along his pale white, hairy legs. There were few sights Martha Gilbert detested more than her husband in Bermuda shorts.

They were personifications of contrast: she was tall, thin, with a schoolmarm's erect posture. Her face wore a tight spinster's smirk most of the time. She had married Joe Gilbert early in life and he had moved right in to take over her father's oil-distribution business. It was her sensible, pragmatic decision that they put off having children during their early married years, and Joe Gilbert rarely contested his wife's decisions.

He had always been easygoing, soft-spoken, chunky, and unambitious. There wasn't an old-timer in Sandburg who didn't remark or believe that Joe had fallen into the best thing possible for himself when he married the daughter of one of the area's most profitable oil distributors. Martha was a strong, domineering, managerial type. It was only natural for her to assume control of the business. Most people thought she had married a man like Joe Gilbert so she could bolster her overbearing ego.

"What time is it?"

"Nearly eleven thirty." She turned off the television set, dropping a curtain of darkness over most of the living room. Light from the hall and the den-office spilled through the doorway. Joe Gilbert got up and shook his head.

"Anything important on the late news?"

"Just like I told you—OPEC's raising the oil prices again."

"I don't know how some of these people are going to make it."

"Well, we can't continue to extend credit to people like the Bakers and the McGees."

Joe Gilbert just shook his head. "I'm tired," he said.

"Tell me something new."

She followed him out of the room. He hesitated for a moment at the foot of the stairway. They had a two-story colonial with eight rooms. It was one of the finest houses in the area, supporting everyone's stereotyped concept of what someone in the oil business should be like.

"Left the light on in the den," he said. He stumbled slightly to the right.

"I'll get it."

He paused and then started up the stairs. Martha threw the light switch in the den and turned quickly to leave. She paused, though, because she had caught sight of the small button light on the telephone. They had three telephone trunk lines into the house: one for the business, one for their private use, and one for Barbara's private use.

Barbara was their only child. When Martha did finally decide the time was right to have children, they had great difficulty because, as it turned out, Joe had a low sperm count. Four years after Barbara was born, they tried again. Their efforts were completely unsuccessful, and eventually they gave up on the idea of a two- or three-child family. Nevertheless, Martha was determined that her one and only child would not be spoiled. Martha wasn't puritanical when it came to Barbara, but she did try to imbue her with a sense of value and responsibility. She granted Barbara her own phone line only after Barbara agreed to work and help pay for it, whether by baby-sitting or summer employment.

She went to the phone and stared at the light for a moment. It was Barbara's line. Here it was eleven thirty on a school night and her daughter was talking on the phone. She was violating one of Martha's most specific prohibitions. Martha was going to turn around and go upstairs to bawl her out. She planned to embarrass her by having whomever Barbara was talking to overhear the chastisement. But she was also curious who that might be. What parents permitted their children to talk on the phone so late at night before school? And what do these kids talk about so much?

She pressed the button down gently and lifted the receiver slowly, looking back at the doorway to be sure Joe had kept going up the stairs. Satisfied, she placed her hand over the mouthpiece and put the earpiece to her head.

"It's not that I don't understand the purpose and the value of what you're doing—"

"We're doing," Lois corrected.

"We're doing. It's just that . . . well, do you think Bernie Rosen really appreciates what you're saying? I mean, all he sees is two naked girls."

"You saw for yourself, didn't you? I mean, did his penis soften or didn't it?"

"Yes, but—"

"And you admitted feeling less sexual stimulation. I know that after a while I didn't even feel naked."

"I don't think I can say that."

"You will, believe me."

"I don't know if I can keep doing this."

"It'll get easier."

"What if he talks, tells other boys?"

"He won't."

"How do you know for sure?"

"Because I understand adolescent male behavior. Right now he's in the midst of a conflict: he's excited by what we're doing, but he's also confused and ashamed. He didn't score, as they would say. His friends would only mock him. To sit naked with two naked girls for over an hour and not even touch one of them . . . don't you see? How can he brag about that?"

"Yes, but . . . he could make up stories."

"He could do that anyway. He's not that creative. Actually, he's a great subject for my experiment. I'm glad you had that 'experience' with him."

"I don't think I could ever let him come near me again. Not after today."

"That's ridiculous. Besides, we're eventually going to begin some physical contact."

"Lois!"

"Don't worry. I have everything under control."

There was a long pause, but Martha couldn't put the phone down yet. She knew they'd hear the click.

"Lois?"

"What? "

"I . . . I can't stop thinking about his thing."

"His penis?" Her voice was melodic. It was as though she were talking to a little child. "That might be penis envy, or it could be a phallic syndrome."

"What's that?"

"Don't worry. It's all quite common. I'll tell you about these things tomorrow. I've got to hang up now."

"I don't think I can sleep," Barbara said. She giggled.

"Masturbate," Lois said. "It'll help." She hung up. Barbara hung up a full second later.

Martha stood with the phone in her hands for a few moments. She had been fascinated, outraged, and shocked, and it took her a few moments to sort out her reactions. She settled on anger and slammed the receiver back into its cradle. Then she headed up the stairs to Barbara's bedroom.

Martha Gilbert lost no time making up her mind how she would handle this crisis. She forbade Barbara to leave her room, even to go to school. "First, I want you to sit here all day tomorrow and think about the things I have said; and second, I don't want you to have any contact with that Lois Wilson until I straighten this out."

Barbara could hardly speak. It was as though her mother had been right there all the time, as though her mother had been standing in the doorway of Lois's room. She felt naked and dirty, but mostly she felt afraid.

"I told . . . you. I told you," she said, her throat aching, "it was just a scientific experiment. That's all it was."

"You're sicker than I think if you believe that. Thank God I found out about this when I did."

Martha summarized the story quickly for Joe. She woke him up to tell him and he listened with his eyes half opened.

"Your daughter's been playing sex games with that Lois Wilson and a boy named Bernie Rosen."

"Sex games?"

"Who would have ever thought it? It goes to show you, you can't trust any of them today, not even the ones with the high marks in school. What do you know about this Rosen family?" she demanded.

"I don't understand."

"What d'ya need translated, Joe?"

"Rosen family?" He wiped his eyes.

"Go back to sleep. I'll take care of this myself, just like I take care of all the important things."

"What are ya gettin' so nasty about?" She began to

ignore him. "Barbara's been involved in some kind of sex thing?"

"Go to sleep," she said. She went into the bathroom and closed the door. Joe thought about getting up to go in and talk to his daughter. He stared at the closed bathroom door for a few moments, and then he shrugged and closed his eyes. It was all probably female problems anyway, he thought. He would let his wife handle it, whatever the hell it was.

Late the next morning, Martha Gilbert walked into Wilson's Pharmacy. Dorothy was rearranging a new cosmetics display and Gregory was behind the pharmaceutical counter. Dorothy saw her, smiled, and approached.

"Isn't this rain depressing?" Dorothy said without considering why Martha Gilbert looked so disturbed. "And we had so much last week."

Martha looked around to be sure no one else was in the store.

"I couldn't care less about the weather this morning," she said sharply.

Dorothy stopped, the smile frozen on her face as her eyes filled with questions.

"You're not feeling well, Martha?"

"No, I'm not feeling well, and I'm not feeling well because of what your daughter has been doing with my daughter. What she's been making my daughter do, I should say."

"I don't understand. Lois?"

"Yes—Lois. If I hadn't heard it all with my own ears, I might not believe it myself, but I assure you, darling, none of this is pure fiction."

"None of what?" Dorothy looked to the back for Gregory, but he was still out of sight.

Martha Gilbert's eyes became small with anger. She pressed her lips together hard and put her hands on her hips. Her pocketbook dangled from her right wrist.

"Your daughter, Lois, has been engineering some sort of sex game."

"What?"

"That's right. With a boy named Bernie Rosen. I'm not familiar with the Rosens," she added parenthetically, "but that's not the important thing."

"You've got to be mistaken. Lois?"

"Yes—Lois," Martha said, wagging her head a bit. "I heard them talking on the phone last night—after eleven thirty, I might add."

"What did they say?" Dorothy was intrigued. She had nearly come to believe that her daughter was asexual. As far as she could tell, Lois had absolutely no interest in boys. They had never had anything resembling a mother-daughter talk about girl-boy relations. She knew Lois was well versed on the biological aspects of sex, probably more informed about them than she was, but she doubted Lois had any inkling of the emotional aspects.

"Apparently," Martha began, looking around to be sure no one was in earshot, "apparently the three of them stripped naked and performed some . . . some experiments, as your daughter termed them."

"I can't believe this."

"Believe it," Martha Gilbert said.

"Greg. Greg, come out here."

Gregory Wilson stood up and looked out at the store. Martha glanced at him and then turned away. She leaned lightly on one of the display cases.

"This thing's given me some headache," she said.

"I can imagine. Greg?"

"What's up?" He walked out slowly. "Hello, Martha. Somebody sick?"

"Yes, your daughter."

"Now, wait a minute," Dorothy said. "From what you've told me, there was plenty of cooperation."

"What's this all about?"

"Martha tells me Lois has been organizing some sort of sex game with her daughter and the Rosen boy."

"Lois?" Gregory smiled and turned to Martha Gilbert, who bit her lower lip.

"I told your wife how I found out. I happened to pick up my telephone last night and accidentally overheard a conversation between Barbara and Lois. It was all about this sex experiment your daughter's creating." The smile left Gregory's face. "Now Barbara's being punished. I've kept her home from school today and in her room. She's not to have anything to do with your daughter after this. I thought about going to the school and talking to the principal."

"Well . . ."

"But there's no point to that. It's not something that happened on school grounds. So I decided I would come down here and let you people know what's been going on. If I might make a suggestion," she added quickly, "I think you should tighten up your control of Lois somewhat. I'm aware of her brilliant school record, but . . ."

"This is really a surprise to us," Gregory said. He looked at Dorothy, who was staring right through Martha Gilbert at this point.

"Yes, well, that might be because you're losing track of her. I don't expect Barbara to be Goody Two-Shoes, but . . ."

"We'll get right on it," Gregory said. "Thanks for coming down. I'm sorry about it."

"That's not the point," Martha Gilbert said, feeling somewhat magnanimous. "I didn't come here to extract any apology from you people. We all know what it's like to bring up children today. I just thought I'd better let you in on all of it."

"We appreciate it," Dorothy said quickly.

"I mean, little kids have been known to play doctor and all that, but I think this has gone beyond that, and at their age . . ."

"We understand," Dorothy said. "We're not complete idiots."

Martha smirked and nodded.

"The fruit doesn't fall far from the tree."

"What's that supposed to mean?"

"All right," Gregory said. "We'll look into the matter, Mrs. Gilbert." She caught his use of her formal name. "Thank you," he added, punctuating the words with a definite finality.

Martha started for the front door and stopped. "Make sure you tell her to stay away from Barbara."

"You don't have to worry about that," Dorothy said. Both she and Gregory stood there looking after her.

"Well," Dorothy said.

"I can't believe it."

"I can. What have I been telling you all this time? You heard her: sex experiments. It figures that Lois's only relationship with a boy would be an experiment," she added and went back to the display.

"I don't know. It still could be something she's exaggerating," he said.

"You'll have to find out." Her assignment of the responsibility solely to him wasn't lost on him.

"Me? Isn't this more mother-daughter stuff?"

"With a normal girl, it would be. She's beyond me. She'll only start on something scientific and I won't know what the hell she's talking about. At least with you she can't fabricate as much."

"All right," he said. "I'll find out about this after school." He started back to the counter when a customer entered. He filled some prescriptions and went back to his inventory, but he couldn't get the incident with Martha Gilbert out of his mind. He kept looking at the clock all day, impatient for the time when the first school bus would come rolling through the village. He made up his mind he would leave the store as soon as Lois's bus appeared.

The incident and the relentlessly cloudy, rainy day depressed him. After a while, Dorothy's "I told you so" looks annoyed him. He was ready to admit Lois was different; he was even ready to admit she was strange; but he couldn't see himself admitting that his daughter was dangerous. After all, all kids did some sex experimentation.

The Gilbert woman had acted as though Lois were in total control, as if she had some kind of power over people. He began to wonder just how true that was.

Lois wasn't surprised or in any way alarmed by Barbara Gilbert's absence from school the day after the experiment. She was vaguely aware that Barbara wasn't much of a student and had a poor attendance record, especially on rainy days. The dark gray morning sky depressed most of the students, who looked bleary-eyed and somnambulistic as they disembarked from the school buses. Lois, who kept to herself as usual, was all business in homeroom, organizing her homework and notes and arranging her day's work. It wasn't until her third-period class that she noticed Barbara wasn't there.

"What happened to the other subject?" Bernie Rosen asked her at lunch. He put his tray down directly across the table and pulled up a seat.

"Other subject?"

"Barbara," he whispered, "the other subject in the experiment. Isn't that what you kept calling us?"

"Oh, Barbara. I don't know. I spoke to her last night and she sounded OK then. I'm sure she just couldn't get up this morning."

"Do you think that's a result of our experiment?" he asked, keeping his voice low.

"Of course not."

"Well, when's the next session?"

"I told you. I'll let you know. I've got to wait for an opportunity when I have my house free."

"What are you doing, Bernie, trying to make a deal for homework?" Bonnie Diller said as she passed their table. The girls behind her laughed.

"Ignore her. She's just one of the Yahoos."

"What's a Yahoo?"

"A smelly, oversexed human creature. It's a term that's become synonymous with those ignorant elements of the population who have disdain for anything intellectual or beautiful. It comes from *Gulliver's Travels*."

"*Gulliver's Travels?* I don't remember that."

"You probably only read Book I. There are other adventures besides the one with the small people."

"How the hell do you know so much?"

"I read, Bernard."

Bernie just shook his head and ate. Lois looked down at her book. He studied her for a few moments, recalling her naked body. She felt his stare.

"What is it?"

"Nothin'." He smiled and she understood. "Perhaps you're right," she said. "Perhaps Barbara wasn't able to face you after yesterday." She thought for a moment. "I really should have considered that possibility."

"Well, what am I supposed to do, forget it?"

"Absolutely not. That would be self-defeating. Keep aware of all your reactions. I'll want to know about them next time."

"Jesus, what ya doin', givin' me a homework assignment?"

"In a sense."

He smirked and ate faster.

"Why don't we try to get some more subjects?" he then said, a smile breaking out again. "There are a number of possibilities I wouldn't mind."

"If we need anyone else . . . actually, one more male would be ideal."

"Male? Who wants another male?" He looked around and then became quiet when Laurie Burack and Mona Saperstein sat down at their table.

"Hope you don't mind the intrusion," Laurie said with deliberate, affected politeness, "but there doesn't seem to be any other seats."

"There don't seem to be any other seats," Lois corrected.

"That's what I said." The two girls looked at each other and laughed.

"Speaking of males," Bernie said, ignoring them, "Mr. Oates stopped me in the hall just before."

"Oh?"

"He wants me to try out for the spring play. Says he never gets enough males to try out. He's always tryin' to pick a play with more females than males."

"Really?" Lois said, exhibiting only vague interest.

"Well, it's his own fault," Mona Saperstein said, wedging herself into the conversation. "Look at the plays he picks. Who the hell ever heard of this one? I can't even remember the title, it's so damn long."

"What is the title?" Lois asked. She was curious now.

"Er, let me see," Bernie said. "Er . . . *The Effect of* something *on the Moon Gold,* I think."

"That's not it," Laurie said. "See, Mona's right."

"*The Effect of Gamma Rays on Man-in-the-Moon Marigolds,*" Lois said softly.

"Hey, that's it."

"Figures she would know it," Mona said.

"I've always been fascinated by the character of Matilda," Lois said. It was more like a thought voiced aloud. "She's the younger of two daughters. Almost pathologically shy, she has an intuitive gift for science. Her teacher encourages her to undertake a gamma-ray experiment with marigolds which wins her a prize."

"Go out for it," Bernie said.

"Lois?" Mona Saperstein said. Both she and Laurie started to laugh.

"I might just do that," Lois said, glaring at them. They stopped laughing, their smiles quickly melting. "I might just do that," Lois repeated, looking straight ahead.

The two girls eyed each other and stifled their giggles. They ate quickly, anxious now to finish and tell this news to others. Bernie studied Lois's expression.

He had never seen such an intense look on a person's face before. Her eyes were so still. She looked as though she had stopped breathing. Her body looked frozen in its purpose; it was as though she had left reality and entered another dimension.

"Well . . ." he said. He looked down at his tray. "I gotta go." He looked at the two girls, who were still working to control their giggles, took another quick look at Lois, who hadn't changed expression, and got up. "See ya later," he said. She nodded blankly and he was gone.

It was still raining at the end of the school day. The steady drizzle had become a downpour and the water ran down the rural highways, turning the roadside ditches into brooks of churning muddy waters. Lois had been unusually pensive during the last couple of periods. She saw the posters announcing the day and the time for play tryouts and she began to consider seriously the possibility of doing it. She recalled the times she had read the play and thought about her favorite scenes. She identified with that girl; she understood her scientific appetites. She was positive she could perform the part better than anyone else. She just might do it, she thought, she just might.

As soon as she got home, she located her copy of the play and began to reread it. She was intensely concentrating when Billy arrived home from elementary school. His voice and his questions were exceedingly annoying to her now.

"You wanna play somethin'?"

"Absolutely not. Go do your homework."

"I don't have any."

"Well, don't hang around here bothering me. Go . . . go look for some more worms."

"Now? It's raining."

"That's the best time to look for worms, stupid. The rain draws them out."

"But . . . will you tell?"

"If I were going to tell, would I suggest you do it?
Where's your sense of logic, for God's sake?"

He thought for a moment. "OK," he said.

She was so happy to see him leave that she didn't
bother to check on what he wore. That wasn't important now. Nothing was important now. Just *Marigolds*.
She could do this, she thought. She could do this.

6

As Gregory turned off Main Street, the rain came down in undulating sheets, pounding the roof of his car and making it impossible to see out the windshield, despite the quickened pace of the wipers. He pulled to the side and waited it out until it let up enough for him to continue safely. But when he came to the driveway of his house, the rain increased again. Just as he stopped, he caught sight of his son crouching under the old maple tree to the left of the house.

"What the hell . . ."

He rolled down the window so he could shout, but the rain attacked with such intensity he had to wind the window up again. He cursed and pounded on his horn.

When Billy heard the car, he instinctively drew his can of newly collected worms closer to him. He debated whether or not he should run for the house. The rain was streaming over the brim of his rain hat and his hands were muddied by the wet earth he had been uncovering. The old overcoat was soaked through. His forehead and cheeks were streaked with dirt because he had been continually wiping his face to clear it of rain. His shoes and socks were soaked and the bottom of his pants was dripping wet.

Gregory saw that his son wasn't moving, so he zipped his jacket up as high as it would go and lunged out of the car. Billy stood up as his father approached. The sight of his father running and crouching added to

Billy's terror and guilt. Gregory grabbed his son's shoulders, squeezing hard, almost lifting him off his feet.

"What the hell are you doing out here? What are you doing?"

"I'm getting worms. It's better in the rain."

"This isn't a rain; it's a flood. Does Lois know you're out here?"

"Yes. She said it was the best time to look for worms."

"Damn it," Gregory said. He straightened up and wiped his face with his jacket sleeve. "You get back into that house and take off those clothes. Then I want you into a hot bath, understand?" Billy nodded quickly, clutching his can of worms as tightly as he could. "All right, let's run for it," Gregory said.

Billy shot forward, his little legs wobbly as he sidestepped puddles and slid over the mud. Gregory followed closely behind but lunged ahead at the front door so they could rush in. He stopped Billy in the alcove and helped him strip off his wet clothes. As he did so he looked for Lois, who obviously wasn't around.

"Lois! Lois!"

The door of her room opened slowly and she emerged as if from a deep sleep. He stood waiting for her, his hands on his hips.

"What's going on?" she said. She had her copy of the *Marigolds* script cradled against her bosom.

"That's precisely what I would like to know. OK, Billy, get to the bathroom," he said. He tapped him gently on the back. Billy started away, looking timidly at Lois. She followed him with her eyes until he was behind her and down the corridor. "Did you tell him to go out in the rain?"

"He wanted worms," she said. She looked as though she would suddenly yawn. "And when it rains like this, it's the best time to gather worms. They come to the earth's surface because the moisture—"

"I'm not interested in worms, damn it. I'm interested in your brother catching cold."

"Oh, Daddy, it's a warm rain, and besides, people don't catch colds from rain. They catch them from viruses."

"I don't want him out there in this kind of weather!" He was shocked by his own explosion. Her calm, rational voice unnerved him. Her condescending attitude made him feel silly for questioning her. He felt his authority challenged.

Lois merely blinked. She stared at him, nonplussed. He pressed his hands against each other in an attempt to put a quick end to the acceleration of his heartbeat.

"It's not too smart to get so excited, Daddy. You know what it can do to your blood pressure."

"Don't tell me about my blood pressure, young lady."

"I'm merely reminding. . . .Did something happen down at the store? Did you have a fight with Mommy?"

"Who the hell do you think you're talking to?"

"I can see you're just not in a good mood," she said and started to turn around to walk away.

"Don't you walk away from me," he said, his teeth clenched. A small pulsating beat had begun in both his temples at once. She stopped, but she didn't turn completely around. "Turn around when I'm talking to you, damn it!"

She turned slowly, her face glowing with anger now. "What is it you want?" she asked, punctuating each word with a controlled indignation.

"First, when we leave you here to take care of Billy, we expect you will take care of him, not push him out into a storm."

"I didn't push—"

"And second, I want to know all about this business with Barbara Gilbert and Bernie Rosen," he said quickly. Any other teenage girl would have been thrown off balance by this, would reveal her guilt, turn red, stammer, look for an escape, and perhaps cry to gain sympathy. But not Lois.

Her expression barely changed. Someone with fingers at her pulse would record only the slightest increase in rate. There was a moment's silence. From the way his daughter was looking at him now, Gregory felt as though *he* had been guilty of the indiscretion.

"What exactly would you like to know?" she said calmly.

"What exactly would I like to know? For your information, Mrs. Gilbert came to our store today. She was very angry, thinking of going to the school authorities. She kept her daughter home all day."

"Oh, really. What did she hope to accomplish by doing that? Barbara's barely passing as it is."

"Look, Lois," he said, trying to regain control of himself. He felt his anger and frustration surging. He was conscious of what this kind of emotional strain could do to him physically. As a man of science and medicine, he was able to visualize the adrenaline flowing into his bloodstream. He thought about the strain on his arteries, the pressure in his circulatory system. He imagined the quick formation of an aneurysm: he saw an artery blow up and explode, the blood rushing forward, the air getting into his system, killing him instantly. He would crumple like a suit of clothes sliding off a hanger and fold up on the floor to die at his daughter's feet. He took a deep breath.

"Look. Mrs. Gilbert accidentally picked up one of their telephones last night and listened in on a conversation you had with Barbara. She heard a lot about some kind of experiment with sex that you've been conducting. Do you deny this?"

"Why should I deny it? I don't like the connotation involved by calling it a sex experiment, though."

"Does this experiment involve . . . does it involve nudity?"

"Yes, but that's—"

"I want it stopped," he said. He said it so quietly, with his eyes so glassy. She was impressed by that. "I don't want to hear anything about it anymore."

"But, Daddy, if you will just consider the scientific value of what—"

"I don't want you doing anything like that in this house or anyone else's house. I don't even want to know the details. I can't tell you how much this has upset your mother."

"I bet."

"And don't you get smart about it either. I'm in business here and—"

"So it boils down to the old profit motive, just like everything else."

"That profit motive is keeping you in fine style and will pay for your college education."

"I'm sure I'll win a full scholarship, Daddy," she said. She said it so matter-of-factly that he nearly smiled. There wasn't a hint of arrogance in her declaration. It was simply a statement of obvious fact. She shook her head. "I would have thought that you, a man of science . . ."

"Forget about this 'man of science' stuff, Lois. What you did was out of bounds because you're involving people who don't see these things as you do."

"I know that," she said, seizing on his reasonable tone of voice, "and I don't expect them to have the same vision. . . ."

"I'm going back to the store," he said, "and I'm going to tell your mother that we had a good discussion about this and the whole thing was simply an idea that got out of hand, that you are ending it right here and now. Do you understand me?"

"I hear you, but I don't understand you."

He stared at her for a moment. Then he shook his head. "I think we're going to have to have a real long talk, you and I, a real long talk. And one of the topics is going to be Demerol." He studied her face, but there wasn't even a quickened eyelid.

"What are you saying now, Daddy? What are you accusing me of now?"

"There is some Demerol I can't account for."

"Why don't you ask Mommy about it?"

"What?"

"Why am I always suspect?"

The cold, piercing look in his daughter's eyes depressed him. It was as though she had become a total stranger, someone consumed by her own intellectual curiosity, a mutation born of science and technology: amoral, indifferent, stoic . . . inhuman. In the beginning it had been cute; then there were moments of pride; but now it was different. It was almost as if . . . he recalled the words of her science teacher in high school: "It's more like fear. The other students act as though they're afraid of her." Was he growing afraid of his own daughter?

"How could you accuse your mother of something like this?"

"How could you accuse me?"

"All right, Lois. I've got to get back, but we'll talk again. We'll talk about all this." He turned quickly and opened the door. She stood watching him. "Make sure Billy takes his bath," he said without looking back. He put his hood up and stepped out, ridiculously happy to leave his own house.

Billy stood in his underwear and waited as Lois dipped her fingers into the water to test its temperature. He was quiet, but cautious and sensitive to his sister's every move. He had heard his father's angry departure: the last statement and the slamming of the front door. He knew that his father was angrier with Lois than he was with him. He expected that Lois would blame him, even though she had told him to go out and look for the worms, so he didn't put up any fuss when she said he would have to take the hot bath now. "Not a half hour from now or an hour from now— now!"

"All right," she said, wiping her hand on the towel.

"It's not too hot?"

"I said all right. Do you think I would put my hand in there if I were going to boil you? I should boil you," she mumbled.

His eyes began to tear. He looked suspiciously at the water and took a step backward.

"I didn't do anything."

"Well, why did you stay out there so long? How can you be so stupid?" She tapped the side of the tub.

"I don't know why I have to take a bath now. I always take it before I go to sleep. I'm not going to sleep," he said, widening his eyes and raising his shoulders.

"Get your underwear off and get in here," she commanded, pointing to the water.

"I don't wanna."

She reached out and pulled him roughly to her. The tears moved freely down his cheeks, but she ignored them and tugged his underwear down his legs and then pushed him back a step so he could walk out of them.

"Get in."

He looked at the water.

"It looks hot."

"That's ridiculous."

He sat down on the edge of the tub and touched the water with his left foot, pulling it back instantly.

"It *is* too hot."

"No, it isn't. Get in there, damn it. Do you think I want to spend my whole life giving you a bath?" She pushed on his lower back and he moved reluctantly into the tub, wailing as his body sank into the water. Then she pressed on his shoulders to force him to sit deeper in the water. He shrieked, but she held him in it. The tears streamed down his cheeks now, then slowly subsided as his body adjusted to the water temperature.

"There, now you see it isn't so bad."

"It is too," he said, but considerably more softly. He was afraid she might let in some more hot water.

"Wash yourself, or do I have to do that too?"

"I can do it." He lifted the washrag and began to move it against the soap.

Lois sat back on the closed toilet seat and stared at him for a few moments. His tiny, methodical motions up and down his arms and over his chest made her think of a cat and the way it worked its tongue over its paws and legs. How was it that a cat had the instinctive know-how to clean itself? She was sure that if children were left to themselves, they would never take a drop of water to their skins.

"Lois?"

"What is it?"

"Why was Daddy yelling about Barbara Gilbert? I heard him."

"It's something you wouldn't understand. Just a lot of confusion."

"Is Mommy going to come home mad, too?"

"Who knows? I imagine there'll be some hysterics," she added, more to herself than to him.

"What's hysterics?"

"Exaggerated emotional behavior. I'm sure it'll take its usual course with her: she'll develop headaches and a stomachache. She might even bring on a fever."

"From hyster . . . hyster . . ."

"Hysterics. Of course," Lois said, assuming her usual pedantic posture. "Emotional upset often causes physical difficulty in the body. The technical term is psychosomatic. I recently read that psychosomatic illness is responsible for over half of all physical illness," she added. Billy had already let his attention drift away, but the next sentence brought him back. "I'm convinced that's what caused Daddy's stroke."

"What's Daddy's stroke?"

"You don't remember when he was in the hospital, do you?" she asked, for the moment intrigued with the depth of an infant's memory.

"Nope."

"I think Mommy told you he went to visit Uncle

George anyway. One of her protective white lies," Lois added with a smirk. "Keep scrubbing."

"Why did she lie?"

"Because Mother is unable to face reality herself, much less force others to face it. Mother suffers from a variety of neuroses."

"I don't know what that means."

"Just wash up and get out, will you? I have things to do."

"Can I help?"

" 'Can I help?' " she mimicked. " 'Can I help?' I told you, when I need your help for anything, I'll ask you. You're not old enough yet to comprehend my projects."

She got up and left the bathroom. For a few moments she just stood outside the door, listening to her brother splash away in the tub. She hadn't counted on her father's sneaking up like that and confronting her with Mrs. Gilbert's story, so she knew she didn't perform the best she could. Now she would have to abandon the project. If there was anything she hated vehemently, it was leaving a project uncompleted.

Billy had settled himself comfortably in his tub now and she could hear him start up his ridiculous game of naval warfare, using the soap as a ship and bombing it with the washrag. His mouth puffed and exploded with the imagined sounds of war. Before she dismissed it altogether, however, she considered how quickly young children, especially young boys, acted out aggressive tendencies. Were we inherently violent? Was it part of our nature to destroy? Perhaps war, violence, was inevitable, even welcomed and enjoyed.

She considered her brother in more detail, recalling how he liked to go outside and "bomb" ants for hours on end. He'd find a place on the lawn where they were abundant and drop rocks on them, accompanying his attacks with the appropriate sound effects. Never once did he think about the fact that he was killing and destroying life wantonly. Lois didn't moralize about that, and she would never lecture him concerning the evil nature of his play. She wasn't thinking of it from a moral point of view. What amazed her now, when she gave it some thought, was the fact that her brother just did it quite thoughtlessly.

She concluded, therefore, that there was nothing innate that would lead man to an essential respect for life or the essence of life. Once it was taught or acquired, however, it could be radically changed. Witness what had happened during the Second World War and how people treated one another, especially in the concentration camps, she thought.

She looked back toward her brother. Wouldn't it be interesting to change one of his attitudes or imprint a new one? Of course, it would be so much easier if he were only a year or a year and a half old. She remembered the way babies were made to hate nature in the novel *Brave New World*. Beautiful flowers were placed just across the room from them and they were allowed to crawl toward them. But when they touched them, they were given vicious electrical shocks. After a while they wouldn't go near any flowers.

Surely there was something like that she could do with her brother. She would give it some thought, but whatever it was, she had to be extra careful about it so her parents never became aware of what was happening. Of course, that wouldn't be too difficult once the summer started and she was left in charge of Billy for so many more hours of the day. Summer was still some months away, but she could plan and prepare for it.

The idea was really starting to excite her. There were great possibilities. The most important thing and the great advantage was that Billy would exist in the controlled environment she created. He couldn't escape from it because it was his home. Why hadn't she thought of this before?

Actually, she owed these new thoughts and new ideas to her father, even to Billy himself. An intelligent person, she thought, always found a way to turn events to his advantage. She was proud of herself and bouyed by the potentials. It had the effect of changing her entire demeanor when she reentered the bathroom.

"Aren't you finished?" Her voice was soft, melodic. It made Billy think of his mother. "Here you told me that water was too hot, and now you won't get out of it."

"It was. At first."

"Come on, I'll help you dry off," she said and took a towel off the rack. He stepped out of the tub and she wrapped him quickly, rubbing him over the back and shoulders vigorously but affectionately, with a motherly concern. "That feels good, huh?"

"Yeps."

"Yep, not yeps. In fact, yes, not yep. I wish I had someone to do this for me."

"I'll do it for you anytime."

She actually laughed. He turned around to be sure she was laughing honestly and not strangely as she often did.

"I'm getting hungry," he said.

"Good, because we're having a great supper. And no nibbling before," she warned, taking on a serious parental look. He didn't mind, because she was smiling, and as she finished wiping his body she was humming.

Gregory Wilson was intensely disturbed by the way his daughter had reacted to the confrontation, but he wasn't eager to discuss it with Dorothy. However, she knew that it hadn't gone well. She could tell from the way he withdrew to the back of the store and busied himself with organizing supplies.

"So? I don't understand," she said the moment the store was empty again. "You told her and she admitted it?"

"Just what I said. It's all over with. Just teenage stupidity, typical young person's curiosity. You know, like 'Let's play doctor.' "

"At her age?"

"People mature at different rates," he replied, but she knew he wasn't telling her everything. He was never a hard man to read, but lately, because of the pressures of the business and the effects of his medication, he had become somewhat irritable. Despite her efforts to prevent it, Dorothy Wilson had grown terribly insecure ever since Greg's CVS. Just last year, Harvey Kaplow had suffered a fatal heart attack at the age of thirty-nine, leaving his wife Miriam and three children. It had been one of the small hamlet's biggest tragedies. Naturally, just like every middle-aged woman in town, she envisioned herself in Miriam's shoes. At least Miriam had a large family to fall back on: four brothers and three sisters, both her parents still alive and in reasonably good health. But Dorothy no longer had her parents and she had been an only child. All Greg's relatives lived far away. She felt totally dependent on Greg; he was her whole life.

They didn't have the type of business she could continue on her own, in the event something happened to him. He was the pharmacist. All she could hope for would be a quick sale of the store and then . . . then what? She hadn't done any other work since high school. There was no way to retool, develop a skill, or go back to college without offending Greg. What would she use as an excuse: "Well, you had a CVS, so I'd better prepare for the fatal moment"? She had never had any other career interests. How could she start to develop them now?

If she asked him too many questions or the same question too many times, if she disagreed with him over anything, no matter how insignificant, and he reacted badly—raising his voice, waving his arms, getting red in the face—she would cringe in anticipation of his collapsing in a cerebral hemorrhage. She felt like someone perpetually tiptoeing about. Her world was filled with shelves of dainty china. A clumsy move here or there or a violent gesture could shatter their lives. Lois knew these things just as well as she did. Why was the girl doing things to provoke him? Didn't she care?

As they started for home at the end of the day, Dorothy sensed that he wanted to talk about what was bothering him.

"It's got to do with Lois, doesn't it?"

"What?"

"Whatever's been on your mind since you came back to the store. Don't tell me you really had a good talk with her."

"I had a good talk. I had a good talk. It's just that this has set me to thinking more about the kids in general, that's all."

"How do you mean?"

"Maybe Billy ought to go to sleep-away camp this summer and Lois ought to be with us more in the store. She stays to herself too much, working on her experiments, keeping her nose in one science book after another."

"Isn't that what I've always said?"

"I'm not saying I don't like her reading and learning, but . . . I suppose she should be around all kinds of people more often."

"I knew that science stuff would get her in trouble. I never liked those animals."

"I'm not faulting her for her scientific interest," he said, his voice a bit more testy. "She's been doing experiments for as long as I can remember. Why, as soon as she could crawl, she was playing with ants and worms. She never cared for the toys we'd buy her."

"Don't I know it."

"But it's not that. . . ." He pulled into the driveway, but he didn't shut off the engine. "I think she spends too much time by herself in general, and with college coming up . . . I mean, being away from home and all, being forced to meet new people . . ."

"They'll think she's a weirdo kid, just like they do around here," Dorothy said quickly.

"Yeah, I suppose so."

"Kind of late for us to be worrying about it, don't you think?"

"I don't know."

"What do you mean? There is something more, isn't there?" She stared at him a moment and then turned quickly toward the house as if she expected Lois to be on the front porch. Gregory shut off the engine. She looked at him again, a realization being born. "You're afraid for Billy, aren't you?"

"I didn't say that."

"You don't have to say it. My God, Greg, why?"

"I said I didn't say that. Now, don't go off half cocked like you always do and let your imagination take over."

"Well, what do you expect me to do?" she whispered. "You act strange all afternoon, and now you hint at terrible things . . . that Gilbert woman acts as though Lois were some kind of monster . . ."

"I haven't hinted at anything terrible. If you're going to start getting hysterical—"

"I'm not hysterical."

"I knew I shouldn't have said anything. I knew it, damn it."

"Why not? Don't you think I ought to know everything about our children? And the doctor told you how bad it is for you to keep things to yourself."

"This is good for me, I suppose?"

"Is there something else going on, something besides what happened with the Gilbert girl? Is that it?"

"No. Look, just forget it." He got out of the car quickly and slammed the door.

"Greg . . ."

He walked to the house quickly. She followed him, but by the time she got inside, he was halfway up the stairs. Frustrated, she walked slowly to the kitchen. Lois had set the table and had the dinner nearly prepared: the roast was in the oven, the vegetables were steaming, the potatoes were baked. Billy was seated at the table, his hair neatly combed. He was wearing a clean shirt and a sharply pressed pair of pants. Even his shoes looked shined.

"Hi," Lois said as she took a jar of cranberry juice out of the refrigerator. "How was business?"

For a moment Dorothy could only stare at her daughter. With everything so perfect, the potential for an enjoyable, quiet meal so real, she considered whether or not she wanted to pursue Greg's intimations, much less discuss the Gilbert incident. Lois looked at her quizzically.

"Something wrong, Mom?"

"You know what happened today at the store?"

"Oh, yes," Lois said, still in a pleasant voice. "Daddy and I had a good discussion about it." Billy was about to say something, but Lois gave him a piercing glance and he went back to playing with his silverware. "Don't worry about it."

"I . . . I think we all better sit down and . . . and take stock of everything," Dorothy said. She clasped her right hand to stop it from shaking.

"Whatever you think, Mother," Lois said. The smile had left her face and she had that penetrating investigative look in her eyes, the look Dorothy dreaded so. It was unnerving.

"Maybe after supper. I'd better go up and change and wash up."

"I took a hot bath," Billy said.

"Oh?"

"Because I was in the rain too long."

"The rain?"

"The little idiot went out there looking for worms and stayed throughout the downpour. Didn't Daddy tell you?"

"No. Weren't you watching him?"

"I was engrossed in this book—"

"One of those damn science books again," Dorothy began. "I—"

"Oh, no, Mother," Lois interrupted, going to the side of the counter by the refrigerator. She picked up the *Marigolds* script. "It's the new school play. I'm thinking about trying out for it."

"Really?"

"Yes, you know, the spring show."

"Well, I was in a few plays. Maybe I can give you some pointers for tryouts."

"Thank you," Lois said.

Dorothy stood there for a moment, feeling totally confused. Maybe Greg was right; maybe she was imagining too much. "I'll be right down," she said.

After her mother left the kitchen, a slight smile returned to Lois's face. It was so easy to manipulate some people, she thought. In fact, it was easy to manipulate most people. She turned and looked at Billy, who was puzzled by her smile.

"Mommy's not mad?" he asked.

"Mommy'll be what I want her to be," Lois said.

He looked at the empty doorway and then back at Lois, who had gone to take out the roast. He didn't know why, but he was feeling afraid again.

What made it worse was that he couldn't tell anyone about it, because he didn't know what he would tell.

7

"It wasn't my fault," Barbara Gilbert whispered. "I'll tell you about it later," she added quickly as Mr. Wasserman, their math teacher, entered the room. He was a strict disciplinarian with a military demeanor. He had actually been a math instructor at a naval officers' school for a few years before entering public education. Lois liked him for his businesslike manner. Most of the kids respected him for his fair and evenhanded ways, but the class cutups had difficulty leaving their more loosely run classes and adjusting to him.

"There's nothing to tell," Lois replied without looking up from her textbook. "Your mother told it all."

"I've got to go right home after school for a week."

"How juvenile."

"Lois Wilson," Mr. Wasserman said. Barbara gasped, expecting a reprimand for talking after the period bell rang. Here she was getting Lois in trouble again.

"Yes?"

"Mr. Van Dancer wants to see you. Go to the guidance office now and maybe you'll only miss the homework review," he added, obviously displeased with the administrative request.

"Maybe your mother's having my schedule changed so I can't influence you," Lois said, rising. The other class members watched her with vague curiosity as she left the room.

When she arrived at the guidance office, Mrs. Stanley, the secretary, told her to go right into Mr. Van Dancer's office. He looked up expectantly, a wide smile on his soft, circular face. He was a pudgy man with hazel-green eyes set deeply under a wide, protruding forehead. His jowls quivered when he spoke, and he had a habit of puckering his lips at the ends of sentences. There were a lot of jokes about him because he rarely came out of his office. He conducted all his business behind his desk. Weighing two hundred fifty pounds at a height of five feet five, he did seem poured into his chair.

Mr. Van Dancer unfolded his short, stubby fingers and pushed himself back in his seat.

"Lois, sit down, sit down," he said. She didn't even look at the indicated seat.

"I'd like to get back to math class as soon as possible. We're going on to new work."

"Of course, of course. Very briefly," he said, looking down at the papers on his desk rather than at Lois, "the school is going to participate in a rather special program with the community college. Maybe you've heard something about it already. I know how fast news travels around here." He smiled and paused to see if she had. Lois only smirked and changed the weight of her body to her other foot. "Er . . . it's called the college-in-escrow program. Have you heard anything about it?"

"I'm afraid I don't have time to tune myself in to the gossip line, Mr. Van Dancer."

"Well, I'm . . . right, and that's why I'm offering this to you. We're not offering it to everyone at the start. We want the program to get under way first and then . . ."

"What is this program?"

"Very simply, we're going to send over some of our high-powered seniors to take some college courses.

This college credit will be accepted by whatever college they eventually attend. We're just starting it now, so you can pick up maybe three, six, even nine credits. You would be able to go during your last-period study hall, for example, and anytime after school or even during the evening."

"I don't know, the community college? I wouldn't expect—"

"Now, don't look down your nose, Lois. First consider some of these courses," he said, lifting the sheet off his desk and holding it out to her. She stepped forward and read the offerings.

"I could take any one of these?"

"Even more than one. During the school day, we're going to arrange for transportation if anyone needs it. Because this is a pilot program, the school will assume the tuition. It really is an experiment of sorts."

"I'm only interested in one course," she said quickly.

"Don't be hasty, now. You could satisfy a number of prerequisites at any of the colleges you've applied to for admission, and—"

"Only one," she said, "and from the times indicated here, I could take it Tuesday and Thursday evenings."

"Which one is that?" he asked, the excitement dying out of his voice.

"Introduction to Behavioral Science with Professor McShane."

"Um." He took the list back and looked at it for a moment. "I don't know anything about this McShane. He's one of their newer teachers."

"I'm not interested in teachers. I'm interested in the content of the course."

Mr. Van Dancer looked at her and nodded, the smile completely gone from his face. Thank God, he thought, that I don't have a daughter like this.

"OK, Lois, if you're sure you don't want any other course . . ."

"I'm sure."

"I see. Well, I'll put you down and make all the

arrangements. You'll be starting next week. I want to
remind you, as I will everyone else in the program, that
you're representing our school in a unique educational
experiment. We'd expect you to give it your full energy
and we'd remind you that the future of the program will
depend on how successful you and the rest of the pilot
group are."

"I don't think you'll have to worry about me, Mr.
Van Dancer. Now can I go back to my math class?"

"Certainly."

"By the way," Lois said, pausing in the doorway, "I
hope you didn't base your selection of high-school
students solely on grades. Functioning on a college
level will require a greater sense of responsibility and
independence."

"Yes, Lois, we have given it every consideration.
Thank you for being concerned," he added, restraining
his desire to be sarcastic. She looked at him for a
moment and then left. After the door closed, Mr. Van
Dancer realized he had broken out in a sweat. He
looked at the community college offerings again. Introduction to Behavioral Science, eh? he thought.

"I don't know who you are, McShane," he mumbled,
"but you're in for an experience when you start this
class next week." He smiled to himself and buzzed Mrs.
Stanley so she would get the next student on the list.

"I heard what Barbara's mother did," Bernie Rosen
said, stopping Lois in the hall between classes. "Does
this mean our experiment is over?"

"Temporarily shelved," Lois replied.

"Well, I just wanted you to know I'm still available."

"I appreciate that," Lois said.

"You appreciate it?" He shook his head. "I see
you're carryin' that *Marigolds* script. Goin' out for it
today?"

"Maybe."

"Good. Maybe I'll come to the tryouts to watch. I
might even try out myself." He kept that wide, idiot

smile on his face. He still had it after school when he sat
in the back of the auditorium at the start of tryouts.
Carl Oates, the play's director, stood behind the po-
dium placed down center stage to explain the rules. He
was a tall, thin man with a pronounced Adam's apple.
When he spoke, it bobbed up and down against his
skin, threatening to tear out and bounce away like a
wayward golf ball. All the girls admired his thick, wavy,
dark brown hair, meticulously trimmed and blown dry.
He taught the twelfth-grade English electives. Many of
the students liked him because he carried his flair for
the dramatic into the classroom, making his daily
lessons performances. Lois didn't like him. She
thought, to use Shakespearean terms, that he was too
much art, too little matter. He never cared much for
her, but he was genuinely surprised by her appearance
at the tryouts and somewhat curious how she would
perform.

"Those of you who are familiar with the play can
read a specific part, if you wish. If you are not familiar
with the play, I would like girls to read pages five
through eight, and boys to read pages forty to forty-
two. You are trying out for a part in a play, so you are
encouraged to accompany your reading with whatever
gestures, mannerisms, or postures you think appropriate. I will be sitting way in the back, so I would
recommend you keep projection in mind. I assume
everyone interested in being in the play has signed this
casting list?" He stopped and looked around the auditorium.

The high-school theater was a traditional structure
with three groups of rows facing the stage. The students
trying out for parts were spread all over the place, with
only the veterans of other plays seated right up front,
eager to read. Lois had taken a front seat stage left. She
sat with her books in her lap, her own script on top.
When she had entered the auditorium, a number of
students looked surprised. Her presence caused much
discussion.

"I'll just read your names off as they were placed on the casting list," Mr. Oates said. He called the first name and started off the stage.

Lois was twenty-third on the list. When her turn came, she stood up abruptly and with such vigor that it looked as though she had been jabbed in the rear with a hatpin. That caused a small tittering wave of giggles across the auditorium. Mr. Oates tapped his pen on the top of the seat before him and the giggles subsided. Lois started toward the stage. She had memorized the section she wanted to read, but she carried her script anyway.

Her posture was as erect and as stiff as always. She approached the lectern as though she were about to make her valedictorian speech. When she got there, she opened the script to her pages, set it down neatly, looked up at the audience, and then, with an unexpected robotlike jerkiness, stepped to the right. To the students in the audience that was comical because it looked as if she had gone up there to satirize students trying out for a play. Even Mr. Oates permitted a slight smile to form on his face.

For her audition, Lois had chosen the little girl's presentation at the science fair, but there was nothing little-girlish about Lois's voice. She sounded even more pedantic than usual. Taking on a lecturer's tone of voice, she recited the speech with her hands hanging dead at her sides. Instead of looking out at the audience, she looked up into the lights. Her stiff, condescending delivery appeared more and more comical to the student audience, which was peppered with kids who were unsympathetic to Lois from the start. Someone produced a Bronx cheer, and that caused a louder ripple of laughter. Mr. Oates tapped his pen again, but another student delivered an exaggerated burp and the audience roared. Lois seemed oblivious of it all, and that made it all funnier. Mr. Oates stood up to see if he could catch the troublemakers. Someone in the back broke a blown-up paper bag. The explosion brought

Lois back to reality. She stopped and looked down at the students in the audience.

They were all laughing now, even Bernie Rosen, who was actually doubling up. She turned to the right and saw Barbara Gilbert covering her fat face, her body shaking with a spasm of giggles. Even Mr. Oates looked ridiculous, pounding his pen on the back of a chair. No one could hear it anyway.

Lois turned abruptly, reached over to the lectern, and got her script. She started off, stopped, and walked to the edge of the stage. When she got there, she took the script in her hand and flung it out like a Frisbee. It sailed into the lights, its pages flapping. A group of kids went for it as though it were a home-run ball hit by a major league star. Mr. Oates ran down the aisle shouting.

Walking off the stage quickly, Lois picked up her books and started up the left aisle. Students were yelling, "Beautiful, Lois," "Great, Lois," "An Academy Award performance, Lois." She closed the auditorium door behind her, shutting out the jeers and laughter.

When she got to Sandburg, she didn't stop at the store as she had promised her mother she would do. Instead, she started walking home, her attention riveted directly in front of her for the first quarter mile. Then she slowed down and eventually stopped. She stood there concentrating on her heartbeat and breathing. She was determined to slow them down. She took longer, deeper breaths, calming herself. When she was satisfied, she started walking again, but at a much slower pace.

Other than her own, there were no voices on this country road. The late March rains had discolored trees, making the white birch gray and the brown maples darker. The world looked muddy and soft. As always, she began to analyze herself, reviewing a list of emotions and feelings she was experiencing.

She had chastised herself for auditioning in the first

place. What if she had gotten the part? It wouldn't have been very enjoyable to work with those other kids, and Mr. Oates most probably didn't understand the play he had chosen to direct, she thought. Now she criticized herself for rationalizing. "I'm simply trying to find a way to explain my own failure," she said aloud. It was as if she had an invisible partner.

Then she thought, I would have gotten the part and done well if it weren't for some of those jealous students who caused a commotion.

"Projection," she said, "just another kind of alibi. You're trying to relieve your own guilty feelings by projecting the blame onto someone else.

"I'm going to face the facts. I'm no actress; it's not in me to be an actress. I have a different genetic plan. I'll be applauded on a different stage and my work will be ten times as significant as any actress's work. People will know my name, and it will be because I have given them a greater gift than a good performance in a play."

Those thoughts revived her somewhat, although ultimately she had to admit to herself that any kind of rejection was painful. She walked on. Her parents had told Billy to get off the bus in town, expecting that she would do the same and there would be no one home for him. The first thing she did when she got home was release her bat. It flew to where the wall met the ceiling and pressed itself into the crevice. She lay back on her bed and watched it shudder and move a few inches to the left, a few inches to the right.

How should it behave? she wondered. It had been shut into an alien environment, ripped out of the world it knew and made completely disoriented. She fed it, but it didn't eat well. That was to be expected. Now, gaining freedom, it was afraid to take much more space than it had been confined to while imprisoned. Would a human being confined or imprisoned for a long period of time react the same way at first? Most likely, she thought. She wished she could put some of those idiots in the auditorium in a world as dark and as confining as the bat's.

The ringing of the phone interrupted her thoughts. It was her mother.

"Why didn't you stop in town?"

"I didn't feel like it."

"But we told Billy to stop here. He's been waiting for you." Lois didn't reply. "Did you go out for the play?"

"Yes."

"How'd you do?"

"I didn't do well. As a matter of fact, I made a fool of myself."

"Oh, I'm sure you didn't do that. You probably did better than you think."

"I walked off the stage, Mother. I don't know what made me think I could do it in the first place."

"Why shouldn't you be able to do it? A girl with your gifts. You'll try again. You'll see, it'll get easier. It's always hard to do something new at first, but once—"

"I already know what I can and can't do. I can't act."

"If you don't try different things, you'll never know what you can and can't do."

"I don't have to make a fool of myself to know," Lois said and quickly added before her mother could continue, "I can't be a cheerleader, and I can't be the prom queen, and I can't be the most popular girl in the class." She was losing control of herself; she could feel it. "And I can't get a steady boyfriend or model designer jeans. And I probably won't get engaged or marry a lawyer-doctor and live happily ever after in Westport. Do you understand?"

"Lois . . ."

"I am me. I do not belong on yearbook covers." She slammed the phone down. The instant she did it she regretted it, not because of what she had done to her mother, but because of what she had done to herself. It was easy to analyze.

"Displaced aggression," she said, turning to the

image of herself reflected in the mirror across from the phone. "You wanted to yell at Mr. Oates and the students, even yourself, but instead, you yelled at your mother.

"She deserves it, though," she replied.

"Good God, what am I doing? Developing a split personality?" She forced herself to be silent. This matter is closed, she thought and walked back to her room. She flopped on the bed again, but it took her a few moments to realize that the bat was no longer cowering on the wall. It was gone. A quick perusal of her room brought her to the realization that it was loose somewhere in the house. It was still loose somewhere when the family gathered for supper.

From the way her parents studied her and eyed each other at dinner that night, she knew that they had discussed her and made up their minds about something. The conversation that was about to take place was predesigned. She imagined her father even saying that he'd do most of the talking. They were unusually quiet during the meal, and when they did speak, they directed most of their words to Billy. She began to prepare herself mentally, finding a strange excitement in the anticipation.

"Billy, you can go into the living room and watch television. Mommy and I want to talk to Lois."

"Why can't I talk, too?"

"Because it's a conversation only adults would understand," Lois said quickly.

Gregory stared at her a moment, shot a quick glance at Dorothy, and then turned to Billy.

"Lois is partially right. It's not a conversation you would enjoy."

Billy got up and Lois began collecting the dishes from the table.

"We'll do that later," Dorothy said. Lois sat down again and looked calmly at her mother.

"Now, your mother told me about your outburst on the telephone," Gregory began.

"I'm sorry," Lois said. "It was displaced aggression. I should have sublimated my anger. I usually do."

"Well, the phone call isn't the entire reason for this conversation," Gregory said, "but since you're so analytical about yourself, let us be also. I think the outburst is really symptomatic of many things. Of course, there are the usual academic pressures. I can sympathize with that, even though you make much more demand of yourself than is being made of you by the school."

"Are you listening to him?" Dorothy asked. From her perspective, it looked as though Lois were smiling and thinking of something else. She was indeed enjoying this so far. She was glad her father had chosen to take a distinctly formal tone. She welcomed the opportunity to intellectualize about herself.

"I'm listening. I'm just not sure what is the point of this entire conversation."

Lois could see that her father did not relish the task. There was a redness about his cheeks. His eyes were small, his mouth tight. The veins in his temples rose against the skin. For a moment she considered his condition and wondered if it was wise for there to be this kind of tension. Usually her mother put an end to such things before they became intense.

"We think we've reached something of a crisis here," Gregory said.

"Crisis?" Lois looked at her mother, who wore a face of stone. "What do you mean,'we've reached'?"

"We, meaning the family. What happens to one of us happens to all of us. Now," he said, trying to achieve a calmer, more controlled voice, "your mother and I have been discussing the situation."

"All this because of Barbara's mother?"

"It's not just that, although that's a manifestation of it."

"Of what?"

"Your fixation on scientific experimentation."

"One thing leads to another," Dorothy said quickly, anticipating Lois's challenge.

"These experiments are educational and interesting, and it's admirable for you to want to do some of them, but I think they're getting out of hand."

"Out of hand?"

"Bringing it all home. You don't take a break from it, Lois," he said pleadingly. "You've closed yourself into your private world so that when you have an opportunity to participate in other things—"

"Like the play? You think I deliberately failed at that. What do you think I am, some kind of Frankenstein?" They were both silent. She saw them as her accusers rather than as her parents. They reminded her of the kids in the auditorium. She regretted worrying about the tension this conversation would cause her father.

"Well, you don't have the self-confidence you should have, Lois."

"That's ridiculous."

"No, it isn't," Gregory insisted.

"It's a ridiculous way to rationalize my failure and to alleviate Mother's feelings of guilt."

"What are you talking about, my feelings of guilt?"

"Yes, you think it's a reflection on you and your glorified years of cheerleading and prom queening."

"That's unfair, Lois," Gregory said. "It's even cruel."

"Nevertheless, it's true."

"That's enough," he snapped. "I've been somewhat blind here, and your behavior right now confirms it. Now, we've decided there will be some changes."

"What changes?"

"First, I'm not going to hire a second counterboy this summer. You'll work in the store with us."

"But what about Billy?"

"He's going to sleep-away camp. Second, there are to be no more experiments with animals in this house."

"I want my pantry returned to being a pantry," Dorothy added. "A house isn't a place for rats and snakes and . . . all sorts of creatures."

"You never complained before."

"She complained. I just didn't listen," Gregory said.

Lois felt a sense of panic. Her eyes moved quickly from side to side. She sat back in the chair. Her parents, sitting across from her, looked threatening. They gaped at her. She thought herself trapped like one of her rats in the cage. Alternatives, options, she screamed to herself. They're putting me in a maze.

"You've got to start thinking about college," her father was saying. She could hear the words, understand and record them, but she wasn't really listening. "You've got to get out more, meet people, become less introverted."

"It's for the best. Believe us," her mother said.

"We're not saying we want you to give up scientific inquiry," Gregory said, "but you've got to develop some other interests too. We wouldn't do this if we didn't think it was important for you."

"Daddy's right."

They were both afraid of silence now, she could see. They had to keep talking. It struck her then just how vulnerable they were, and that gave her a renewed sense of confidence.

"All right," she said. "If this is what you want. I'll take my stuff out of the pantry."

"You won't regret it," Dorothy said, cheered by Lois's quick surrender, but Gregory wasn't as believing.

"It might be a good idea for you to start spending an hour or so in the drugstore now," he said.

"I'll try," Lois said, "but I should tell you that I've been chosen to participate in a pilot program involving college courses for college credit."

"I know," Gregory said. "We received a call from the school. It's a good idea. What are you going to take?" he asked, but before Lois could respond, they heard Billy's scream. He came running into the kitchen.

"The bat! The bat!" he shouted, pointing toward the living room.

"What bat?"

"A bat? Oh, God, in the house?" Dorothy said, cringing.

Gregory got up and went out. Lois followed slowly, Billy right behind her. Lois's fugitive bat had found its way into the living room and settled itself on the far wall, just above the television set.

"How the hell . . ." Gregory went for the broom. "Keep your eye on it," he said. He returned quickly and swatted it hard. It practically bounced off the wall and onto the rug. "Get the dustpan," he ordered. Billy went for it and brought it back to his father. Gregory swept the crushed animal off the rug. He looked at Lois for a moment and then took it outside to dump it into the garbage can.

"There must be more," Dorothy said when he returned. She was close to hysteria. "How can I sleep, thinking about them? We've got to get a professional exterminator."

"I'll call one in the morning," Gregory said softly, eager to placate her. "Don't worry."

"Go up and check our bedroom. Go on."

"Take it easy. I'll do it," he said. He looked inquisitively at Lois. "I thought we had gotten them all."

"I thought so, too," Lois said.

He knew she was lying. Despite her inscrutable face and her unquivering voice, he knew. She was something different, his daughter, something colder, harder, tougher than he imagined. Perhaps it was too late. He looked down at Billy, who bit his lower lip and stared up at him.

"You see," Dorothy said, her voice high-pitched

now. "You see, you and your damn animals. They think they can all live here."

"That's silly, Mother."

"It's not silly. It's not silly!"

"Dorothy, get hold of yourself."

"It doesn't matter, Mother," Lois said. "I'm not going to have any animals in the house anymore, remember?"

"Oh, God," Dorothy said. "Oh, God. Go up ahead of me, Greg. Go on."

"I'm going, I'm going." He paraded toward the stairs, pounding each step in his anger and frustration as he ascended. Dorothy, still cowering, followed slowly behind. To Lois, they looked somewhat comical.

So they didn't want her working with the animals. Her mother wanted her pantry, and her father wanted her in the store. Yet they wanted her to keep her scientific interest. How interesting. How quaint.

She could do that—she could stop working with animals and yet experiment and learn. Her smile caught Billy's attention. She was looking at him in the strangest way.

"Boy, that was scary."

"It shouldn't have been," Lois said, reaching out and putting her hand on his head. "You should have remembered what I told you about bats and you should have been unafraid."

"I couldn't help it," he said.

"Yes, you could, Billy. You will. I'll help you. I'll show you more."

"Now?" he asked.

"Not right now, but soon. Soon."

She drew him a little closer to her, and they both stood there listening to their mother's hysterical ranting upstairs.

8

       Professor Kevin McShane believed in coming late for his own classes. As an expert in behavioral psychology, he realized that anticipation whetted the appetite and the expectation. He especially enjoyed his first class with new students, comparing and contrasting them with animals in a maze.

"You're in a controlled environment and I'm in total control of it. But don't get too depressed about that. I'm about to show you how you move from one controlled environment to another all day, every day of your life," he added, the twinkle in his powder-blue eyes complementing the tease in his voice, the dimples in his cheeks. He wore his thin red hair short, nearly military style. At six feet tall, he had a medium frame with athletic shoulders and arms. All of his gestures were gracefully slow, suggesting that he was rarely an impulsive man. Everything about him was neat and well organized. He had that old-fashioned Joe College look with his pullover sweaters and corduroy jeans.

Overwhelmingly popular with the student body, other faculty members, and staff, the thirty-year-old McShane would have been the most sought-after bachelor on campus if it weren't for his serious and ever-growing relationship with Sherry Madeo, a tall, slim, Lauren Bacall type who was a four-year veteran of the drama department. Jealous secretaries had to admit they made a handsome couple as they walked over the campus or sat drinking coffee in the commons. Those who sat in on their conversations often witnessed a continual but friendly debate about the values of the sciences versus the humanities.

His developing romance did not prevent McShane from being a flirt in class. He loved to tease his female students, many of whom developed their own fantasy relationships with him before his classes were two weeks into session.

"You are all probably familiar with the love relationship between the male and the female black widow. The female works hard at attracting a male to fertilize her eggs, and once this is done, she kills him. Is not the lesson clear? Men, don't overlook nature as a primer. Remember Hamlet's speech to Ophelia," McShane would say and then look at the most sexually attractive girl in his class and recite: " 'I have heard of your paintings too, well enough. God hath given you one face, and you make yourselves another. You jig, you amble, and you lisp. You nickname God's creatures, and make your wantonness your ignorance. Go to, I'll no more on 't; it hath made me mad. . . .' "

He filled the class with laughter, but just as quickly as he had driven them to hilarity, he would change expression and drive home a serious theme: the behavior of animals in nature give us clues to human behavior. Nothing must be overlooked. The perceptive mind sees some truth in the life processes of the smallest insects. He challenged his students to be aware and to be alive. "For what distinguishes you from inanimate objects? Surely not the mere pulsation of protoplasm."

Normally, his classes were jammed; his registrations were quickly filled, so it was not without a certain amount of persuasion that the dean of students finally convinced him to participate in the new pilot program with area high-school students. Often resembling a marine recruiter, Bob Stigman hammered home his arguments.

"Our enrollment has been steadily declining. The

community college system has been growing everywhere. Our out-of-towners are finding it less expensive to remain in their own areas. Staff cutbacks are inevitable. This is a way to slow the attrition.

"And besides, it's the first function of a community college to provide educational opportunity for its community. Don't look down your nose at these high-school students, Kevin. They're the choice. Right now they're being selected carefully. You're going to find them more challenging than what you've got now."

"What I've got now are humanoids, not humans. Sometimes I think I've slipped into the land of the dead. Do you know in some classes I'm answering my own questions? What I do is ask a question, wait a significant amount of time, and then point to the back or the side of the room and say, 'That's right,' and then give the answer. They turn around to see who spoke. They don't even know if someone had or hadn't."

"Exactly. That's why I know you're going to enjoy this more than anyone else. These are the kids that are destined for the Ivy League, scholarship winners, the gifted. You're going to love it."

"A high-school kid is a high-school kid is a high-school kid."

"Just give it a chance."

"I must be crazy. Put me down," he said. "Maybe I can use it for a paper on the adolescent's learning problems."

And so it was with something less than cautious optimism that Professor Kevin McShane walked toward his classroom to begin his part of what was now known as the college-in-escrow program. He decided to be even more unorthodox than usual in a quick effort to weed out the "babies."

This class consisted of fourteen students. He noted immediately how they were scattered over the room:

groups of three and four, probably unified by their common schools, and one solitary student up front by herself. Without even introducing himself, he threw out a question.

"Why these little clusters all over my classroom?"

There was a moment of stunned silence. Then Lois Wilson looked up from her book.

"It's simply a ramification of the herd theory. Man is by nature gregarious. This is a new, and therefore threatening, experience," she added, turning slightly and gesturing toward the remainder of the class, "so they clump to face it with a greater sense of security."

Most of the other students grimaced at being referred to as a clump. McShane's eyes widened as he looked hard at this pedantic-sounding girl. With her wide-rimmed glasses set on the bony bridge of her thin nose, her mouth turned down at the corners, her hair pulled tightly behind her head, she looked like the classical sexually frustrated scholarly type. And yet there was something about the way this girl main-tained her posture and held her gaze that led him to believe she was different, more confident, stronger. If only Sherry could see her. He made a mental note to point her out.

"And you don't have that need, Miss . . . ?"

"Wilson, Lois Wilson. Of course. What I've done is subdue it."

"Conquered instinct, eh?" He started to smile.

"Put the lid on it. I don't believe we can conquer instinct in the sense that we can literally destroy it. Of course, we can and do sublimate, but under the right conditions even the most so-called civilized man can regress into purely instinctive behavior."

"Why do you say 'so-called civilized'?" This girl was going to offer some challenge, he thought.

"In context, the word is judgmental. We've given it a positive connotation, but there are some, if you'll excuse me," she said in an obviously condescending tone of voice, "so-called uncivilized people who might very well be living more fruitful lives."

He stared at her for a moment, trying to imagine the parents who had produced this kid. Probably loaded her room with encyclopedias and forbade her to watch any television but *Sesame Street* and *National Geographic* specials. McShane was about to go on when he realized the rest of the class had turned into an audience. He quickly gazed at his registration sheet.

"Well, now, what do you think of all this, Mr. . . . Arnold?"

A short, black-haired boy in the back smiled slowly, looking at his companions on the right and on the left. He shook his head.

"I don't even know what the hell she's talking about," he said, and the class roared.

McShane noted that Lois Wilson seemed completely undisturbed by the remark. It was as though she had already written them off.

"Well, we're going to have to do something about that, Mr. Arnold. We're going to have to get you to the point where you do know what the hell she's talking about. Do you think that's possible?" Arnold shrugged, still smiling. "What do you think, Miss Wilson?"

"You're in a better position to judge that, Professor McShane. Check his IQ scores, his reading level, his academic achievements to date. Academic prognostication has become a more exact science, has it not?"

"What Miss Wilson is suggesting, Mr. Arnold, is that I take your mental temperature," McShane said. The class laughed again. Lois smirked.

"Long's she's not doin' it," David Arnold said. There was more laughter.

"OK, then. Let's begin at the beginning." McShane took out a small pile of ditto sheets. "I'll give you your outside readings and your syllabus today," he continued and started down the aisle. "You'll notice that I'm requiring one paper," he said. The groan that followed brought him back to reality. Except for the Wilson girl, things weren't going to be that much different after all.

To the extent that she would permit herself to be infatuated, Lois Wilson was infatuated with Professor Kevin McShane. She found herself growing excited when he went on to say that Shakespeare was wrong, the world's not a stage, "it's a controlled environment. We don't act; we react. Some of our reactions are automatic; some of them are learned and developed. There is stimulus and response. 'That is all ye know on earth and all ye need to know.'"

Perhaps he was overly dramatic, but he was right. After that initial class, she felt more of a kinship toward him than she did toward any member of her own family. It was as if she had finally found one of her own kind. Here was someone who apparently was as much of a purist as she was in viewing the world as a setting for behavioral patterns. He was able to convert almost anything into its simplest and clearest description, whether it be national historical events or daily activities carried out by every human being. He had the perception, the vision, the freshness; and those students who left his class complaining about his work requirements and his topics were simply myopic. She detested them and dreamed of being alone with Professor McShane so they both could be unencumbered by those with a lesser vision. Accordingly, she was quick to make an appointment for a conference about possible topics for her paper.

As for McShane, after only two classes he was intrigued with this girl. In a mere pair of classroom discussions, she had made references to the works of Spengler, Freud, Pavlov, and Skinner. Although he had been a college teacher for six years, he had yet to encounter a college student who was as well read and as verbal. That was all interesting and exciting from an educator's point of view, but there was something more to this girl. She had an unusual sense of purpose and determination. Her questions and answers so definite, her gaze so intent, she forced him to concentrate and think harder. He began to do more research, plan more, and think of topics he would never dream of discussing with the classes he had had in the past. In fact, he had just sat down to restructure his next class with this special high-school group when Lois Wilson came to his open office door.

The teachers' offices in the community college were relatively small. Some teachers, mostly the instructors, shared office space and crowded in two desks and file cabinets, leaving minimal space for visitors. McShane's office was one of the larger ones. His desk was set directly in the back facing the doorway. He had two file cabinets to the right, a wall of shelves to the left. To the immediate left of his desk, he had a small couch. There was an extra hardwood chair in the right corner, and a small window right behind his desk chair. He had a view of the front of the campus and the long, circular driveway that joined with County Highway 201.

"Excuse me," she said, "but I saw from your schedule that you were free this hour in the afternoon."

He stared up at her, speechless for a moment because of the way she had simply appeared as he was thinking about her. He was in awe for a few seconds, because he had been developing her in his mind as someone so extraordinary she was almost unreal, and here she had simply appeared.

"Er, come in, come in, Miss Wilson. Or do you prefer Ms.?" He smiled as she entered.

"The only title I'll be seeking is Ph.D.," she said. She had no textbooks, but she carried a notebook in her right hand. Dressed in a light blue down coat and dark blue slacks with fur-lined shoe boots, she didn't look much different from other coeds on the campus. Her individuality came from her eyes: their fixed intensity, their burning determination. Some people look at you, he thought; some people look through you; but this girl looks into you. He felt as though he were being X-rayed.

"Touché. Lois? Sit down, sit down," he said, indicating the couch. She did so quickly. "What can I do for you?"

"I wanted to make an appointment to discuss my paper."

"Uh-huh. And have you centered in on some topics already?"

"I had topics long before I entered your course, Professor."

"Oh?"

"Actually, I've been interested in behavioral science for some time now."

"I gathered." He sat back in his chair and took a longer look at Lois Wilson. "What got you so interested in the subject?"

"It wasn't a teacher," she said, pulling the corners of her mouth up.

"Oh, it hardly ever is," McShane said, enjoying an opportunity to be sarcastic with this girl.

"What I mean is, high-school teachers are so superficial when it comes to these things. I don't fault them for that. They have curricula to follow, and few students want to go into any depth anyway. . . ."

"Very understanding of you. But you haven't answered my question: What got you so interested in the subject?"

"A realization at an early age that the behavioral sciences hold the most promise for a real understanding of the world, that is to say, the life forms."

"Including man?"

"Especially man."

"How early?"

"Excuse me?"

"How early an age was it when you came to so grand a conclusion?"

"I think around the fourth grade," she said. He could see she was deadly serious.

"Well, that's a little earlier than me. So," he said, sitting forward and leaning on both forearms on the desk, "what are some of your topics?"

"You mean, we can talk about them now?"

"I think so," he said, nodding. "What I have to do can wait." She looked at him for a moment and then opened her notebook on her lap.

As McShane listened to Lois's possible topics, he grew mystified and awed. A mind like this comes once every twenty or so years, he thought. He didn't come to that conclusion on the basis of her ideas alone, but the ways she presented them. Her insights and organization, her systematic arrangement of facts and concepts, excited him. He hadn't felt like this about his subject material since he himself was studying and having tutorials with his professors.

Then he experienced a sinking feeling. Was he equal to this girl? Could he provide for her needs, especially in the context of his classroom structure as it now existed in this community college? For a moment he regretted his decision last year not to apply for that position at Columbia. When he rationalized about it, he blamed the decision on his romance with Sherry; but when he was more honest with himself, as he was now, he blamed it on his own sense of inferiority. If there is anything that can underline that sense of inferiority, he thought, it's a student like this who is light-years ahead in her insights and mental quickness.

"I must say," McShane began when she had finished her presentation, "you have really done your homework. I don't think I could have a finer introduction to topics from a graduate student."

Lois felt herself blush. She liked the feeling, and she could see that McShane's appreciation of her was sincere. It wasn't at all like one of her high-school teachers giving her a pat on the head for an "excellent answer," and then making her feel like some kind of weirdo for knowing it all and being able to anticipate any questions he or she might ask.

"Thank you."

"I'm going to have a hard time deciding which of those you should center in on. As far as I'm concerned, they're all worthwhile."

"I'll probably do more than one anyway."

McShane's eyes widened. To have ability, enthusiasm, and drive, to be self-motivated—she was the dream student. Imagine having a classroom filled with her kind. It would be a pleasure to teach; it would actually be exciting to go to class.

"Let me think about it all and we'll talk about it again, OK?"

"Of course," Lois said. She smiled. This man respected her the way she should be respected. It made her feel more secure and more confident.

Later on, on her way back to the high school, she couldn't help but continue to make comparisons between the two educational experiences. Too bad she couldn't have gotten into something like this back in the ninth grade, she thought. Her education had been such a waste ever since—the classes moving so slowly, the teachers, unlike McShane, limited and unappreciative. Here in college she could flower, she could grow freely; there were no rigid boundaries, no stupid statements like "That's not in our curriculum." Too bad only an hour and a half of her day was assigned to the college. She had to work for more time, somehow get them to expand this experimental program.

"The cast list is up for the play," Bernie Rosen said, coming up behind Lois in the hall. She didn't stop walking, but he sped up to be beside her.

"I'm no longer interested."

"Barbara's a prompter and first understudy. Can you believe that?"

"Yes, I can," she said, stopping and turning to him. Students moving to and fro bumped and pushed into them, but Lois ignored it. "I don't think Mr. Oates has an inkling of the meaning of that play."

"I didn't get a part," Bernie said, smiling even wider than ever and disregarding Lois's bitterness. "He asked me to come out and then he doesn't give me a part." Bernie shrugged as they continued on down the hall. "But I thought you were great."

"Oh, I was fantastic."

"No, really. That was one of the funniest things I've seen."

"Well, it wasn't meant to be."

"Everyone thinks you did it deliberately."

"Everyone's an idiot. Anyway, I'm glad I didn't make the play. I wouldn't have had time for it."

"What are you working on now?" He touched her shoulder to stop her. "You didn't go and get new subjects, did you?" His teasing eyes communicated the innuendo.

"You know, I don't understand why I even started with someone like you or Miss Obesity. You have nowhere near the capacity needed to appreciate my work. You're a good pair—she has fat wrapped around her body and you've got it wrapped around your brain." She turned quickly and continued down the hall. For a moment he just stood there with his mouth open.

"Excuse me, Madam Einstein," he called. A few other students stopped to watch. She didn't look back. "I didn't know the rest of us mere mortals were so inferior." There was some laughter. Bernie looked about to suck up the appreciation and compensate for his ego loss.

Lois turned into the guidance office and stood before the secretary's desk. Mrs. Stanley had her back to her, filing papers away. She waited, but Mrs. Stanley did not turn around. She knows I'm here, Lois thought, and that started her mind in another direction.

What is it about bureaucracy that hardens people against one another, that dehumanizes us? People who are polite and compassionate in their daily lives become monsters of rules and regulations, inflicting pain and hardship on other people, disregarding feelings, sub-merging themselves in a crust of procedures. Under such circumstances, morality could be pushed aside. It was easier to make "good people" do negative things. From Professor McShane's syllabus, she could see that the topic was going to be one of his future units.

"Excuse me," she said finally, "Mr. Van Dancer asked me to stop in between classes."

"Oh. Just a moment," Mrs. Stanley said. She turned back to slip a few more sheets into the file. Just to keep me in my place, Lois thought. "Now, then, I'll buzz him and let him know you're here."

"That would be very nice," Lois said. Her blank expression confused the secretary for a moment. She quickly buzzed the guidance counselor and sent Lois in.

"Well, now," Mr. Van Dancer said, actually standing up behind his desk, "you've made quite a hit over at the community college, it seems. And in such a short time."

"I've only had contact with one teacher and a librarian over there."

"Well, he's spread the word." Van Dancer slapped his hands together and turned a page on the desk before him. "Now, through their dean of students, Professor McShane has requested that you be permitted to audit the remainder of his course in abnormal psychology. Quite an honor, quite an honor. I hope you appreciate it."

"We've discussed it. I understand his objectives."

"Yes, well . . . still, you should appreciate the honor. . . ."

"I don't consider it an honor to do what I'm capable of doing. I consider it an obligation," she said dryly. He stared at her a moment. Her gaze was steadfast, her posture stiff. She held her books against her right side. He felt himself becoming intimidated and resented it.

"It's still an honor to have the opportunity," he insisted. She could see he was intent on having the last word, so she remained silent and looked to the side.

"Now, then, what we will do for you, not because we are obligated to do it, but because we want to do it," he added, "is rearrange your gym class so you can have the sixth period free and go to the college in time to make Professor McShane's afternoon class. Starting tomorrow, report to Mrs. Fini's third-period gym class instead of your usual study hall. That's a tenth-grade class, but there's no other way to do it."

"With something like this, I should be able to waive my physical-education requirements."

"Well, you can't. There are state regulations."

"Do you think the time will ever come when we'll stop dealing with one another as items and start dealing with one another as people?"

"I'm doing the best I can. Look, Lois, this is all in the way of a favor for a college teacher who is cooperating with our new program and a favor for you. I don't see—"

"I'm sorry. Thank you, Mr. Van Dancer. I'll take the third-period physical-education class." She walked out of his office before he could reply. Mrs. Stanley was typing at her desk.

"I need a late-to-class pass," Lois said, this time in a more demanding tone of voice. The secretary stopped immediately and began writing the pass. "Thank you."

As she left the office she considered the way the secretary had become instantly obedient. It was as though she had pushed the right button. Manipulating people was really only a matter of utilizing the right combinations. People are really a lot like the machines they operate. The idea struck her as ironic. It also made her feel superior, for she knew something few people knew: anyone could be controlled.

She resolved that from this time forward she would submit to no one's authority unwillingly, including her parents'.

During the weeks that followed, Lois developed a closer relationship with Professor Kevin McShane. She remained after class on just about every Tuesday and Thursday night to continue discussing a question or concept brought up during the class session. For the most part, he enjoyed the extended periods. He began to see their discussions as a sort of intellectual sparring, realizing that Lois Wilson was searching him out, looking for his soft spots. Where did he weaken in his view of the world as deterministic, filled with patterns that led to inevitable and predictable results? Was he corrupted by any sentimentality? He was amused by her relentless pursuit. It was as though she were testing him to confide some great secret.

On the other hand, he could put her on the defensive easily, simply by asking her personal questions in an attempt to discover what her family life was like or how she enjoyed school and other students her age. Her answers were always quick, offhand, monosyllabic. She never hesitated to indicate how insignificant all that was.

"Your parents don't object to this career interest of yours?"

"My father's a scientist."

"That doesn't answer my question. Your mother?"

"You talked about auditory discrimination yesterday."

"You simply shut her out, is that it?"

"Yes. Now, you didn't answer my question today."

He smiled widely. This was one helluva clever kid, he thought and sat back in his seat. He pressed his fingers into a cathedral and pressed the point of it under his chin.

"Go on."

"You said if the subject can be made to believe the ends justified the means early on in the process, he will rarely go back to question his first step. And once he does something he considered evil, he will do something else he considers evil or even more evil?"

"Sure. The first act reinforces the second and the second reinforces the third . . . so on, so on. That extract on the Nazi SS trooper. After he had helped gather up the Jewish family, an act he actually deplored, he was willing, even eager, to see them shipped to the camps. Remember his quote about getting them out of his sight so he could place the blame up the ladder. Someone else would be more guilty and diminish his own responsibility for what happened."

"So in obedience control, the first step is the most important and the most significant."

"Absolutely. The greater the degree of evil, or rather negative action, you can get the subject to commit, the better is your prognosis for control and success. Those people who were paid to participate in that obedience experiment—you know, the ones who were told to deliver an electrical shock to the subjects in the other room when those subjects gave the wrong answers—they're a prime example. Those who continued to give the shocks, up the voltage, defended the experiment afterward, said it had importance and significance."

"They were easing their own sense of guilt."

"Right. Now it would be much easier to have them do a second experiment which supposedly complements the first, even though the second experiment might be more cruel and more sadistic. You've been thinking a lot about obedience control lately. Are you planning to change your topic for the paper?"

"No," she said quickly—too quickly, he thought. "But I am interested in the subject. I think it holds the key to a great deal of what goes on in society."

"No doubt. If you want to get into persuasion, though, you'd better start with *The Image Makers*."

"I took it out just before I got here." She revealed the book in her carryall bag.

"That's a nice bag. A present?"

"My father sells them in his store."

"Sounds like a big store."

"It isn't. It's crowded . . . cluttered, I should say."

"You know, I've never really stopped in Sandburg.

I've driven through it, but I haven't stopped and gone into any of the stores."

"There's nothing to stop for."

"Outgrown your hometown, huh?"

"The day I was born," she said. She began to thumb through her notebook.

Kevin McShane found himself growing more and more determined to know this girl. She was so good at hiding her feelings and beliefs that he began to see it as a challenge for himself. They had met privately a half a dozen times, besides all her classes with him, and he had yet to see her smile or laugh. He watched her when he joked. She acted as though she were thinking, This is something he has to do to keep the attention of the others. In fact, that's the way he began to feel about it. Her attitudes and her intensity infiltrated his subconscious to the extent that he felt guilty for wasting class time. He told himself that was ridiculous. After all, she's the student; I'm the teacher.

"Do you know," he told Sherry when they met for lunch at the Old English Pub, two blocks from campus, "it's as though this kid's beginning to possess me, manipulate me toward her goals."

"I'm beginning to think so. Should I tell you how much time you spent talking about her last night? I don't want to say I'm growing jealous, Kevin dear, but when I spend a good part of my afternoon getting the duck à l'orange as crisp as you love it and I spring for your favorite rosé, you could at least leave your classroom behind."

"Was I like that?" She nodded, smiling. "Why didn't you say something? Why didn't you shut me up? Why—"

"Because you were obviously so wrapped up in her. I didn't have the heart to bring you down. I've never seen you so interested in your students and your work. It was refreshing for a while. After all, you know how I've been criticizing you for treating this more like a nine-to-five job than a profession of love."

"Well, until now . . . with the students they've been sending me, it has been a nine-to-five grind. Even though I don't work nine to five. I wish you could meet this girl and see for yourself. I've been attempting things I never dreamed I'd do."

"Well, I might just pop into your next class. I am free that period on Thursdays. Maybe I'd intimidate her, though."

"No, I think not. The president of the college could come in and she'd behave and speak the same way."

"Do I detect something negative in your tone of voice? You didn't sound as though you were giving her a compliment just now."

"It's not exactly a criticism, I suppose."

She could see his mind drifting.

"Then what is it? Tell me, O most stable, well-adjusted man of science."

"I deserve that. This will sound like a humanist talking, not a scientist."

"You've got my complete attention." Her hazel eyes dazzled him for a moment as she leaned forward on her elbows, her lips inches away from his.

"I'm losing my train of thought."

"Sorry." She sat back and folded her arms across her breasts. "Proceed."

"It's an irrational feeling of gloom. At times she's exhilarating, but at times she's depressing as hell. Then there are times when she's simply . . . "

"What?" Sherry's smile froze. McShane shook his head.

"Simply neutral, like something nonhuman, an objective, unbiased force."

"That sounds like your definition of God, Kevin. Are you sure you're not confusing the two?"

"I'm serious."

"Well, from the way you've described her, she looks like some stiff, puritanical schoolmarm."

"Yeah, but it's more than just that . . . something."

"Are you sure she's not infatuated with the handsome young professor, just as so many other coeds are, and she's not just trying to impress you? It's a unique approach, I know, considering the scholastic achievement of some of our students, but—"

"No, no, she doesn't appear driven by any of those motives. I wish she were," he said, his eyes widening. "It would make her more . . . more . . . human. She needs that."

"You're not going to give it to her, are you?"

"Of course not."

"Well, I'm just going to have to meet this girl. There are no two ways about it. You've succeeded in getting my interest up, but in the meantime, can we order some lunch?"

"Huh? We haven't ordered yet? Damn, I've got to meet Fred Madden in a half hour to discuss our negotations position on salary. Damn."

"This girl really has gotten to you, McShane," Sherry said, "and for a behavioral scientist, that's a sin."

He met her eyes for a moment and then smiled. They talked of other things after ordering and during their meal, but Lois Wilson's questions, comments, and insights peppered his mind increasingly during his quiet moments. He was finding it more and more difficult to escape.

One night he dreamed about her eyes. They were pools of blackness with a candle burning in each. The tiny flickering flames fascinated and hypnotized him. Her face drew closer. He could feel the small sensations of heat. It grew hotter and hotter until he awoke with a start, his own eyeballs aching. He pressed his face with his palms. His forehead was so warm he thought he might have a fever. It took him a long time to fall back to sleep. It was almost as though he were afraid of it.

9

Lois sat across from the couch and stared at Billy's cherub face. He had fallen asleep halfway through the story, just as he always did when she read in that deliberately soft tone of voice. Her parents had gone out—her mother finally talking her father into a movie "just to get the hell out of the house."

Watching Billy in sleep always fascinated her. There was just the smallest, almost imperceptible movement of his eyeballs against his closed lids. His little chest rose and fell under the pajama top. His fingers were curled slightly inward on each hand, and his lips were parted just enough to reveal the tops of his lower teeth.

It would begin tonight. The idea had been boiling in her for some time, but she had always kept it repressed out of the moral considerations. They weren't as important anymore, especially when placed against other priorities. Her parents thought she was a freak anyway. Why should she consider their feelings, their beliefs? They didn't have the capability of understanding the things she was able to do.

But someone like Professor McShane did; he could appreciate her fully, and in time, when he learned about this experiment, he would appreciate her even more. Perhaps even respect her as an equal, as more than an equal. Would it not be wonderful, be—and she hated to use the word because it really was a distortion

—be romantic for both of them, she and the professor, to work together on a project of equal importance someday? Maybe, when he learned to respect her more, he would confide in her and tell her his ideas, his secret concepts and thoughts. It was something to look forward to.

Her idea was based on two observations: for as long as Lois could remember, her mother had eagerly passed off her maternal responsibilities in relation to Billy to her, thus diminishing Billy's dependence on his mother and increasing his dependence on Lois; and secondly, both of Lois's parents offered her rewards in front of Billy for caring for him. Consequently, Billy envisioned himself as a burden.

Could she actually get him to hate his mother because of this and then take some negative action? Wasn't it possible, as Professor McShane explained, to build the intensity of the negative acts by causing him to feel less and less guilty only when he became more and more committed? Each succeeding act would justify what came before.

She got up quietly and walked softly out of the room and down to his bedroom. She snapped on the lights and stared coldly at the twin black-and-white teddy bears on both sides of his *Star Wars*–pattern pillow. There was only a moment's hesitation, a twinge of conscience emanating from the hitherto dormant memory of her first rag doll. At the age of eight, she had destroyed it with one deep incision from the neck to the pelvis in a search to discover what gave it a stiff form. She actually thought it might contain a spinal column.

Scooping both teddy bears up quickly, she put them under her left arm and walked out of Billy's room. She took the stuffed animals upstairs to her parents' bedroom, opened the master closet, and hid them securely behind a carton of her mother's old shoes, which she was forever promising to donate to the Salvation Army.

Billy was still asleep when she returned to the living

room. She waited a few moments and then nudged him gently. His eyes flicked open and he sat up quickly, rubbing his cheeks.

"It's getting late," Lois said. "You've got to go to bed before Mommy gets home and finds you still up."

"OK." He swung his feet around and put them in the Mickey Mouse slippers. He stood up and started out of the room. Lois followed closely behind. The second he entered his bedroom, he noticed his teddy bears were missing.

"Where's Mick and Nick?"

"Gone."

"Gone?" His sleepy, thin voice cracked, so he repeated the question. "Gone?"

"Mother says you shouldn't be sleeping with baby toys anymore. She says that might be why you wet the bed last week."

"Where are they, Lois?" He rubbed his eyes to get himself more awake. "I want them."

"She took them away. I don't know. She might have thrown them in the garbage for all I know."

"But I want them."

"Well, what can I do about it? They're gone. You're just going to have to forget them. And I wouldn't ask her about them either. I promised her you would start acting grown up."

"I don't want to act grown up."

"Just get into bed. They're thinking of sending you to sleep-away camp this summer. You've got to act grown up. You couldn't take two baby toys with you, could you?"

"I never go to sleep without Mick and Nick," he said. His face was collapsing quickly, his cheeks lifting and his forehead wrinkling. His eyes watered and he pulled the corners of his mouth back.

"What do you want me to do? Mother's the boss, isn't she?"

He started to cry. She pushed him firmly but gently

toward the bed. He got in obediently, but he didn't stop crying.

"Listen," she said, sitting down on the bed, "if you stop crying, I'll sit here for a while until you fall asleep."

"I want Mick and Nick."

"Um. Well, you know how mothers are. They want their children to be grown up and on their own, then they don't have to do much for them."

"Can't I be grown up and have Mick and Nick?"

"No. Do I have stuffed animals to sleep with?"

"Where did she put them?"

"I told you, she might have thrown them out."

"Can I go see?"

"What if you found them? She'd only get mad."

He started crying again.

"I'll tell you what," she said, standing. "I'll go outside and look into the garbage cans to see if she put them there, OK?" He nodded quickly. "Just stay in bed until I come back."

"OK."

She walked out, put on her coat, and went out the front door. Standing on the porch, she considered the next step in the behavioral modification procedure: she wanted him to think of her as an ally. That way he would be less reluctant to carry out her commands. There were numerous studies that proved people were more prone to be commanded by leaders they respected and trusted, even if those commands were contrary to established beliefs and morals.

After a sufficient amount of time, she went back inside, taking her coat off in Billy's bedroom doorway to emphasize the effort she had just made in his behalf.

"Not in the garbage," she said.

"Then where are they?"

"Somewhere in the house. I'll tell you what. Tomorrow, when you come home from school, we'll both look for them."

"What if we find them?" He wiped the tears off his cheeks. A search was an adventure. Strategy was involved.

"You'll hide them where you want them. But we can't let Mommy know we're going to do this. Listen carefully," she added, coming farther into the room and lowering her voice for dramatic effect. "Don't even mention that they're missing. Don't ask her about them." He nodded. "That way she'll be off her guard and she'll leave them wherever she's hidden them. Understand?"

"Yeps."

"OK, OK, let's both get some sleep." She went out to hang up her coat, leaving his door slightly opened. When she came back to go to her own bedroom, she heard him whimpering softly.

He's filled with sorrow and fear right now, she thought, but that will soon convert to anger. When it does, I will have step one completed.

She went to sleep, satisfied.

Lois almost forgot about her next steps in the procedure the next day when news came of her full scholarship award to MIT. Mr. Van Dancer was very excited. She was called down to the superintendent's office for his personal congratulations, and the principal had it announced over the public-address system. All of her teachers made a point to mention it in her classes and wish her luck. Teachers she didn't have for classes stopped her in the halls during the passing between classes and congratulated her. By the end of the day, she had had her ego stroked so much she felt like a national celebrity.

It was interesting to note the reactions of the other students. For most it confirmed their image of her as something alien. It reinforced their beliefs that she was different from them: unmoved by the things that would move them, moved by things they would never understand. Old *Star Trek* fans who watched the reruns religiously called her the female Mr. Spock.

But Mr. Wasserman slowed down some of the negativity when he remarked, "It's nice to see the colleges applauding scholarship with the same enthusiasm they applaud sports." Some of the students reevaluated Lois. Perhaps she was a superstar of academics, comparable to someone who would eventually make the NBA or the major leagues. After all, they had known her—she came from their school. There was some pride to be gained from that.

Gregory Wilson was extremely proud. The announcement couldn't have come at a better time, as far as he was concerned. His views and hopes for Lois had been challenged by so much lately that he was terribly confused about her. He had really become very depressed about his daughter. He had trouble sleeping nights, thinking about the fact that he didn't like his own child. All of the ways he defended her against Dorothy's accusation were paled and weakened by her recent activities.

Mr. Van Dancer, the principal, and the superintendent all made personal calls to the drugstore that day to congratulate him and Dorothy. Each call puffed him up a little more. Dorothy's initial reaction to the news had been something less than enthusiastic.

"MIT? What kind of a name is that for a college? She *would* want to go to a school with a name that sounds like some kind of chemical. I'm surprised she didn't apply to DDT. Is there a DDT?"

"You don't know how stupid you sound. MIT is a top institution. Just to be accepted is honor enough, but to be given a full four-year scholarship by the institution—that's a national honor. Don't you know what such a thing says about their confidence in Lois's future and Lois's abilities?"

"I suppose so," Dorothy said, with some sadness still in her voice. "I just know she'll miss out on all the fun in college, just the way she did in high school."

"Well, she's a different kind of kid, damn it. She's not you and she's not me. She's . . . "

"She's closer to you."

"She's beyond me," he said, forcing a smile. "I was nowhere near the student she is."

Dorothy reluctantly accepted Greg's evaluation. She subdued her own attitudes about the college and the honors and openly and enthusiastically accepted all the congratulations from various customers during the day. She saw that most people were genuinely impressed by the financial award. As the day progressed she began to modify all her attitudes. At least we don't have to finance Lois's weird career interests, she thought.

Lois was in something of a daze when she came home that day. She went to her room and sat with her back against the headboard of her bed and thought about the future. There were so many things she wanted to learn, experiments she wanted to be part of, teachers she wanted to meet. She had recently read abstracts by a number of professors still at MIT. She would be there, with them, in their presence.

She didn't hear Billy come home, but he had been thinking about these moments all day. In fact, he couldn't wait for school to end, and he was impatient with the school bus's slow progress on the return trip. When Lois wasn't right there waiting for him the moment he came through the front door, he felt let down. He called, but she didn't answer, and he was afraid she had forgotten and wasn't even home. He found her in her room, looking as though she had been hypnotized.

"I'm home," he said, coming in slowly. It was always dangerous to walk into Lois's room without her inviting him to do so. He moved tentatively toward the bed. She looked at him without speaking. "You said we would start as soon as I got home."

"Start?"

"To look for Mick and Nick. Don't we gotta do it before Mommy gets back from the store?"

"Oh, yes, yes." Her face came back to life, and he felt relieved. "Take off your coat and hang it up by the door, you idiot."

"I was lookin' for you."

"All right, come on." She followed him out of the room. She stood with her hands on her hips as he hung up the coat. "All right," she said, "where do you think Mommy might have hidden them?"

"I don't know."

"Think, will you? If you were Mommy, where would you hide them?"

"I wouldn't hide them," he said innocently.

She smirked and shook her head. "Well, you're not Mommy and she did hide them. Now, if you're not going to help, I'm not going to do this."

"In the kitchen?"

"In the kitchen. All right, we'll try the kitchen. I work in the kitchen, so I know there are only a few possible spots. Follow me."

After a quick search, she turned to him again. It was her theory that he would be more impressed by his mother's action if he found the hiding place himself. This would reinforce the statements she would develop and strengthen his negative feelings toward his mother.

"Now where?"

"You think the basement?"

"She hates going down there. Especially since the bats. She wouldn't go there."

He looked around, thinking.

"Her room, maybe, huh?"

"Maybe. Let's try it, but whatever we disturb, we'd better set right or she'll know."

She stopped in her parents' doorway when they got upstairs.

"I'll look under the bed," she said.

"Where should I look?"

"Where do you think?"

"Maybe in the closets."

"OK, but don't mess up the clothes."

She watched him go to the closet and walked slowly to the bed, kneeling down for a quick pretend search. He opened the closet and looked in, gently separating the hanging dresses and pants suits.

"I don't see anything," he said.

"She wouldn't hang them up. Look on the floor. They're not under the bed." She stood up and waited. He got on his hands and knees and crawled farther into the closet. His shouts of joy made her smile. She came around the bed as he sat back, clutching the two teddy bears to his body. "Good going," she said. "You're a good detective."

"They didn't like bein' in the closet." She was happy to see his face register some anger so quickly.

"Who would?"

"Where am I going to put them?" he asked with real worry. He stood up, keeping them tightly pressed to his chest.

"You've got to give that some serious thought. She's going to eventually realize they're no longer here and she's going to figure out that you found them."

"So I'll tell her I don't want her to take them."

"She'll do it just like she did it this time—without telling you."

"She better not." He looked determined.

"Well, just to be sure, find a good hiding place in your room, and if she comes in and asks you where they are . . . "

"What should I say?"

"Say . . . say you don't know." She smiled slyly. "That will really confuse her. Say you've been wondering about them, too. She won't know what to say because she won't want you to know she took them like a sneak."

"What will she do?"

"She'll probably ask me and I'll say, gee, I don't know. Then she'll just forget about it after a while and you won't have to worry."

"We're going to have to lie to her a lot."

"So what? She lied to you by taking them without telling you first. That's a bigger lie." He nodded. "Come on," she said, putting her arm around him. "I'll help you find a place to hide them every morning after you wake up."

"Thanks, Lois."

"That's OK," she said. "Adults sometimes do stupid things. Just because they're adults doesn't mean they're always right."

"Yeah, like making you take your experiments out of the pantry."

"Like making me take my experiments out of the pantry. I'll tell you a secret," she said, stopping at the top of the stairs. "Someday I'm going to have my own laboratory and I'm going to have free rein over what I do with as much of a budget as I need. People are going to want me to have that."

"What's a budget?"

"Money."

"We coulda gotten money for the worms," he said.

"I'm talking about a lot of money—thousands and thousands of dollars. I already won many thousands."

"You did?"

"From the college I'm going to. I'm going to it for free."

As they walked down the stairs, Billy Wilson clung to his two teddy bears and looked up at his sister with more admiration than he had had for anyone else in his whole life. Not his father, not his mother (now especially not his mother), not his teachers, not even television stars looked as big, as important, and as powerful. Lois could do anything she wanted; she could get anything she wanted.

His little mind was too undeveloped for him to intellectualize or philosophize. His thought process was quick and simple. I should be more like her, he thought. I should be more like my sister.

She kept her hand on his shoulder. He felt very secure and very safe.

"I think we ought to celebrate this weekend," Gregory Wilson said at dinner. "We'll go out to eat in honor of Lois's scholarship."

"Yes," Dorothy said. "Why don't we try that new Chinese place in Liberty?"

"Nope. It'll be lobster and steak. The Old Mill," Gregory said. Dorothy's smile widened. She reached over to brush Billy's hair from his forehead, but he leaned away.

"I was just going to get the hair out of your eyes."

"I can do it," he said, moving the strands back himself. Dorothy's smile froze on her face, but she could sense that her son was acting differently toward her. Instinctively, she turned to Lois. Lois was always the first to realize when Billy had a fever or a stomachache. She knew if Billy had gotten into any trouble in school.

"He needs a haircut," Lois said quickly.

"Yes."

"I do not."

"Come on, Skipper. You'll get it for our celebration," Gregory said. Billy edged closer to his father but looked down at his plate and played with the peas around his fork.

"Well," Dorothy said. "I'll wear that new pants suit I bought and those earrings you got me last Christmas. I haven't had much chance to since."

"Now, don't start that."

"I'm not starting anything."

"Billy and I will do the dishes," Lois said. "I have no homework tonight."

"No homework? That's a first," Gregory said, winking at Billy.

"Nothing due tomorrow. I do have some reading, of course. . . ."

"Naturally. Come on, Dorothy, we'll watch an

Archie Bunker rerun or something," he said. Lois started taking the dishes toward the sink disposal to scrape off the leftovers. Billy gathered the silverware. He stood next to her and waited as she rinsed off the dishes before putting them into the dishwasher. She turned to see if her parents were out of earshot.

"I don't want to go for a haircut."

"Forget about that. There's something else I think you should do."

"What?"

"You know those earrings Mommy just mentioned— the big gold ones with that jewel at the bottom of each?"

"I don't remember."

"They're gold rings and big as this," she said, making a circle with her forefinger and thumb. "How could you forget them? Don't you remember the big deal she made when she got them?" He shook his head. "Well, that doesn't matter. I thought of something to teach her a lesson for what she did with Mick and Nick."

"What?"

"I want you to go up to their bedroom, go to her jewelry box on the dresser, and take those earrings out."

"What for?"

"You'll bring them down here and hide them."

"Where?"

"When you come down with them," she said slowly, pronouncing each word with controlled vehemence, "we'll think it out. Keep them in your pants pocket. Now go do it."

"Now?"

"Well, they're in there watching television. It's the best time. Just don't let them hear you going up the stairs."

"I'm scared to."

"You weren't too scared to go sneaking in her closets, were you?"

"That was when she wasn't here."

"You can do it," Lois said, glaring at him. He turned and looked at the doorway to the living room. The sound of the television could be heard and his parents' voices just over it. "Hurry, while they're distracted. Now," she commanded. He turned and moved quickly. She waited a moment and then went back to the dishes.

It took him so long to return that she was afraid he hadn't done it. She stopped wiping off the table and stood up as he reentered the kitchen.

"Well?"

He drew the two large gold earrings out of his pocket. She looked toward the living room and then pushed his hand back toward his pocket.

"Go hide them in your room."

"Where in my room?"

"Where you hid Mick and Nick," she said. He nodded and ran out again. Her mother's loud laughter made her smile. That was easy, she thought. Now she had to be sure that he didn't break when her mother discovered they were missing and went on a hysterical search.

"What's going to happen when she can't find them?" he asked when he returned.

"Oh, she'll feel sad," Lois said, putting away the coffeepot. "Just the way you felt when you couldn't find Mick and Nick," she added. He nodded; any remorse he had started to feel quickly subsided.

"Hey, aren't you two finished in there?" Gregory shouted from the living room. Lois steered Billy toward them. Their parents were seated on the couch—Dorothy leaning back against her husband's chest, his right arm draped over her. She looked back at them without turning her head.

"Just finished up," Lois said.

"Come on in and watch the evening news. You can tell me the behind-the-scenes reasoning for everything," Gregory said. "No sense having a resident genius in the house if we don't use her," he added. Dorothy laughed.

"Nothing very interesting happened today," Lois said. "I want to do some reading."

"You gotta learn to relax some, kid. Don't take after your old man."

"That's for sure," Dorothy said. They both laughed. "How about you, Billy? Wanna sit by Mommy? C'mon." She pulled her legs up to make a spot on the couch.

"No," he said quickly. "I wanna work on my puzzle."

"You can bring it in here, son," Gregory said. From the way Dorothy tightened up against his body, he could sense she was upset by Billy's rejection.

"I wanna work in my room," he said and followed Lois out.

Dorothy sat up slowly, folding her arms across her chest.

"I don't care what you say. Scholarship or no scholarship . . . "

"Now, don't start in, Dorothy," he said. She didn't say another word about it, but she didn't have to—the sentences lingered in the air about them, diluting their happiness and wedging them apart. They remained seated on the couch, staring at the television set. They went to sleep when they finally grew bored with each other's silence.

10

It happened the night they were to go out for the dinner of celebration. Later on, Lois would see much irony in that. Dorothy, during her own hysterical moments, would actually voice the belief that her missing earrings and the subsequent frantic search for them had much to do with what happened. Lois would have found that ironic too, if it weren't for the depths of guilt such an idea was to instill in Billy. That would create complications for Lois—nothing she couldn't handle, but still, complications.

She was in her room dressing when Billy came in to tell her how Dorothy was screaming about the earrings.

"Daddy went down and up the stairs twice. She's still wrapped in a towel. I was in the hall watching."

"If she asks you anything, you act like you don't know what they look like. You ask her to describe them."

"She pulled a drawer out and everything fell on the floor. I heard it."

"Don't worry about it. Go play with something."

"Should I give them back?"

"Of course not. How can you do that without showing her you took them?" Reinforcement, she thought, reinforcement. "What you did was good, because we're helping her learn a lesson. You didn't steal them, because you're going to give them back someday."

"Daddy's mad. He's yelling."

"That's OK. He's not yelling at you; he's yelling at her. He's trying to teach her a lesson, too. We all have to teach each other lessons all the time." She could see her brother considering the ideas.

"She could never find them in my room."

"Good," Lois said, making her voice as nonchalant as possible. Diminish the intensity, she thought. She made a mental note to take the earrings out of his room when he wasn't around so he couldn't return them on his own. That way she would have an even firmer control over the experiment. She heard her mother on the stairs, calling her. "Don't say anything," she said, walking past Billy. "Just listen."

"Lois!"

"Yes, mother."

"I can't find my new earrings. Did you take them?"

"Hardly. Adorning my body with jewelry has never appealed to me."

"Damn it. I can't believe this."

"I'm sure there's a logical explanation for it," Lois said. Her calm tone of voice infuriated Dorothy more, and she rushed back up the stairs. When Lois turned around, Billy was standing right behind her, his hands in his little pockets. "It's working," she whispered. They heard the slamming of doors. Gregory raised his voice again. Then there was silence. "She's gone into the bathroom to finish her hair. Going out has always been a Broadway opening for Mother," Lois said dryly. "Come on, I'll play you a game of checkers while we wait."

At least fifteen minutes passed; Lois was quite sure of that. She was on her fourth game of checkers with Billy when the scream began. This time it was a long, shrill sound that evolved into a series of hysterical pleadings: "Greg, Greg, Greg . . . "

They both stood up and went to the living-room door. By then Dorothy was shouting for Lois. She moved quickly up the stairs, with Billy stumbling behind her. Dorothy, in a slip and bra, her hair blow-dried and wavy, stood outside her bedroom door, her arms up, her hands opening and closing as she clutched the air.

"He's out . . . your father's passed out. . . . " She closed her eyes and shivered with each word. Lois thought she was about to foam at the mouth. She turned away from her in disgust and looked into the bedroom. Her father was sprawled out on the floor by the side of the bed. He was on his back, but leaning toward his right, his right arm caught under his body, the right hand sticking out just below his waist. His left arm dangled behind him, the fingers of his left hand just touching the floor. His face was pressed against the carpet, his eyes shut.

She knelt down beside him and took his right arm into her hands, feeling for his pulse. Billy stood in the doorway, holding on to the frame and gaping, wide-eyed. Dorothy had pressed her right fist into her mouth. She bit down on her knuckles. Lois handled her father with a confidence characteristic of clinically experienced personnel. The pulse she finally found was weak and indistinct.

"What's wrong with him?" Billy asked. He looked up at his mother, but that frightened him more. He decided to step farther into the room and be closer to Lois.

"I'd say it's another stroke. Call for an ambulance," Lois ordered without turning from her father. Dorothy didn't move. She seemed to be gagging on her own hand. "Mother, get hold of yourself! Call an ambulance! Call the police! Do something!"

"Oh, God," Dorothy moaned. "Oh, God, oh, God." She moved to the phone, but when she lifted the receiver, she dropped it to the table. She fumbled with the dial. Finally, Lois got up and took the phone from her.

After the phone call, Lois put a pillow under her father's head, loosened his shirt buttons, and went for a cold washrag. She told Billy to wait downstairs and holler as soon as the ambulance arrived. Dorothy sat on the bed by Gregory and sobbed.

"That's going to really help him," Lois said. "At least get dressed. We're going to have to go to the hospital behind the ambulance."

"Oh, God, yes." She got up and groped in the closet for her pants suit. As she dressed she tried to avoid looking down at Gregory. Her chatter took on the rhythms of a chant. It was as though she were using idle talk as a prayer. "I didn't hear him fall. He didn't shout or say a word. There wasn't a warning, no warning. Of course, with the hair drier . . . you can't even hear the phone ringing . . . . I have no idea how long he was lying there. I didn't hear him fall. If he would have banged on the door . . . "

"From the looks of things, I don't think he had a lot of time to think about what he would do."

Dorothy hopped about the bedroom to get her shoes on. When she was dressed, she leaned against the wall and closed her eyes. "I told him he was working too hard, I told him."

"They're here!" Billy shouted from the bottom of the stairs. "They're here, Lois!"

Dorothy stayed out in the hall as Lois went downstairs to let the attendants in. Sandburg had a volunteer ambulance squad of ordinary citizens who had taken the necessary first-aid courses. They were well organized and dedicated, keeping their duty roster with a military efficiency. Patty Morganstein, the hamlet's policeman, accompanied Bert Herman and Charlie Davinport up the stairs. They moved quickly, all business.

"Now, take it easy, Dorothy," Patty said, moving right to her. "We've contacted Dr. Bloom. He'll meet us at the hospital." The moment Patty spoke to her, she burst into tears. When they carried Gregory out of the room, she wailed louder. "Are you going to be able to drive?" he asked her.

"She'll drive," Lois said. He looked at her for the first time since he had arrived with the squad.

"Well, someone should go along with her." Patty started down the stairs after the attendants and stretcher.

"Get yourself together," Lois said in a loud whisper, her teeth clenched. Dorothy stopped sniveling and went for her coat. Lois got Billy, and the three of them were in the car and going only a minute after the ambulance. They sat in silence, following the sound of the siren, hypnotized by its rhythmic screech in the otherwise quiet country night.

At the hospital, the attendants worked quickly to get Gregory rolled into the emergency room. Dorothy and Lois caught a brief glimpse of Dr. Bloom heading in after it. One of the emergency-room personnel showed them to the waiting lounge. Dorothy sat stone-eyed, her body rigid. She's going into a form of shock, Lois thought, as a mental defense mechanism. Billy thumbed through a stack of magazines, looking around periodically with the eyes of a frightened deer. He was intrigued and curious about everything going on around him. He wanted to ask questions but sensed that it was wiser to remain unobtrusive.

It was nearly an hour before the doctor joined them. Dorothy looked up expectantly, her cheeks quivering. Bloom pulled a chair closer to her and sat down.

"It's what we feared the most," he began. Lois appreciated his directness, but Dorothy's body began to tremble, her face quickly collapsing into the Greek mask of sadness. "I don't know the full extent of damage, but it's severe. He's regained consciousness." Bloom paused, his gaze automatically moving from Dorothy to Lois, who looked attentive and calm. He sensed her strength and stoic demeanor. "At this time the entire right side of his body is incapacitated. I can only find a small motor capability on the left: a little finger movement, almost imperceptible movement in the left leg and foot."

"Oh, God," Dorothy said.

"Unfortunately, that's not all. He's . . . he's lost speech and can only utter a monotone guttural sound."

Dorothy broke down completely, sobbing uncontrollably, her face in her hands. Dr. Bloom looked to Lois. Seeing she was not moving to offer her mother any comfort, he got up and slid next to Dorothy on the couch. He embraced her and she leaned into him.

"What's the prognosis?" Lois asked. Bloom, surprised at the cool, calm tone, merely stared at her a moment. Then he shook his head.

"We'll see," he said, but Lois didn't need any more information. She nodded knowingly. Too knowingly for the doctor, who was annoyed by the arrogant ease with which this girl could accept the sentence her father's body had passed on him.

"There's no point in our staying here any longer, Mother," she said. "We've got to get ourselves together and go home."

Dorothy wiped her face quickly.

"I want to see him," she said.

"He's still in the emergency room."

Dorothy stood up with the doctor. Lois got up reluctantly. Billy slowly joined them and they all proceeded to the room. The nurse who had set up an IV stepped back as they approached. Gregory Wilson, his eyes closed, lay there looking almost as white as the sheet.

"Greg," Dr. Bloom began, "it's your wife and children. Greg. C'mon, Greg."

From the amount of effort it seemed to take, it appeared as though moving his eyelids were a nearly insurmountable task. He did not move his head. Dorothy leaned over the bed. He began to blink rapidly.

"Oh, Greg, Greg. Please, get better, please." She pressed her face against his.

Billy tugged on Lois's jacket.

"Why can't Daddy talk? Huh, Lois? Why can't he?"

"Just be quiet."

Dr. Bloom knelt down beside him.

"Talking is a motor skill controlled in your brain. That part of your father's brain has been shut down."

"When will it start again?"

"We're not sure, Billy. In the meantime you've got to help your mother out, OK?" Billy looked to Lois for confirmation. She smirked and turned away. "I don't like being in here," he said.

Bloom stood up. "Why don't you take him out and I'll finish talking to your mother."

Lois took Billy's hand and started out of the room. The doctor caught up with her at the door and spoke in a loud whisper.

"You might just be the strong one now, Lois. Your mother's going to need all the help she can get."

"She always has," Lois said.

"I don't expect this will be easy on any of you," he said in a much harsher tone of voice.

"We'll adjust. It's a matter of adapting ourselves to new conditions. That's what living is all about," she added, her voice drifting. For a moment she looked melancholy and philosophical to the doctor. This is probably the closest she can come to showing emotion in front of others, he thought and nodded. He turned back to Dorothy.

Dorothy didn't speak until they drove out of the hospital parking lot.

"What are we going to do now? We're lost, lost."

"Don't be silly, Mother."

"Oh, don't be silly. Well, you tell me what I'm supposed to do with two children, a house, and a drugstore without a pharmacist. And here it is only seven weeks to July fourth and the season." Dorothy stopped sniffling, her voice growing harder as she outlined her difficulties. She nodded to assure herself that she was right in her view of the world as it now stood.

"Number one," Lois said, sitting up stiffly, "you'll advertise to sell the store. It's the best possible time for it, since the season isn't that far off. Number two, you'll activate Daddy's disability insurance policy immediately. You can also apply for social security disability. Number three, you'll check into that mortgage insurance policy Daddy bought when he took the mortgage with the United National. I believe there was a rider for disability. The house could be paid for."

Dorothy slowed down and turned in amazement.

"How do you remember all this?"

"I pay attention when people talk. Tomorrow, I'll go to the store and make an inventory of things we can use, things we should take home."

"But maybe we should hold the store until your father . . . in case your father . . . "

"We couldn't maintain the overhead without any income coming in. There's no sense living in delusion anyway."

"But in time . . . " Dorothy smiled, tilting her head, drawing up a fantasy for herself.

Lois sighed. "So he can work for someone else. He'd rather do that anyway," she said.

"Yes," Dorothy said. "Yes. That's very sensible, Lois. Very sensible." She looked at her daughter and nodded. "I can see I'm . . . we're going to be very dependent upon you, Lois. You've got the mind for times of crisis."

"It's merely a matter of reacting intelligently to the changes in one's environment, adapting and adjusting. It's characteristic of any species that's survived. There are some insects and underwater creatures that have lived hundreds of thousands of years."

"Insects?" Dorothy began to sniffle again. "Insects and creatures?" She released a short laugh. "You think of that now? Your father is paralyzed, possibly for the rest of his life, and you compare us to insects?" Her laugh turned into a sob. "Help me, O God."

"Don't you know that God helps those who help themselves, Mother?" Lois looked back at her brother, who was sprawled over the back seat. His eyes were closed and he was clutching his own body as though to protect himself. "What God has done, if there is indeed a God, is given us the ability to be like him, to be godlike."

Dorothy didn't seem to hear her. She had withdrawn to deeper thoughts.

"I knew," she said a few minutes later, "that when I couldn't find those earrings something terrible was going to happen. It was a bad omen."

Lois didn't respond: she didn't smile or change expression; she looked out at the night, watching the hood of the car wash through the glow of streetlights as they moved into Sandburg. Life really was a series of mazes, she thought, and just when you feel you've got it figured, God, her mother's concept of some powerful force, changed things. This whole thing, creation, was one big experiment. She saw it as a challenge. So, rather than feeling any great sorrow after having deposited her father in the emergency room of a hospital and learning that the world as they had known it had crumbled, she felt a new excitement. She was to face a new test, and she was eager, she was actually eager.

"What got you so interested in the psychological effects of color?" McShane asked. He was having what could be his next-to-last private conference with Lois Wilson. She had presented him with yet another paper, this one just as well researched and well written as the others.

"Something that was done up at the hospital."

"The hospital?"

"You remember I told you they had my father up on that floor with the terminally ill and the senile who are waiting for placement in the county infirmary?"

"Yes."

"Well, obviously such a section is inherently depressing for most people, especially the patients who can think about it. The old antiseptic white would reinforce a view of the hospital as a place of sterility and death.

What they did, however, was paper the rooms with bright, lively colors. The windows have attractive curtains instead of shades. Some of the rooms have fairly nice pieces of furniture in them. It all helps maintain an illusion and makes it less depressing for visitors."

"Well, there's a lot of validity to color therapy and influence. We all have our favorite colors and colors we dislike."

"My mother hates anything green. Fortunately for her, my father wasn't put in the room just down the hall from him. It's a bright lime."

"How's he doing?"

"He's made absolutely no progress," she said and then looked up quickly. "But I'm not disappointed, because I'm not expecting him to. Of course, it's different for my mother. She insists on seeing progress."

McShane was taken by her extraordinary detachment. He nearly smiled, thinking about Sherry and the way she kidded him during their lovemaking for being a detached scientist. Of course, she did it just to get him more riled up and he played along, but if she witnessed this . . .

"Can't blame your mother."

"It's unrealistic. I finally got her to advertise the sale of the store. We've placed it with a real-estate agent."

"I'm sorry."

"We'll manage. Adversity often makes an animal stronger, more determined." She leaned toward him, her eyes small and penetrating. "When I was a little girl, I was amazed by the energy of a laboring ant dragging a dead fly or something across the sidewalk. I'd let it get more than halfway and then lift it gently and put it back where it started. It never gave up. It worked harder, faster."

"But, with little intelligence, it didn't ponder its plight; it couldn't get depressed and discouraged. It worked on instinct. You can't compare man to—"

"Who really has the advantage, then?" She smiled, but he felt it was a very mechanical smile.

"It depends. If you're only goal-oriented, then the ant."

"Precisely. It has no sentiment; it has no emotion. Success will satisfy some instinctive need."

"Um. But without sentiment and emotion, you can't have art and beauty; and without art and beauty, you have a very mechanical world. Is that what you want?"

"To paraphrase you, I don't think we have a choice. We think we do."

"Some people need to think that, though, Lois. Take your mother, for example . . . "

"In time, she won't need it. She'll face reality and go on."

He studied her a moment, sitting back with his arms folded across his chest.

"What if she doesn't?"

"Oh, she will. I'll help her. I know I can," she added, this time smiling with obvious self-assurance and pride. It was at that moment that McShane permitted himself to admit to himself that he disliked this girl. He had fought it all this time because she so personified all the things he believed in and subscribed to, and in disliking her he was actually disliking a large part of himself and what he felt he represented. He resolved to bring about some changes in Lois Wilson, important changes.

What Lois Wilson needed, he thought, was a sense of balance between science and humanism. What good was all the invention and discovery if it didn't improve the quality of life as well as the quantity? It was Sherry's argument and he'd often deliberately oppose her just to tease her, but of course, she was right. Maybe he should turn her loose on this Wilson girl? Then again, no, he couldn't do that to Sherry.

"What are you going to do this summer?"

"It depends. If the store is sold, as I hope it will be, I'll have more freedom to try some projects and read. Why?"

"I'm teaching a six-week sociology course. Just introductory material, but you might find it interesting. Why don't you audit?" This could be a way to get some of those humanistic concerns across to her, he thought.

"I might just do that."

"We can throw some ideas about."

"I'd like that. Thank you." She was flattered. Obviously, he was very impressed with her.

"Oh, by the way, whatever happened to that paper you were going to do on obedience?"

"I'm still working on it. It's become somewhat more involved than I originally intended."

"Well, stick with it."

"I will. I'm more like that ant when it comes to behavioral concepts," she said and offered him the warmest smile she was capable of giving.

That night, more aggressive than usual in his love-making, he told Sherry he was behaving like an ant and laughed.

"What's the joke?"

He told her, and then he told her about his conversation with Lois concerning her father.

"I mean, it's almost as though she feels absolutely no blood relationship. Can you imagine how this kid must've been brought up?"

"I get the feeling it wouldn't have mattered how she was brought up."

"What d'ya mean?"

"From what I've seen of her and from what you've told me, she's just . . . emotionally disabled. I think it's genetic."

"Doesn't sound like your interpretation of things."

"I know, I know. It's frightening. You're going to laugh again, but I think such a girl, such a person, is dangerous. Don't you dare call me a romantic," she added quickly. He didn't say a thing, not a thing.

When Lois returned home that afternoon, she found her mother in the darkest corner of the living room.

Her posture was so stiff and erect that she looked like a clothing-store manikin. Her hands were folded in her lap. One of the side-table lamps was on, but it succeeded in throwing only a pale yellow glow over the room, silhouetting the furniture and other lamps on the far wall. The curtains were drawn tight, permitting very little of the dull gray afternoon light to enter the room. Lois stood in the doorway for a moment and then walked into the room.

"Why are you sitting there like that? Mother?"

"What?"

"I asked you why you were sitting in the dark like that."

"Is it dark? It wasn't this dark when I first sat down."

"Where's Billy?"

"In his room, I guess. Lois, you'd better come sit down. I have some rather bad news to tell you," she said. She spoke as though hypnotized, a tone of voice Lois recognized from previous occasions when her mother was faced with some difficult emotional problems. It was her retreat from hysteria.

"Is Daddy dead?" She sat on the couch and put her books beside her.

"You've got such strength, such strength. I should be more like you," Dorothy said and laughed a silly little laugh. "No, your father's not dead, although he'd probably be the first to say he's as good as dead. I'm sure he'd rather be dead."

"All life is relative. I'm not a moralist, but I oppose euthanasia. There is always something to be learned and—"

"Please, Lois, please." She held her hand up like a policeman stopping traffic. "I just can't deal with your lectures right now."

"Well, what is it? What's the bad news?"

"I had a long talk today with the doctor—as a matter of fact, with all the doctors taking care of your father. They don't hold any hope of his making much improvement."

"I could have told you that long ago."

"What do you mean? Do you think you're a trained doctor too?"

"The incidence of complete recovery from such a massive stroke is simply—"

"I don't want to argue about it." She paused and lowered her voice. "I don't have the strength. They don't want to keep him there anymore. They don't think there's any point to it."

"I see. What does that mean?"

"They want me to institutionalize him. I realize now that it's going to have to be done . . . eventually."

"What do you mean, 'eventually'?"

"Well, one of the doctors said he could make some progress faster if he were in his own home, in a familiar environment."

"Of course, the environment is terribly important for any behavioral changes, even in his case. Perhaps especially in his case," Lois added, more to herself than to her mother. "It's very interesting."

"Interesting? I'm talking about your father. Don't you understand?"

"Of course I understand. So what are you planning to do?"

"I got a call from Bob Peterson an hour ago. He's got a buyer for the drugstore."

"That's great. I knew we would sell it."

"So with that out of the way . . . I think we can bring your father home, at least for the summer. I've learned how to handle his therapy, and the therapist did say he would stop in shortly after we bring Greg home. He'll review everything with both of us." She paused and took a deep breath. "I'm still thinking about sending Billy to sleep-away camp. It'll make for less responsibility for both of us."

Lois's thoughts went immediately to her obedience paper.

"I don't know if he'd be that much of a problem, and there *is* the added expense."

"With your father here in the condition he's in . . . I don't know if I can handle it . . . we might have to give up after a week or so."

Lois thought about her father upstairs in his room. He was like a large one-celled animal with a man's intelligence. What an object of study. What potential for understanding and developing concepts. She might do her greatest paper before she even entered college.

Of course, her mother could be something of an obstacle. If that should happen, she could work around her or perhaps (and this possibility held out even greater potentials) work on her.

"Well, what do you think?"

"Think?"

"About all that I've been saying. I'm going to need your help."

"I'd have to agree with the doctor. Bring Daddy home. Let's try. Let's give him the best care we can."

"And Billy?"

"I don't see him as a problem. If he is or becomes one, we can always take him to the camp then. He can even be of great help."

"O God," Dorothy said, wringing her hands some, "give me the strength. I hope we're doing the right thing."

"We're doing the right thing," Lois said. She got up and left her mother in the shadows. It was better that her mother didn't see the light burning in her daughter's eyes.

11

The arrival of the ambulance bringing Gregory Wilson back to his house was traumatic for each member of his family for different reasons. Billy was excited at the sight of it, but he was also frightened by it because he had known it only as a sign of illness, death, or accident. Its siren quickened heartbeats. No matter where he was or what he was doing, all play would stop, the movement from fantasy back to reality was instantaneous, and the images it brought to mind lingered to haunt him the rest of the day. When he saw his father emerging on the stretcher, he felt as if a movie he had seen before were now being played backward. His father's eyes were shut, his face was pale and gaunt; he looked just as small and as helpless as he did when the ambulance came to take him away.

"Is he dead, Lois?" Billy whispered. "Did they bring Daddy back dead?"

"In a manner of speaking, maybe," she said and then looked at him. "No, she said. "He's not dead, but he's not completely alive either." Billy remained confused but asked no more questions.

Dorothy Wilson stood with her hands pressed against her cheeks. She looked like a woman watching furniture movers, afraid they might damage a family heirloom. Greg was placed on a stretcher with legs that unfolded. It had wheels at the bottom, making it possible for the attendants to roll him toward the front door. She had the sensation that she was receiving a delivery. In this case it was her husband on a slab. Confronting him like this, out of the hospital environment where there was all that equipment, the security of nursing personnel nearby, where she could go to visit and then leave him behind, confident that what could be done was being done, she suddenly felt terribly afraid.

Because of his condition, there was very little happiness to be felt in his homecoming. Instead of being washed in joy, ecstatic and lightheaded, she experienced the impression that a great weight was now being lowered onto her shoulders. Panic began to set in—she had taken on too much. And now it was too late. Could she start to shout "Stop"? Tell them to put him back in and take him away again? What had she done? She turned to Lois for confirmation of her fears, but Lois looked as intent and as calm as usual. In fact, she looked even satisfied.

Lois had determined that from the beginning she would avoid thinking that the man on the stretcher was her father. She would deliberately repress the thought in order to avoid any emotional obstacles. He wasn't much like the father she had known anyway, so it wasn't that difficult to do.

Her concern at this moment was to catch her father's reaction to being brought home. She wished she could follow alongside the stretcher, taking his pulse, observing his physiological reactions. She could see from the way his eyes were moving from side to side that he was trying to take in as much of the familiar scene as he could. No doubt he wanted them to stop the stretcher, lift him up, and permit him to look completely at the front yard and the front of the house. He was hungry for the past, desperately reaching back for the way things had been.

All the while she considered his homecoming, Lois wondered about the way someone in her father's condition reacted to conflict. Who could be at a higher frustration level than a man who was once very active and was now almost a vegetable? There were a number of ways in which people reacted to their frustrations. How many of them would her father now exhibit? He couldn't continually deny the problem. He could pretend he was asleep and this was all a terrible nightmare, but he couldn't sustain that pretense long.

Of course, he must be going through great fear and anxiety, she concluded. That could easily lead to a distortion of the reality he now knew. Certainly not able to blame himself for his condition, he was surely going through a defense mechanism known as projection: he was shifting the blame. Perhaps he blamed Dorothy or faulty medicine. Perhaps he blamed the doctors. She was eager to find out.

Someone in his condition had to embrace fantasy eventually, she thought. Perhaps he would envision himself a futuristic creature who had gone beyond the body, a creature who existed only in the mental process. She determined that she would keep her father aware of his body for as long as she could. There were plans that depended upon that.

"Easy, now," one of the attendants said as they lifted and tilted the mobile stretcher to go up the small front-porch steps. Dorothy moved closer to the action. Billy hovered around Lois, who remained aloof.

"Takes a lot of courage to do this," Patty said, coming up behind Lois and Billy. "Your mother's got a lot of guts. Let's hope it works out for the best."

"It will."

"If you need me for anything, don't hesitate to call. No matter what time of the night or day."

"Thank you."

Billy followed Lois into the house. She and her mother had determined, after some conversation, that it would be of greater psychological benefit to keep Greg in his own bedroom, even though it was upstairs and that meant a lot more difficulty for them. Lois had agreed to give up her bedroom if it proved too difficult.

Throughout the conversation, Lois could sense that her mother was somewhat hesitant about sharing her room with Greg now that he was in this condition. Lois relieved that problem somewhat when she suggested they buy a motorized hospital bed for him.

After they rolled him through the entranceway and to the foot of the stairs, the attendants stopped the mobile stretcher and lifted Greg off it. The walk up was obviously very difficult because of the stairway's narrow width. After he was finally secured into the bed, they raised him to a sitting position. The attendants said their goodbyes to him. Greg's mouth moved, but no sounds emerged. He closed his eyes and struggled to utter his indistinct guttural noise. Each attendant squeezed his hand and left.

Dorothy stood to the left of the bed, smiling stupidly. Billy was so close beside Lois he continually touched her with his head and shoulders.

"Well," Dorothy said, slapping her hands together, "it's so good to get you home. The children . . ." She turned to Lois and Billy. "The children are so happy. Come closer, Billy, so your father can see you."

Billy hesitated, but Lois pushed him forward. He inched up to the side of the bed. Lois thought she detected a definite smile on her father's face now, although it was difficult because of the slack-muscled look he now wore.

"Say something," Dorothy prompted. Billy looked to Lois and then shook his head. "Go ahead; he wants to hear your voice."

Gregory's eyelids closed and opened slowly.

"I don't wanna," Billy said and ran back to the doorway.

"Give him time, Mother," Lois said, approaching her father's bed. "The doctors told us you've been saying yes and no with your eyelids: once for yes and twice for no. Is that right, Dad?" He closed his eyes and opened them. "Good."

"I don't want you to worry about any of the financial problems," Dorothy said. She sat herself at the foot of his bed and took his limp left hand into her hands. "We've done everything we had to do. Lois has been a great help. She remembered so much about our affairs. You can be very proud of her. We've considered everything very carefully." Gregory looked away from Dorothy. He seemed to be searching Lois's face for some confirmation.

They had decided not to tell him about the sale of the drugstore just yet, figuring that might be too devastating a blow. The doctors had agreed. Despite Gregory Wilson's medical knowledge, he would cling to hope for himself.

Later, Lois elaborated for her mother. "His mind won't permit itself to think in terms of finality. He's like a man about to be hanged, dreaming that the rope will break. The imagination provides some respite. If we shut off all avenues of escape he might withdraw into a complete coma."

"What'll we do?"

"Lie to him. Tell him we've hired a pharmacist until he gets well enough to take on his responsibilities again."

"But he'll wonder why I'm not at the store anymore."

"You'll stay away from him enough during the day to give him the impression you do go to the store, and we'll tell him we've hired more help, responsible help. He'll let you lie to him. You'll see. He doesn't want to face the truth."

That was just what Dorothy set out to do. Lois observed that she wasn't very good at it, and every time she turned to Lois for support and her father studied her face, she knew none of it was very convincing.

"The bottom line is we won't starve; we're provided for until you get well again," she concluded. She held his hand, but there was no change in his facial expression. He stared with watery eyes. "It's so good to have you home, Greg. It's so good." She kissed his hand.

"I'll go down and work on supper," Lois said.

"Good." Dorothy straightened up and nodded, wiping her cheeks. "I'll just keep him company. You can stay if you want, Billy."

"I don't wanna. I wanna help Lois." He followed Lois down the stairs eagerly. "Maybe I should give her back those earrings now," he whispered. "Maybe that'll help make Daddy better, huh?"

"What?"

"You know, those big earrings."

"That doesn't have anything to do with it. He was sick for a long time before that. I told you that. Forget about those earrings. And why are you so afraid of him? He's still your father."

"I don't like the way he looks. When will he talk again?"

"I don't know."

"He will, though, right?"

"Maybe," she said, taking on that dreamy, far-off look he had grown accustomed to. "He'll change, I guarantee that."

She said it with such certainty it made Billy feel reassured. Still, he wondered if he shouldn't give back those earrings. Maybe he would just sneak them back. Maybe.

"I was thinking about Helen Keller and Annie Sullivan the other day."

"Yes?" McShane said. He couldn't help but notice a subtle but definite change that had come over Lois recently. Although it would have seemed impossible to him before, she appeared even more confident, more assured, more (and he hated to use the word even though it fit) powerful to him. It was as though she had quickened her steps to maturity. What brought it to his attention was the fact that she wasn't asking as many questions; she was making more definite statements. Analyzing the moment, he felt as though he were sitting with one of his peers, someone else who taught in the department. To go even further, he felt as though Lois were the teacher now and he the student.

"I'm sure you've read or seen the play *The Miracle Worker.*"

"Of course. What's your point?"

"I don't think there can be too many better situations or conditions for obedience control than the one Annie Sullivan finally had in relation to Helen Keller."

"How so?"

"She got Helen's family to the point where they agreed to permit a situation whereby Helen was dependent on Annie for everything, even her bodily needs. It was through control of those needs that Annie conquered her."

"I don't know if *conquered* is the right word."

"It isn't. I should have said *controlled.* Because she could control her, she could manipulate her, which in this case was for her own good."

"Um. I see what you mean."

"It's basically what we do with our laboratory animals: we starve them and feed them in order to get them to do what we want or change what we want. We heat them, freeze them, shock them." McShane nodded. He decided to simply wait for her conclusions. "Complete obedience control can come, therefore, if one has complete control of the subject's basic needs."

"True, but you could be describing a form of slavery as well as a scientific experiment."

"I'm not interested in slavery," she said with some disdain.

"Does any of this have to do with your valedictorian speech next week?"

"In a way. I want to show how everything—political, social, whatever—boils down to basic behavior modification."

"I might just come to hear that speech."

"I hope you do. I gave you what would have been my father's invitation."

McShane changed expression and sat back. "How's it going?"

"As is to be expected."

"Your mother holding up?"

"No, but that was to be expected." She said it dryly, without the slightest note of sarcasm or sorrow. It made him think of Sherry's comment: "The girl's emotionally disabled." Was Sherry right? Did this make Lois Wilson dangerous in a unique way, a way not easily detected?

"I suppose, in some ways, you see your father in Helen Keller's state before she was able to communicate."

"Precisely," Lois said, her face coming alive with an excitement he had seen only on rare occasions. "You see that, too?"

"Give your senile old teacher some credit," he said. She neither smiled nor laughed. "I suppose all this is part of that obedience-control paper you've been dangling before me continually."

"Yes, as a matter of fact, it is."

"How much longer before I see something?"

"Most of the summer. But don't worry, you'll read it before I leave for MIT."

"Looking forward to it. Well," he said, looking at the wall clock, "I've got to do some shopping in Middletown tonight." She gathered her things quickly. He thought for a moment and then stood up. "You know, I could just as easily go through Sandburg to get to the main highway. No problem dropping you off, if you'd like."

"I've got to drop these two books off at the library."

"Meet me in the teachers' parking lot."

"Thank you. I appreciate it."

He watched her leave and then sat back again. Why was it, he wondered, that Sherry's admonitions were growing louder and louder? It was ridiculous, silly, to read such romanticized horror into this girl. It's just a characteristic of her brilliance; she's the personification of science, as pure as an idea.

"She'll never cry at sad movies," Sherry had told him.

Was that such a great sacrifice in the name of progress? he had asked. She had said yes, but she was wrong. Wasn't she? He was still arguing with himself when Lois joined him in the parking lot.

"What have you been working with for this paper on obedience?" he asked after they had started out. "Laboratory animals?"

"Some."

"Something additional?" He waited, but she didn't reply. He looked at her and then out at the road again. "Top secret, eh?"

"For the time being. I don't want any outside input just yet. It might influence my thinking."

"I see." The rest of their conversation was small talk until they reached Sandburg. She wanted to be dropped off in town, but he insisted on taking her to her house, driven by his own curiosity concerning every aspect of Lois Wilson's life. He regretted that he couldn't meet her father now, but hoped to meet her mother soon, just so he could get an idea about the home environment that had produced such a girl.

"This is it," she said. He pulled into the driveway.

"Interesting house."

"Belonged to Dr. Fleur. Ever hear of him?"

"No."

"Sandburg's most famous citizen." She opened the door.

"That your little brother on the porch?"

"Yes. He hasn't reacted well to my father's being an invalid. He's actually acting out aggression because of it."

"Understandable."

"I haven't had time to deal with it, but I will."

"Keep taking on more and more, don't you?"

"Not any more than I can handle. I'd invite you in, but my mother would panic. She's developed the idea that waiting on my father like a full-time nurse is taking its toll on her, causing physical degeneration."

"I'm sure it's not easy."

"She's always been neurotic about her looks. It's a classic example of a neurosis on the way toward becoming a psychosis." She stepped out and started to close the door. "Thanks for the ride," she said. He watched her walk toward the house, noting how the little boy was digging at a wooden column with a small pocket-knife.

He backed out and continued down the road. As he drove on he felt as though he had gone in and out of some strange nightmare. He couldn't imagine what life inside that house must be like, with an invalid father, a neurotic mother, and a daughter peering about with microscopic eyes. The little boy looked tormented. How could anyone grow up normal under those conditions? He felt sorry for the kid, but he didn't know what he could do about it. How much more involved could he become? Sherry thought he was too involved as it was. Maybe she was right. He used scholastics as an excuse for his interest.

"Maybe I'll write a paper about her," he had told Sherry. "She is a phenomenon."

"You're just as bad as she is," she had replied. He laughed, remembering.

Forget Lois Wilson and think about what you have to buy, he mumbled and drove on.

He thought he had succeeded in pushing her to the back of his mind when suddenly, for no apparent reason, he conjured up the image of her little brother. He had looked out at them with a face characterized by blankness and lack of interest. Children were usually curious about strangers. It was as though her brother were blind or . . . in a spell.

It gave him the chills, so he rolled the window up to

cut down on the incoming breeze. Then he turned the radio up to help drown out his thoughts.

"What's going on?" Lois asked.

"The therapist was here again. Mommy was mad you weren't here to listen. She did a lot of work and then fell asleep on the couch." He went back to gouging the column.

"Stop that. Why don't you find something constructive to do?"

He folded the knife quickly and put it into his pocket.

"She started yellin' at me for nothin'. She said I was makin' too much noise. I can't even play with my cars."

"Just ignore her. That's displaced aggression."

"I don't know what that means," he said in a belligerent tone. Lois was amused by his anger.

"She's not happy taking care of Daddy, but she can't yell at him, so she yells at you."

"That's not fair."

"Who ever said things had to be fair?" she replied and went inside.

Heavy silence greeted her. The gloom that had been part of the old Fleur mansion, a heavy, depressing atmosphere that Dorothy Wilson had never succeeded in removing despite her efforts at redecoration, had intensified the day Greg was brought back from the hospital. The laughter that had once existed between them was smothered in the silence of Greg's eyes. His presence, without the sound of his voice, amplified her own sounds, making her aware of her own breathing. She had started talking to the walls, catching herself in the middle of monologues. The new, deeper, more permeating quiet caused every ordinary sound to take on a shriller, higher note. The banging of pots and pans, the clink of dishes, the hollow echo of footsteps on the wooden floors, the creaking of banisters and doors, the scraping of chair legs—all conspired to tear at her, bringing her to a more hysterical frame of mind. And Lois was of little help.

Her daughter continued to stay to herself. Their conversations were one-sided and short. Dorothy was even willing to discuss some of the girl's scientific projects, but Lois would have none of it. She contributed to maintaining Greg, she cooked and cleaned and looked after Billy with just as much vigor as before, but she provided no substitute for the absence of small talk. She disliked watching television and thought most parlor games a total waste of time.

Billy was no help either. She recognized that he was going through some sort of psychological upheaval, but his avoidance of her was intolerable. He was treating her as though she were to blame for what had happened to Greg. She wondered if Lois could have put such a thought in his mind. In any case, she realized that what she had succeeded in doing now was isolate herself terribly. Since she was no longer working in the store, her contact with the outside world was limited to shopping for food and going to the post office and the bank. It couldn't go on; she had to think of some changes.

Lois found her mother, as Billy had said, asleep on the couch. She studied her for a moment. There was some physical degeneration. Lois could recall when her mother had worked on her hair, babying each strand. Now her hair was wild and stringy. It looked greasy and dull. Instead of taking the time each morning to select her day's wardrobe with an eye to fashion and color coordination, her mother threw on housecoats and wore them from morning to night. All of her makeup went unused; she didn't even open a lipstick tube.

The work and the mental strain were reflected in her complexion as well. Gone were the rosy cheeks, the glittering eyes, the dazzling white teeth. She was pale and dull. One thing fed on another. Because of her self-imposed isolation, she neglected her appearance; and because her appearance degenerated, she reinforced her isolation.

For a few moments, as Lois studied her in sleep, she

felt genuine pity. Despite her own attitudes about cosmetics and fashions, her mother's attention to them often brought a shine and cheerfulness to an otherwise dreary world. Granted, it was a surface gleam and liveliness, but it was, nevertheless, something in contrast. Her mother was a flower without sunlight now, and Lois sympathized with her as she would for any living thing transplanted out of its natural habitat.

But after she analyzed this reaction, she sensed an even deeper sorrow, one that touched on feelings and thoughts so dormant they were nearly nonexistent. She remembered how it was, even as a little girl, to walk in the streets with her mother beside her. She recognized that she felt a certain pride in the way other people looked at her mother, appreciating her good looks, her fashionable appearance. Perhaps—and she fell back into the role of psychoanalyst again—because her mother shone so brightly, eclipsing her, making her aware of her own physical inadequacies when it came to good looks, perhaps because of this Lois had become so hardened against her mother's continual attention to physical beauty.

All these thoughts passed through her mind as she stood there in the doorway staring in at her sleeping mother. They came and went with the same telegraph-like, electric pattern most of her thoughts took on. And when they were finished and she became fully conscious of the moment again, she rejected conclusions that would lead her away from her purposes. For an instant she thought of herself as a modern-day Dr. Jekyll and Mr. Hyde. However, she quickly rejected the voices that told her she was like someone possessed and out of control. That was ridiculous. If anything, she was someone with more control. Determined, she turned away from her pathetic mother and started up the stairs to her father's bedroom.

He was awake, but if he was happy to see her, it did not register in his eyes. His gaze followed her into the room and to his side. He had been left sitting up.

"Daddy," she began, "I've got to talk to you about Mother. I know you've probably seen the change that's come over her since you were brought home from the hospital." She waited, and he blinked once. "She just isn't adapting well; she doesn't have the right attitude about all this," Lois said. She walked to the foot of the bed and touched his right foot. "We've got to help her," she went on, not looking at him as she spoke. It was more like someone voicing her thoughts. "It's simply a matter of adjusting the image she has of herself and the image she now has of you. Why, even this room, this entire setting, the whole house, have changed in the way she perceives them. Understandable, I know, but, nevertheless, not good. You see what I'm trying to say, don't you?" He blinked twice and then he blinked twice again.

Lois straightened up and smirked with impatience.

"If you don't see, it's because you simply don't want to see. You're smarter than that." She took an even more pedantic posture. "Mother is caught in what we term an approach-avoidance conflict. The same goal both attracts and repels her. She wants to help you, serve you, cure you. She wants to be the wife who lives up to her moral responsibilities. You know the stuff: 'for better or for worse.'

"But she is repelled by your condition, by this situation, and by what it's doing to her. Thus we have approach-avoidance. People caught in such conflicts often develop behavioral problems. She's headed that way, I'm afraid.

"Consequently, as soon as school ends next week, I'm going to change things somewhat. I want Mother in here less and less. It'll be better for everyone." He blinked twice and then blinked twice again. "That's selfish, Daddy. That's not like you. Don't worry, I know what I'm doing. There are things I want to do, things she'd never understand. She'll only get in the way. You'll see," she said, nodding.

He opened and closed his mouth. The guttural sound

emerged, but she wasn't interested. She was looking about the room, thinking of changes, thinking of arrangements.

"I'll talk to you about this again," she said and started out. He blinked his eyes rapidly, but she was already gone. In the silence that followed, a tear emerged from his right eye. It traveled a crooked path over his cheek and down the side of his jawbone, after which it fell and was lost in the sheets.

There was nothing for him to do but wait.

12

It began the day after Lois's graduation ceremonies. They had hired a nurse to stay with Greg while Dorothy and Billy attended the festivities. Lois's speech was as many had predicted: esoteric, filled with scientific jargon, long; the wrong kind of speech to deliver to excited parents and grandparents. Few people actually listened, and when it ended, the sharp, hard applause was more because it had ended than in appreciation for what was said. There were some graduation parties, but Lois didn't go to one.

Although her daughter was the recipient of so many honors and awards, the graduation exercise was a terribly depressing event for Dorothy. She kept looking at the stranger on her right, imagining that he was Greg, that all that had happened was just a terrible nightmare. But no amount of fantasy would change things.

Afterward, she could see the sympathy and the sorrow in the eyes of those who congratulated her. She shook hands and accepted the plaudits like one resigned to punishment. Later, she was grateful for her chance to escape and go home. On the way to the parking lot, Lois introduced her to a rather good-looking young college professor.

"I was eager to meet you, Mrs. Wilson," he said. "It's anticlimactic to tell you that you have an amazing daughter, but I must tell you she stimulated my class and my own work this spring."

"Thank you." Dorothy could feel the way his eyes searched her. He had the same analytical quickness as Lois, and that made her exceedingly nervous. "I'm sorry," she said, "but we've got to get back to the house. I was able to get a nurse for only a few hours today."

"Of course." He saw how hard she was clutching her little son's hand. She walked quickly to her car. Lois lingered for a few moments as they exchanged some thoughts on her speech.

After they left, he remarked to himself how hypertense Lois's mother was. She was nothing like what he had imagined. He had pictured a stereotyped schoolmarm type, actually an older version of Lois. He certainly hadn't visualized a soft-faced, emotional woman with an attractive figure. It made him wonder more about her father. He wanted to meet him, even in his present condition.

As Dorothy approached the house she felt her body begin to shake. Lately this was happening every time she left and returned to the old Fleur mansion. The graduation exercises and all those people had turned out to be more of a strain than she had expected. Mentally and physically exhausted, she wasn't looking forward to dealing with Greg. What she did contemplate was a good stiff drink, a highball or two. It would be a good way to calm down from her emotional stress.

Lois didn't go upstairs to show her awards to her father until after the nurse was paid and left. In the meantime, Dorothy made herself a drink and settled on the couch in the living room. She contemplated herself in the wall mirror over the mantel. At the last moment, before going to the graduation ceremony, she had opted for pinning her hair back as a way to hide its poor condition. She told herself she just had to get to the beauty parlor soon and resurrect her good looks, or at least what was left of them. She rubbed her cheeks to stimulate some color. Her skin felt dry and tough. All this made her angry.

In the morning she called Nikki's Salon and pleaded for an early appointment. She was promised one if she rushed right down, so she skipped breakfast and left everything for Lois to do. Of course, Lois offered no resistance, but this time she had other reasons to want her mother to leave.

Dorothy was pleased with herself. Nikki himself took charge of her hair. He moaned and groaned and bawled her out for letting it go so long. Then he saw her as a challenge, and before long her hair became center stage for the whole beauty parlor. He lectured as he worked, and the other women, who normally chatted and read magazines while they waited, gathered around and watched him revive Dorothy Wilson's good looks. She was flattered by the attention and her spirits soared. It never even occurred to her that her husband could show his appreciation only with the blinking of eyes. She was singing along with the car radio as she pulled into the driveway.

Her first disappointment came when neither of the children met her at the door. It was quiet as usual and there were no lights on downstairs. She took off her thin white sweater and stood admiring herself in the mirror in the entrance hall. With her face glowing with a smile of satisfaction, she walked in farther.

"Lois," she called. "Billy." She waited, but there was no response. "Lois?" Something was different, she thought, and then she recognized a strange new odor in the air. It was emanating from upstairs. "Damn, where are you two? What's going on here?" she muttered and started up. The odor was very strong at the top of the stairs. When she turned into the master bedroom, she froze in the doorway, for a moment too shocked to utter a sound. Lois, dressed in one of her lab robes, was on a footstool completing some window-trim painting.

Billy was just below her, sprawled on his stomach, painting a strip of molding. All of the walls of the bedroom had been repainted a bright green.

"What are you doing?" All of her facial features became distorted in the rubbery movement of her mouth, the widening of her nostrils, the exploding of her eyes. She clutched at her new hairdo, her fingers digging right through the sculptured strands and into her scalp. Greg was laid out flat, his bed lowered totally so he could only stare up at the yet-to-be-painted ceiling. Lois turned and paused, holding the small paintbrush like an artist disturbed at her easel. Billy was so intent on what he was doing that he didn't bother to stop.

"I'm changing Daddy's negative environment. This is the room in which he suffered his stroke. The room has a bad connotation for him in that respect," Lois said. Dorothy could see tiny specks of green on Lois's eyeglass lenses.

"But why green? This green is so . . . ugly. I hate green. I've always hated it."

"We're not doing this for you, Mother. I've done a thorough study of color," Lois said, turning back to her work. She continued to paint as she spoke. "Green has been found to benefit the nervous system as well as increase vitality. The late Col. Dinshah P. Ghadiali wrote a compendium of color therapy based on many years of research with patients from all over the world. His book *Spectro-Chrome-Metry* contains an immense amount of information on color therapy. He considered green the master healer."

"That's ridiculous. How can a color make any difference?"

"Oh, but it does," she said, stopping her work again and turning back. "Color therapy is centuries old. Each color has its own specific frequency or wavelength which is a valid source of energy. I'm not saying it can do things all by itself, but in conjunction with other factors—"

"But I can't stand green. This is my bedroom too," she said, as though she had just realized it.

"Mother, I'm surprised at you. Really, this isn't a time for us to think of ourselves," Lois added and looked at her father. Billy stopped working and looked up at his mother. Dorothy was taken with his very real look of hatred.

"But I . . ."

"Why don't you move into one of the other bedrooms up here? That would solve the problem."

"There's such an odor from that paint. Don't you think it bothers your father?"

"We'll air it out. You want to help with this?" she asked, holding up the brush.

"Absolutely not."

"Your hair looks terrific," Lois said. Dorothy realized she still had the fingers of her right hand pressed into her trimmed and sculptured strands. She lifted it out quickly and patted herself behind the ears gently.

"Think so? Everyone at Nikki's thought so. Do you like it, Billy?"

"It's nice," he said, but he was obviously more taken with his painting job.

"I just felt that I had to do something. I just felt . . . I needed it." She moved farther into the room, grimacing at the odor of paint and the color. "I'll sit you up, Greg, so you can see," she said, moving to the bed's controls.

"No point in doing that now," Lois said without turning around. "He's asleep."

Dorothy studied her husband's face. His eyes were indeed closed. He looked like a man suspended in time—immobile, hardly breathing, yet still possessing enough of a complexion to look alive.

"How did you know without even looking at him?" Dorothy asked, still staring down at Greg.

"He's been asleep ever since we started painting," Billy said, obviously sounding proud that he knew something Dorothy didn't. In fact, she thought he sounded as arrogant as Lois did at times.

"It works out better that way," Lois said. "By the time he awakens, we should be finished here."

Dorothy stood there, watching the two of them work. Then she walked to the doorway.

"I'm going to get myself some lunch. I'd better eat before this stink destroys my appetite. I haven't had a thing all day."

"Fine. Which of the two bedrooms do you want, the farthest or closest?"

"The closest, of course."

"OK," Lois said, a slight smile on her face. "As soon as I finish here, I'll help you move some of your things. I'll make the bed and get the room aired out for you."

Dorothy didn't respond. She went downstairs quickly, all the while feeling a terrible sense of nervousness. She was shaking again. Here she had finally left the house and come back without feeling that terrible sense of doom when she drove into the driveway, and now she was all in a tremor. It wasn't food she needed; it was a stiff drink—a highball, quickly. She made one and retreated to the living room. She forcefully sat herself in the easy chair. After a moment she began to chastise herself for going into a sulk, but she did feel that the limits of her tolerance were quickly being reached. She consumed her drink quickly and made herself another, stronger one. Soon a warm, relaxed glow came over her. She knew it would happen quickly because she had no food in her stomach. Kicking off her shoes, she put her feet up on the hassock. She was calming down; it was going to be all right. She took a deep breath to suck in the long-missed odor of hair spray. That, too, helped revive her spirits.

"I suppose," she muttered, "Lois is right." After all, she thought, the girl was brilliant. Who knows, maybe she would come up with something that would help Greg and bring about a real recovery. How could she stand in the way of that? As long as she didn't do anything that was downright harmful to anybody, there was no reason to stop her. Dorothy was sure Lois had Greg's best interests at heart. So she would sleep in one of the other bedrooms. No real harm in it since they didn't have to heat it. In fact, she secretly applauded the idea.

It had been difficult sleeping in the bedroom with Greg. What could she do—hold his hand while she masturbated? It was like being alone anyway. Even worse than that, it was like being beside a different kind of creature. Oh, God forgive her for thinking such a thing, but it was true. She couldn't help the way she felt. If things were reversed, he'd feel the same way. She was sure of that.

Still, she didn't like the way Lois was taking over. She was too smart, she thought, and then she reconsidered. "No," she said aloud, "this is probably Lois's way of showing her love. At least she cares." Dorothy had been worried lately that Lois was totally indifferent to what had happened.

Greg's stroke had certainly not changed Lois's life much. It meant she wouldn't have to work in the store for the summer and it meant that Billy would stay home and remain her responsibility, but Lois didn't make any real changes in her daily life. At least, not as far as Dorothy could see. She was still into her work and into her schooling. She continued to read a great deal and stay to herself as usual. No, Dorothy thought, she couldn't chastise her for painting the room. In doing that, she was coming out of her shell somewhat and doing something for someone else.

All this reasoning, plus the third and fourth drink, put Dorothy into a happier frame of mind. She put the stereo on and moved to the music. She got up and danced about the room, giggling and laughing to herself, subduing and bawling herself out for making too much noise.

"You want to wake Greg up?" she said and laughed.

It was so silly, but it did feel so good. After a while she got very dizzy and had to catch herself on the arm of the couch. At that moment she looked into a wall mirror and caught sight of herself—staggering, her clothes a little disheveled, her new hairdo a little messed. It brought tears to her eyes. She sat down, unable to prevent herself from sobbing. But even that felt good. Then she began to feel nauseated. She clutched her stomach, hiccuped, and rushed to the bathroom.

Upstairs, Lois and Billy had completed their job.

In Lois's mind, moving her mother to another bedroom was essential for the success of the project. A description of the project, activities making up the project, and the results of those activities were all a major part of what would be the paper on obedience she had been planning and writing since she had met Professor McShane. She had been planning a series of traditional-type experiments using lab animals, but on the day her mother first brought up the idea of bringing her father home, she conceived of something so innovative it nearly drove her mad with excitement.

She would turn her father's bedroom into a Skinner box. B. F. Skinner, the famous psychologist, made a science of using operant conditioning on animals in the laboratory. Operant conditioning was sometimes referred to as the carrot-and-stick method of modifying behavior. Rewards were given for desired responses, and punishments were used to discourage repetition of undesired behavior. A Skinner box gave a caged animal an opportunity for reward or punishment. What was her father now, if not a caged animal?

What scientist could take a human being and place him or her in a caged environment so he could experiment with operant conditioning? No university would approve of such a project; no fund would finance it. But think of the things that could be learned about the human mind and human behavior, she reflected. Her father was already imprisoned by his stroke. He was already in a kind of Skinner box. What harm could there be in taking advantage of that fact? There was certainly much to be gained. She might even enter college with a publishable study all completed.

Now a second possibility had suddenly emerged. In manipulating her mother out of the bedroom, Lois had discovered the potential for an even larger Skinner box: the entire house. The paper was practically writing itself. She was very glad now that she had gone to the drugstore and had done the inventory before they sold the business. Her mother thought she had only brought home sundries, cosmetics, minor medications, and the like. But she had had more foresight than that.

Her father hadn't just fallen asleep at the beginning of the painting of the bedroom and coincidentally slept through the work. Now she would have other uses for those sleeping pills. And what of the other drugs she had collected and cached in the house? Some of them would prove to be carrots for her experiments with operant conditioning. She would need them for both her father and her mother. Her mother was a veteran of uppers and downers anyway. Her sudden interest in booze was symptomatic of how she handled most of her anxieties.

Yes, Lois thought, all the ingredients were here. She could maintain control over all of them. She was confident of that. After she had completed her experiments, she would return things to their "normal" state. She could handle everything in such a way that no one would really understand what had taken place. The therapist was finished with his instructional visits, and with the doctor being available only when needed . . . no one from the outside should interfere.

At times when she planned and dreamed, she felt she could grow giantlike and lift the roof off. She'd peer down on her family and move them about. She'd have the all-knowing, omnipresent point of view; godlike, she'd determine futures, map out destinies. This was her fairy tale. It was her Jack and the Beanstalk, her world of Oz. She was the age-old storyteller who began, "Once upon a time . . . ," but unlike him, she worked in the real world.

After Lois and Billy had finished the molding and window trim, she put her father into a sitting position. His eyes were still closed, but she expected he would awaken shortly. His response to the new room color might be interesting, she thought. To go to sleep in one world and then wake up in another had to be traumatic. He'd probably think he had been moved out of the house.

"Take the brushes and the paint out carefully," she commanded.

Billy began rolling the paper up from the floor. "We still got a lot left, Lois."

"I know. I have other uses for this green."

"We're gonna paint some more?" he asked excitedly.

"Yes."

"But what if Mommy gets mad?"

"She won't get mad; she'll get indifferent."

"What's indifferent?"

"Never mind. Just put everything away carefully. Make sure the lid on the paint can is tightly closed." He worked quickly, obediently. She watched him for a moment and then studied the room. It wasn't going to be hard. She had a good mind for mechanics.

She would put a hook in the ceiling right above the left side of his bed. A pulley would be placed on the hook. There would be another hook by the door. The cable would run from his bed to a gong attached to the wall, right by the door. At the end of the cable by his bed she would attach a tiny flat bar. The bar would dangle just above his left hand. All he would have to do would be to raise his fingers and pull down on the bar. That would pull on the cable and ring the gong. Thus she would have a typical Skinner box response mechanism. It was important that he hear the sound of the gong, too. Later on, she would use that sound to establish various conditioned reflexes. She had so many ideas. Her mind was simply exploding with them.

After she arranged the response mechanism, it was simply a matter of shaping the behavior. What was to be the stimulus? Why would he pull down on the bar? What would be the positive reinforcement? She determined she would start with the most basic of needs, food itself. Now he was on a regular schedule fit to his biological clock. She would have to change that by putting him on what was known as a variable interval schedule. He would learn that the only way he could get food would be by pulling down on the response bar, but she wouldn't reinforce this every time. He would know that he couldn't get food without pulling on the bar, but he would not command food. He would get it when she gave it to him, at intervals she would determine, intervals she would vary. Of course, she would keep as exact a record as possible of how often and when he made the gong ring.

It occurred to her that she should give Billy some role in this. She would make him aware of the gong and have him record when he heard it too. That way, if she missed the sound and he didn't, the gong would still be recorded. She decided she would place the chart right up on the wall just outside his door. She would show Billy how to mark it.

Once all this basic work was completed, she could begin her important experiments. To what extent could she control his physiological functions: cause him to be hungry when she wanted him to be hungry, for example? What would be the effects of a vitamin deficiency over a specific length of time? How would that affect operant behavior? She hadn't been just kidding her mother before. She was fascinated with the effects of color. She had all sorts of ideas for experimenting with that. And perhaps with sounds too. Then there were the drugs.

She had taken all sorts of mood modifiers from the drugstore. How would they affect appetite and other physiological functions? How soon could she get him into an addiction and then get him out of it? In short, she believed she could control his body at will, determine the rate of his heartbeat and breathing, the cycles of his ingestion, digestion, and excretion. Perhaps she could even get into his sexual fantasies. The potentials were enormous; her problem was limitation. She had just so much time to work, and everything she did had to be done well, accurately, with proper documentation and replication. Unfortunately, she had to be selective and realistic.

His eyelids flickered and then opened slowly. As he focused and took in the new green color, he moved his head from side to side to see as much of the room as possible. His mouth opened and closed. The fingers of his left hand moved up and down. Then he made his guttural noise.

"You're still at home, Daddy. I've just painted your room. How do you like it?" He blinked twice, indicating the negative. "Oh, I bet you're thinking more about Mother and her opinion than your own. Is that it?" He blinked once. "No problem, Daddy. She's going to sleep in one of the other bedrooms." His eyes widened. "That's by her own choice too.

"You see," she said, moving closer to his bed, "I've made a study of color and the positive and negative effects different hues have on people. Green has definite medicinal benefits." She paused and then put on her quick, mechanical smile. "Just have patience and trust me. Everything I'm doing, I'm doing for your benefit. And the benefit of science too," she added. That made him turn more toward her.

"Remember when you and Mommy made me get rid of my lab animals? At first I thought, Well, there goes all my experimentation with behavior modification. Then I realized behavior is all around me, all the time—the behavior of people, my own people, my family. Why couldn't I just study that? I've already started working with Billy. He's a perfect subject, you know, because he's so dependent on me. I can thank you and Mommy for that." This time her smile was warmer.

"Well," she said, running her forefinger over his left wrist, "now this terrible thing has happened to you. It's horrible and I feel bad about it, but it would be foolish if I didn't take advantage of it and try to learn something from it. You'd be the first to say that, I'm sure," she said. Her face was filled with sincerity. Greg's eyes moved back and forth quickly as he searched it, looking for meanings between her sentences.

"You and I can understand this, but we can't expect Mommy will. In time, she might understand some of it, but we can't be concerned about that. Anyway, your illness is having more of a psychological and emotional effect on her than she cares to admit. She went absolutely berserk this morning and ran off to get her hair done at Nikki's. When she comes up to show you, try to make a big deal of it. As big a deal as you're capable of making, I mean.

"So, you see," she went on, "I think it would be better for her anyhow if I relieved her of most of her responsibility toward you. She's really not strong enough for all this. Don't get me wrong," she added quickly. "I think it was admirable of her to want to bring you home and take care of you. But it's simply another case of expectations exceeding capabilities. We see it every day, don't we?

"All right," she said, starting toward the door, "I'll go down and let mother know that you woke up. Want to sit up a little higher?" He didn't blink once or twice. "Now, you can't sulk, Daddy. That's not a mature response." She waited a second or two, but he continued to simply stare. "OK," she sang and walked out of the room.

Downstairs, Dorothy had fallen asleep. Her new hairdo had already begun to come apart. With her head collapsed to the side in a drunken stupor and her jaw dropped, opening her mouth enough to reveal the tip of her pink tongue pressed against the inside of her lower lip, Dorothy appeared just as paralyzed as her husband. Lois shook her head in disgust as she stood looking down at her. Then she poked her sharply in the shoulder.

Dorothy's eyes struggled to stay shut. After a few moments she opened them and confronted her daughter. She grimaced and pushed herself into a sitting position and then rubbed her face as vigorously as she could.

"What time is it?"

"Daddy woke up. He wants to see you and your new hairdo. I told him about it."

"Did you?" She yawned and felt the sides of her head to see how badly the strands had broken free of their mold.

"Yes. I'll go up and start preparing the other bedroom for you. Then we'll move your stuff."

"Why . . . why would I move my stuff?"

"Do you want to keep running back and forth for clothes every morning? I just assumed you'd want the convenience. . . ."

"I guess you're right. Let me just wash my face in cold water before I go upstairs," she said, struggling to stand. "I feel so warm."

Lois backed away. "I'm going back upstairs." She met Billy in the corridor. He had just finished putting all the paint and brushes away. "Tomorrow," she said, "we're going to build a little machine for Daddy, something that will make things easier for him."

"Wow."

Lois looked behind her.

"But don't say anything to Mommy about it yet. She'd only get in the way and make things more difficult."

"I won't."

"Good," Lois said. "Help me fix up the other bedroom for her. If you keep helping me like this," she said, "I'll do something special for you."

"You will? What?"

"I'll show you how to make a worm farm."

"Oh, boy! I'll help you, Lois, I'll help you all the time."

"I know," she said. "I know you will." She gave him a curt smile and started up the stairs quickly. There was work to be done and she never liked wasting time.

13

In the morning Dorothy went to the supermarket to buy a week's worth of food. Lois encouraged her to do so by complimenting her on her newly revived good looks and got her to the point where she was eager to be seen in public again. As soon as she left, Lois began building the Skinner box response mechanism. She had what she needed in her inventory of materials from her previous projects with animals. Gregory Wilson watched with a look of surprise and terror on his face as his daughter and small son constructed the cable and gong. When they were finished, she asked him to try it, but he didn't move his fingers a bit.

"That's the wrong attitude, Daddy. I was hoping you would be cooperative from the start. We don't have that much time to work, you know." She waited, but he simply stared and blinked twice.

"Why is he saying no?" Billy asked. Greg turned to his son and repeated his message. Lois stepped between them.

"Because he doesn't understand yet," she said. "Don't worry about it. He will."

Lois didn't tell Dorothy about it until later when they helped her bring in the packages and unpack the groceries.

"We've built a device for Daddy so he can call us when he wants us," she said.

"Yeah, it really works good," Billy said.

"Oh?"

"Want me to go upstairs and ring it, Lois?"

"Sure, go on."

"Just listen," he said and ran up to his father's room. Dorothy waited. They heard the gong vibrate.

"Why, that's amazing. And your father can do that?"

"Whenever he wants to," Lois said. She continued to organize the foods. Her mother had fallen for this part easily, she thought, but what would follow would be more difficult to do as long as her mother played such a major role in taking care of her father. Her next step, as she saw it, was to direct her mother away from her father and away from the house. She had to get her to see the situation as totally threatening to herself; she had to get her to reject it all.

"Did you see a lot of people?" Lois asked.

"Some. Everyone asked about Greg. I don't know whether it's more depressing to stay in or get out."

"Oh, by all means you should get out more. Take in a movie, visit someone."

"I wouldn't feel right without your father," Dorothy said.

"That's ridiculous and unrealistic, Mother."

"Maybe, but right now nothing like that interests me. I'm satisfied with my soap operas," she added, smiling, and headed for the living room.

Lois thought for a moment. It was clear to her what she had to do. Although it was important to be subtle, it was equally important to be assertive. She didn't have the time for intricate strategies. Thank goodness she didn't need them; her mother was already tipping in the right direction. It only required a gentle shove. She made her a stiff drink and brought it into the living room.

"What's this?"

"I know what it's like to do battle in the local supermarkets. Figured you'd like to calm your nerves."

"I didn't even eat lunch," Dorothy said, a smile frozen on her face.

"So? Cocktails before a meal are always in order."

"I've got to feed your father."

"Already done." She was lying, but there was no chance of her mother's discovering that. "Of course, it's time for his bedpan."

"Oh," Dorothy said, taking the drink.

"But why spoil your appetite? I'll take care of that."

"Would you? Thank you, Lois. I know I couldn't have brought him home without your help." She took another long sip from her drink and settled back in her chair.

As soon as Lois walked into the bedroom, Greg's eyes snapped open. She could see he was expecting food.

"Mother came back from the supermarket, but she's exhausted. Doesn't have the same stamina she used to have. I thought you'd press the bar and ring the gong. Aren't you hungry?" He blinked once. "Well, you're going to have to press the bar, Daddy. That's the way it's going to be now. I don't have to go through the procedures to establish a conditioned reflex with you, do I? You want food, you press the bar; food, bar, that's the association. You have the intelligence to make it with verbal directions." He blinked twice. "That's stubborn and disobedient. I really didn't expect this."

She looked at the bedpan that was on the chair beside the bed.

"I can't give you the bedpan until you eat," she said. She turned to the door and then looked back at him. "I hope you don't wait too long. If you mess the bed, God knows how long you'll be lying in it." She left, a smile of determination on her face.

She was only halfway down the stairs when the gong vibrated. Billy came charging down the corridor and up the steps.

"He did it? He did it?" he asked, the excitement bringing a full red flush to his face.

"Of course," she said and walked back up. Billy went down again and hurried into the living room. Dorothy was absorbed in her soap opera. She had her feet up, her nearly emptied glass held high.

"Did you hear it? Did you hear it?"

"Hear what?"

"The gong. Daddy rang his gong."

"No, I didn't. What did he want?"

"Lois went to see."

"Good," she said and turned back to the television set.

Upstairs, Lois gave Greg his bedpan. He looked angry and worked hard at expressing it through his guttural noises.

"I know," she said, "I know. But this reaction will pass. You'll get so you like the system, you'll see. The more dependent you are on it, the more you'll like it. It's a common phenomenon, evidenced in the behavior of hostages who develop positive relationships with their captors. Remember the poem 'The Prisoner of Chillon' by Byron? Oh, you probably don't. You had a poor literary background, Daddy. I meant to tell you that a number of times.

"Anyway, in the poem, when his saviors come and finally free him, he says—and I always remember these lines because they illustrate an interesting behavioral reaction; Byron was ahead of his time with the concept. He says, 'Fetter'd or fetterless to be,/I learn'd to love despair./And thus when they appear'd at last,/And all my bonds aside were cast,/These heavy walls to me had grown/A hermitage—and all my own!/And half I felt as they were come/To tear me from a second home.' Later on, he says, 'My very chains and I grew friends. . . .'

"So, you see," she said, with a voice as cheery as any she could express, "in time, you're going to absolutely.

love this little Skinner box bar. Now I'll go down and get you something to eat."

Lois had a new motive for bringing animals back into the house. Dorothy discovered it when she came upon Billy entering the house with a small garter snake captured in a jar. Before she could turn him out with it, Lois was on the scene.

"I need it," she said.

"What do you mean, you need it? I thought we all agreed you weren't going to experiment with animals in the house anymore."

"That was before Daddy got so sick." She took the jar from Billy, opened it, and lifted the snake out. Dorothy backed away. Lois stretched the snake its full length.

"That's ugly and disgusting. I don't want it in here. What if it should get loose?"

"It won't get loose."

"What does your father's illness have to do with your bringing animals back in?"

"Well, if I'm going to be tied to this house for a considerable part of the summer, I won't be able to carry out my work someplace else, now, will I?"

"What work? Why can't you experiment with something else?" Dorothy asked, keeping her distance. Her voice was already weakening.

"I don't see why you're being unreasonable, Mother. I wasn't unreasonable when you asked me to make sacrifices."

"Just keep them away from me," Dorothy said. "Don't let me know about them. You can have the pantry back again."

"I'm using the study," Lois said. She put the snake back into the jar.

"What?"

"The pantry is just too small."

"The study?"

"We don't use it, Mother. It won't make any difference."

"All those dirty creatures in the study?"

"They're not dirty. You hardly ever go in there, so what's the difference?" Lois held her ground. Dorothy looked at the snake in the jar and then walked on to the living room.

"It was easy to catch it, Lois. What else do you want?"

"I want field mice, lots of field mice. We'll use my traps. Go get them and set them up in the backyard."

"All right," he said eagerly. He started, but stopped when they heard the gong. "What's Daddy want?"

"Never mind. Go get the traps." They heard the gong again and then again.

"Is it time for his lunch?"

"No," she said. "Go get the traps, I told you."

He walked off, turning back when the gong was sounded and then continuing on when Lois glared at him. She took the small pad out of the back pocket of her jeans and made a notation. The gonging stopped. She smiled to herself and went into the living room. Dorothy sat sulking in the easy chair.

"What did he want?"

"What do you mean?"

"I heard him gonging."

"He wanted the bed rolled down," she said, sure she had left it that way.

"How can you tell what he wants? He was hitting that gong all through the night last night. Nearly drove me crazy. I'm exhausted from lack of sleep. I went in there and asked him if he wanted a drink or food. He had no bathroom problems. All he did was make that horrible throat sound. He was trying to tell me something, but there was no way I could understand him. I thought about calling the doctor."

"There's no need for that."

"He kept putting his fingers on that bar thing you

created and blinking no and making that sound. It's just a mental torment for me. This was a mistake, a terrible mistake." She shook her head and buried her face in her palms. Lois studied her for a moment and then, in a very contrived manner, put her hand on her mother's shoulder.

"I know it's hard," she said, "but we can't give up on him so quickly. You should have just left him and gone back to sleep."

"I did." She raised her head slowly. "I shut my door too," she added, a look of guilt on her face.

"That's all right. I would have done the same thing."

"Would you?"

"Of course. You've got to relax, Mother. It's not going to do anyone any good if you have a breakdown, too."

"I know. I worry about that all the time."

"Take a Valium."

Dorothy looked at her and then shook her head quickly.

"I've taken so many of them lately."

"That's all right. If you need it, take it. I'll get it for you." She didn't wait for her mother's reply, and when she returned with the pill, Dorothy took it obediently. Lois put the water glass on the table beside her as Dorothy laid her head back.

Lois stepped back and then sat on the hassock and watched her. It was interesting how quickly mental anguish would write itself into a person's face. The lines that had been there were deeper, darker; and new lines had recently appeared. She looked older, tired, worn. The color in her lips and cheeks had dulled. Sacks under her eyes, that had hitherto been only a suggestion of age to come, now were fuller and more distinct. Despite her session at the beauty parlor, her hair no longer had its gleam and look of softness.

But the most remarkable thing was her hands. Fingers that had always been dainty and feminine, manicured and youthful, now looked arthritic. They had always rested straight and gentle; now they were curled, bony, the nails nibbled into uneven shapes.

Lois imagined an animal within her mother, gnawing away, draining her of youth and beauty, feeding on the same light that had once caused her eyes to glow with a sexual energy that Lois envied. Dorothy no longer had the look of a woman who was once prom queen. Her mental anguish had drawn a blanket over her face, leaving her in shadows more characteristic of the aged.

"I'm constantly doing battle with my thoughts," Dorothy said, keeping her head back, her eyes closed. "I fight to keep myself from hearing them. I'm afraid of what they'll tell me. I'll do anything to avoid thinking, anything."

"That's only natural." Lois's voice was close to a whisper.

"There's a voice inside of me that wants to tell me life as I once knew it is dead. There's a voice that wants to end all hope."

"We've got to adjust, Mother. You've got to learn to accept what is factually true."

Dorothy shook her head. She was fighting tears, struggling to keep her face from collapsing.

"I can't be that strong. I'm not your father; I'm not you. I come from a world filled with rose petals and bubble baths. I used to brush my hair two hundred strokes a night. Do you know how long it's been since I've done that?" She straightened her head and sat forward. A new look had come over her, one that resembled anger more than sadness.

"I know that I should go up there, be with him more often, talk to him, hold his hand, do anything . . . but I can't. It's hard. It's not him," she said, shaking her head. "There's someone else in that bed," she whispered. "Your father went to the hospital, but someone else was brought home. It smells in there, and that noise he makes . . ." She covered her ears. "I hear it in my sleep."

"I think you'd better start taking sleeping pills, Mother. I don't like your not getting enough sleep."

"It won't help."

"Yes, it will."

Dorothy stared at her for a few moments. Then she nodded softly.

"Why don't you go lie down in my room, Mother? Take a short nap. You won't hear his gong so much if you lie down in my room. I only hear it because I'm listening for it."

"Yes, maybe I will. You're so strong, Lois, so strong. I guess that's a good quality after all. I didn't think so, but I see now that it is."

"That's OK, Mother; I knew eventually you would."

Dorothy got up, steadying herself on Lois's shoulder for a moment.

"I'll just take a little nap. Wake me and I'll help with supper."

"It's all arranged. Don't worry about it." Lois watched her walk out. Then she got up and went into the study. The large piece of oaktag paper was spread on the desk. She looked down at it. Satisfied it was done the way she wanted it done, she took the tacks out of the desk drawer, picked up the oaktag, and went upstairs. Just outside her father's bedroom door, she pinned the chart up. Then she took out her marker and her notepad. Carefully she transferred the information onto the chart. When that was completed, she stepped back to admire her work. Billy's shouting interrupted her.

"What is it?"

"I got one. I got one," he said, proudly displaying the trap. A rather large field mouse sniffed at the bars. "So fast."

"Good. I knew that was a good spot."

"Where should I put it, Lois? In the study like you said?"

"No." She walked down a full step. "No, take it quietly, very quietly, and set it just inside the door of my room. But make no noise," she warned. "Mommy's gone in there to take a nap."

"She has?"

"Just set it down quietly and leave," she repeated. Billy nodded and practically tiptoed down the hallway.

The sound of the gong turned Lois's attention back to her father's room.

As soon as Kevin McShane entered his classroom, he searched the group of faces for Lois Wilson. She had missed the last two sessions, and he wondered if that meant some major problems at home. Perhaps Mrs. Wilson had suffered the emotional breakdown Lois had been predicting. He wondered just how much Lois had helped to prevent it.

"Maybe she's finally becoming a typical high-school or college kid, Kevin, and decided to cut your class to do something that's more fun," Sherry told him when he mentioned Lois's absences.

"No, it can't be that. She's so self-motivated, and the subjects: Mass Media and the Public Mind, Peer Pressure as a Force for Good and for Evil—they were right down her alley. It's hard to believe she would deliberately miss them."

"I'm surprised you didn't call her up."

"I thought about it."

"Oh, that's ridiculous."

"No, something's cooking over there. She suggested to me that her mother was in a bad way and getting worse and worse."

"Why shouldn't she with a daughter like that? Don't be surprised if the kid's half responsible for her mother's problems too."

"What do you mean, 'too'?"

"Did I say 'too'? Funny, when I think of her and the situation at that home the way you described it to me, I somehow see her as to blame. It's not like me to be so—so suspicious."

He laughed, but he couldn't put Lois out of his mind.

So when he entered his class and saw her in her usual front seat, he felt relieved. She gave him a quick glance of hello and opened her notebook. Only auditing the course, and yet she was ready to get down to business. He looked over the other students: some still half asleep, others wearing totally uninterested expressions.

Afterward, he called her aside. The rest of the class emptied out as quickly as usual, some of the students practically running over others in their haste. Well, it was summer and a beautiful day. He could sympathize somewhat.

"Missed you. Thought you might have dropped out."

"No, I've just been busy. But I've done all the reading."

"Things working out at home?"

"To a certain extent. It's hard on all of us, but I'd have to agree with the doctors: the home environment has got to be more conducive to recuperation."

"Oh, no question. I gave you that piece about prisoner home privileges, didn't I?"

"Yes. I agree. The reinforcement using a tangible stimulus has got to be stronger motivation."

They both started out and down the corridor. He noticed that she was wearing her hair differently. She had let it grow longer but kept it tied back tightly. Her complexion was even paler than usual and her eyes were glassy.

"You look tired, if I might say so. Keeping late hours?"

"Trying to do a lot. I'm developing a project that I think might just be of some significance."

"Oh?"

"And of course my mother is getting to be less and less of a help and more and more of a burden."

"I'm sorry. She did seem quite overwrought the day I met her at your graduation."

"You don't know the half of it. She's not eating right; she's drinking too much. The worst part of it is that she is withdrawing, becoming more and more introverted.

She's closing up into a tight fist," she added, demonstrating with her right hand.

"You don't have any other relatives in the area?"

"No."

"Perhaps you should think of professional assistance."

"No, I'm capable of handling it. The therapist has shown us what to do."

"Don't take on too much."

"It's just for the summer."

They stopped at the head of the stairs. He half expected her to turn with him toward his office, but she was obviously on her way out.

"If there's anything I can do . . ." He stopped, not even sure why he had made such a suggestion. Surely if the family didn't have relatives nearby, they had close friends.

"You know that point you were making when you spoke of television figuratively as a drug . . ."

"Yes?"

"Well, I agree; and, you know, it gave me an idea, something that will help me with my project."

"Oh? How so?"

"It's too complicated to discuss right now, but you'll read about it," she added, moving down the stairs quickly. He watched her exit through the front door and walk hurriedly down the sidewalk.

She was going to use television like a drug in her project? What could she be doing? He thought about it as he walked on to his office. His curiosity had been very much aroused, and despite his determination to finish grading some student extracts he had assigned and collected, he found himself continually stopping to think about her statements.

He couldn't help but think about that gloomy house as well, situated off the road with those overpowering weeping willow trees casting it in shadows. Her little brother's face came back to him too, and the way her mother was gripping his hand so fiercely that day.

Into that environment Lois's father had been deposited—a man helplessly dependent on the services of an obviously high-strung, somewhat neurotic woman —and Lois. He got chills just thinking about it. It made him even more grateful than ever for his own good health.

He looked at one of the extracts again, but his mind kept wandering and he read the same lines over and over before he understood them. This was ridiculous. He was better off just putting the papers away and coming back to them later on in the evening. He chastised himself for having such poor concentration. He didn't want to bring this work home. Now he would have to. He put the papers back into his briefcase, shut off the desk lamp, and started out of the office. He saw Sherry crossing the campus and chided himself for forgetting they had the same hours today. He ran to catch up.

"You look worried."

"Something Lois Wilson just said."

"Oh, not Madam Test Tube again. What did she say this time?"

"Something about using television as a drug . . . part of her project. She was working on a paper about obedience, and I keep thinking about her little brother. He looked so timid, so subdued."

"Wouldn't you be with a sister like that? Maybe she's trying to turn him into a robot."

"I'm serious."

"That's been your problem from the start. That girl has no sense of humor, and now you're losing yours. She's making you more like her every day."

"That's ridiculous."

"Is it? Why worry about it? She has a mother."

"I told you what she's like."

"Other people go there, I'm sure. What about the doctor or therapist?"

"After early instruction, they leave therapy to the family for a time."

"Are you saying that family is isolated, invalid and all?"

"I don't know. I get that impression. I do know this: if for no other reason than just to satisfy my own curiosity, I'm going to pay a visit to the Wilsons. Somehow, some way, on some pretense, I'm going into that house."

"Dum, de-dum dum," Sherry sang and put her arm through his. He welcomed her closeness.

14

"Hurry," Billy said, meeting Lois at the door. "Mommy broke the dishwasher. It's leaking all over the kitchen floor. Hurry," he repeated as Lois continued at a normal pace. "It's going all over the place." He ran on ahead of her.

When she entered the kitchen, she found her mother on her hands and knees. There was a small pile of soaked bath towels next to her and she was dipping another one into a puddle that extended nearly to the middle of the floor.

Dorothy was, as usual, dressed in one of her housecoats; it was only on a rare occasion now that she got dressed up, or even put on an ordinary skirt and blouse. Her hair hung down the sides of her head in thick, greasy-looking strands. She wore no slippers and the bottoms of her feet were black with grime and dust.

"What happened?" Lois remained in the doorway, her hands on her hips. Dorothy continued to dip the bath towel into the water, moving in a slow, lethargic motion. She seemed hypnotized by the activity and hadn't heard Lois's question. "Mother, what's going on?"

Dorothy turned. She was smiling weakly; her eyes were glassy, and she didn't look directly at Lois. It was as though she were blind and could only turn toward the sound.

"Lois, I think something happened with the dishwasher."

She's into the Seconal on her own, Lois thought. She had started her with them as a sleeping pill, but now she was using them as a tranquilizer. The Valium had become insufficient. Her body had built a tolerance for it.

"Obviously. So why don't you shut it off? As long as it runs, it leaks," she said and turned the control.

"Oh. I didn't think of that. We'll need a plumber now," she said, dropping the saturated towel onto the pile beside her. "Your father used to do all these minor repairs," she added, sitting back on her own legs.

"Maybe I can fix it," Billy said. He got down on his knees and opened the cabinet door.

"Now your pants are all wet," Dorothy said and added a short, empty laugh.

"Come on, Mother," Lois said, scooping her under the left arm and lifting. "You'd better take a rest."

Dorothy cooperated enough to get to her feet. Still dazed, she looked around and shook her head. Lois squeezed her upper arm to get her to turn toward the door.

"I just hate it when things go wrong in the house. I always hated it. Your father was so good at keeping those kinds of things unknown to me."

"Well, he's unable to do that now. You're going to have to face up to that."

"I don't want to face up to that," Dorothy said in a little girl's voice. Lois nearly laughed.

"Then stay in your room, Mother. Maybe that's better for you for a while anyway. I'll bring one of the television sets up there. I don't need the one in my room, and the cable connection is in the wall."

"Yes, that would be nice." She stopped at the foot of the stairs. "I'm so tired; I don't even think I can make these steps."

"You can make them. C'mon. You'll rest, and I'll send Billy up with your supper later."

"That's nice of you, dear. So nice of you. You're really a considerate girl," she said, moving up the stairs now. "I wish we'd gotten along better. I know it's partly my fault, but I try. I try to understand your animals and your projects." She stopped and leaned toward Lois. The aroma of the morning's booze still lingered on Dorothy's lips. "But I'm not as smart as you and your father."

"That's all right. C'mon, keep walking."

When they got to the top of the stairs, Dorothy stopped again. She swayed a little and then steadied herself against the wall. Lois watched her without saying anything. Dorothy wiped her forehead and peered at the wall chart by Gregory Wilson's door.

"Why did you do that? I still don't understand."

"It's to keep track of things Daddy does so we can see if there's any improvement."

"Is there any?"

"It's too early to tell. Go lie down, Mother."

Dorothy nodded and then walked on toward her bedroom. She stopped but turned only halfway back.

"Don't tell your father about the dishwasher," she whispered. "It'll only upset him, and it's not good to upset him in his condition."

"Of course I won't. Don't worry."

"Good girl, good girl," she said and went into the bedroom. Lois looked toward her father's bedroom for a few moments and then went downstairs. Billy was struggling with something in the cabinet.

"I found it, I found it," he said as she entered. "It was simple. The hose was just disconnected."

Lois smiled. "My, but you are mechanically inclined, little brother."

He finished and stood up.

"I wonder how it could get loose like that," he said.

"I wouldn't know." Lois picked up all the wet towels. "I'll have to mop this up. Go change your pants and then come back. I need you to help me bring my television set upstairs."

"Upstairs?"

"I'm putting it in Mother's bedroom."

"Is she always going to stay in that bedroom?"

"Not always, but probably for the rest of the summer."

"She was acting real funny, Lois. She made me get all those towels."

"It's all right. She's not feeling well. Later, you'll take her supper up to her."

"She's not going to get like Daddy, is she?" Lois could see how terrified he was at the thought.

"No, it's not that bad. It'll pass."

"You can make it pass, can't you?" he said.

"What do you mean?"

"You're helping Daddy; you'll help her too. Won't you, Lois?"

"Of course," she said. She felt the wetness of the towels penetrate her blouse. That cool, damp feeling brought her back to the moment and she hurried out of the kitchen to get the mop.

She didn't turn the field mice randomly loose in the house. She had carefully planned out feeding places so they would return to those spots regularly. It was simply a matter of reinforcement. One of those spots was just outside her mother's bedroom door. After Dorothy saw the first one, she was terrified of walking out there in the dark. When she saw the cheese, Lois told her it was filled with poison. She was satisfied with the explanation, but the whole affair was just another thing to turn her against the house. Now that she had her own television set and her meals catered for her whenever she wanted them, she began to withdraw even more. Lois rationed out the Seconal, carefully including the narcotic in foods she prepared. The liquor supply was maintained as well.

The Catskill resort area was well into its summer season, and all of the local businessmen had most of

their energies taken up with the daily pressures result-
ing from a swollen population. Everyone knew that
Dorothy Wilson had her hands full, and no one expected she would be spending a great deal of time in
town. Lois had taken to carrying out all the errands.
Most who saw her doing all this complimented her on
being such a great help to her family at so obvious a
time of need. She thanked them and answered the
questions almost automatically:

"Yes, my mother has her hands full. We're managing. We still think it's the best thing we could have done
under the circumstances."

Some people told her they would stop by as soon as
they had a chance. Lois wasn't encouraging. She always
made a point of telling them her mother wasn't anxious
to see people just yet.

"Caring for my father has taken its toll on her. She's
not up to visitors. You know she's very self-conscious
about her looks."

People nodded because they did know that was so.
Few of them really intended to pay a visit anyway. They
knew it was a depressing scene and they didn't think
Gregory Wilson wanted them gawking in at him in his
condition. Summer business was a convenient and
logical excuse. They would come as soon as they got a
free moment. Lois was satisfied that none of them
would, at least until she was finished with her work.

Some did phone, and when they did get Dorothy to
talk to them, she reinforced the impressions Lois had
left in the village. She didn't sound as though she
welcomed their interest, and she hardly carried on a
conversation. Once someone called and spoke to her,
he or she never called again.

Theirs was a quiet road, even in the summer. Occasionally, they could hear the mumur of voices—tourists
taking an after-dinner walk from Rosenfield's Guest
House. Lois kept few lights on. The tourists would look
in at the house but continue walking as though the

house were a vision from the nether world they would rather ignore.

So Lois felt little or no threat of discovery. Not that what she was doing had anything but a good connotation for her. It was just that she knew other people, less informed, ignorant people with small vision, would never understand the importance of her work and what such a project could mean to science. Romantic concepts of morality were responsible for the slow progress of science anyway. Imagine the audacity, the gross stupidity, of the people who challenged the work in genetic engineering, for example. No, she just couldn't permit those people to interfere with her.

Every few days Dorothy Wilson would attempt to revive herself. She would get up in the morning determined to "clean up" and "get back into the swing of things." She'd start to brush her hair but soon become discouraged with the knots in the strands. When she came downstairs, she would inform Lois of her plans to get her hair done, a wash and trim. Lois would nod and listen while she prepared her father's breakfast. Billy would go up with it while Dorothy ranted on about what had to be done to get the house back in shape.

"I think it stinks in here; I think we have odors. Your animals are messing in the house."

"No, Mother. I'm very careful about that. None of my lab animals are loose."

"I think we've got to air out your father's room today."

"I did that yesterday, but if you think we should do it again, we can."

"Well, if you did it only yesterday . . ."

"Hungry?"

"Yes, I'm starved."

"I made batter for blueberry pancakes. Billy loves them."

"That's good," Dorothy would say and grow silent. She'd sit in a daze and wait as Lois worked. "I'm gaining weight," she'd conclude. "I'm losing my shape. Aren't I?"

"Go on a diet."

"I need exercise. Maybe I'll go for a walk. I might even walk to town."

"Good. I think you should."

Lois would put the pancakes on her plate. Dorothy would cut lethargically, nibble on a small piece or two, and then finish her coffee.

"I don't know why I'm so tired all the time."

"You need vitamins. Everyone needs some vitamins. Maybe you're anemic."

"Your father always tells me that."

Lois would put an iron tablet on Dorothy's plate. After a moment or two, she would take it.

"I think I'm too tired to go for so long a walk today. Maybe tomorrow."

"All right, just rest up today."

"Yes. Tell your father I'm resting today. I . . . I don't feel up to spending time with him."

"It's OK. He watches television and I'm taking care of his needs."

"I know you are, Lois. I don't know why I feel so tired all of a sudden. I felt so energetic when I got up."

"Maybe you're coming down with a summer cold. Be careful. I'll make you some tea with booze later. You like that and you always say it's good for a cold."

"Yes." Her face would brighten some. After a little while, she would go back upstairs to her room.

Sometimes she would meet Billy in the hall or on the stairs and pet his hair or straighten his shirt. He would wait obediently as she handled him, but he did little more than tolerate her. She was growing more and more distasteful to him—looking the way she looked, smelling the way she smelled. Even the sound of her voice had changed. It was always high-pitched, as though she were nearly hysterical. And she always tilted her head to one side and looked as though she were gazing through him instead of at him. He was always relieved when she would finally stop and walk back up to her room.

"Why is Mommy acting so funny all the time now?" he'd ask.

"I told you before. She's tired and depressed about Daddy."

"What's that mean?"

"Sad, very sad."

"I'm sad, but I don't look like that."

"She's a woman; that's the way some women react. Forget about it. She'll get better."

"I thought you were going to help her, Lois."

"I *am* helping her."

"Daddy was crying just now, Lois."

"Crying?" She became more attentive. "What do you mean, crying?"

"I gave him his breakfast drink, just like you showed me to, and he kept blinking no, no, so I stopped."

"What?"

"I guess he just didn't want it today."

"Damn."

"Then he started crying. Tears came down his face. You better go see."

"I swear, everyone's falling apart in this place. When I tell you to do something, do it."

"But . . ."

"All right. Go clean out the rat cages. I'll take care of it."

He left quickly, eager for the opportunity to escape her wrath.

That's wrong, Lois thought, considering what Billy had just described to her. He shouldn't reject what I give him when I give it to him. I don't want to include any narcotics just yet, because addiction would cloud my experiment in obedience. Getting him to behave in a certain manner through physiological dependence like a drug craving is not a pure exercise in behavioral modification to me, she mused. I'll have to consider a proper punishment for disobedience—something that won't be that harmful but will instill fear. What could it be?

She thought about a lesson Professor McShane had once taught. He had used Edgar Allan Poe's short story "The Pit and the Pendulum" as an illustration.

"What frightens and terrifies us the most—the threat of something terrible or something terrible?" He waited, that wry smile on his face. "I see I have many of you confused—even Miss Wilson."

"I'm not sure I understand your question."

"Let me simplify it. Everyone here, including myself, has some particular fear. Some of you might hate being in the dark or being closed in; many detest spiders and snakes. All of us have a fear more terrible than any other. How we came upon this fear isn't the question right now. Accept the fact that we all have at least one."

"Agreed," Lois said. She was the only one who spoke, and once again McShane felt as though he were alone with her rather than in a classroom with twenty other students.

"Now, Edgar Allan Poe used this simple truth to develop a terrifying mechanism: the pit in his short story 'The Pit and the Pendulum.' A prisoner, you'll recall, is placed in a cell that has a pit in the center, and all that he is told is that something terrible, the thing he hates the most, is at the bottom of that pit. He cowers in fear as the walls of the cell close in on him, pushing him closer to the pit. But that's not what makes Poe a genius. By not telling his character what's in the pit, he doesn't tell us; and what does each and every one of us do?"

"We imagine our own worst terror at the bottom of the pit," Lois said.

"Exactly. Mr. Poe has forced you to add the most important ingredient of horror—your own worst fear.

And so, this is a case where the threat is worse than the thing itself. Understand?"

She did, and she was happy she remembered it now. She would bring up a wooden box—something she would make very simply and quickly. She would paint it black for the obvious color connotation and psychological effects. And she would tell him:

"Now, Daddy, when I send something up for you to eat, you must eat it then. You must do what I tell you to do. If you don't, I'm going to place your hand—the one that you can move a little—into this box. It won't be pleasant, but you will learn not to disobey," she would say.

And she would leave the box there in the room, place it in a spot where he could see it easily, all the time.

That would be enough. She felt confident of that.

In the beginning it was as though he had been trapped in a dream. He was a man in the middle of waking up when suddenly the process had stopped. His mind sent continuous commands to all parts of his body, but nearly all of those commands were turned back. It was a mutiny. His first reaction was to be angry with himself. The most important part of him was being let down by all the lesser parts. Reports of failure were coming in from everywhere along his spinal column. As all the avenues and roadways became blocked he found he was shut up within himself. His anger turned quickly into terror.

In his mind he could hear himself screaming, but all he could actually hear was an indistinct guttural noise that disgusted him. He hated making it. Because he could see and hear without being heard, he often experienced the strange sensation that he was looking into the world. It was as though he were another person inside his shell of a body. He longed to break out and be free again.

Gradually, as time passed, the two "hims" merged

and he evolved into a new creature. He called himself a man-thing. He could dream, think, imagine, just as he had always been able to do. Now, however, he could go little beyond that.

He had developed an odd relationship with his bed. Lately he had begun to feel he was an extension of it, or it was an extension of him. When he was taken out of the bed, for whatever reason, he became disoriented and weightless, like an astronaut on a space walk. He didn't like it. Most of the time, he would keep his eyes closed.

Sometimes, when he fell into a deep sleep, he would dream he was back in the store. He would see himself working, hear his conversations with customers, and even experience the fatigue he would have from standing on his feet all day. The names of various medicines would pass through his mind on a ticker tape, like stock quotations.

When he awoke from such a sleep and such a dream, he would consider the real world his dream, his nightmare. How often had he thought about being in this condition; how often had he envisioned it. Perhaps that was all this was now. Soon he would awake and be back in the store.

Considering his confusion, he remembered the Japanese print he had on the back wall by the prescription counter: a picture of a man asleep under a tree with the outline of a butterfly superimposed over the man's face. Under it was the caption: "I was a man dreaming I was a butterfly. Or was I a butterfly dreaming I was a man?"

After they brought him home, there was never any question. His first confrontation with Lois ended that. She was cold reality, as tangible as anything solid in the physical world. He searched her eyes for signs of compassion and sympathy but found only her analytical, penetrating gaze. She wore the faces of doctors probing, searching, testing. He felt naked, but even more, he felt microscopic, under glass. The nucleus of

each and every cell in his body was exposed. He could
cover nothing. She would be at his amino acids; she
would scratch his bones and pluck his tendons.

Oh, God, he thought. How he wanted to touch his
wife again, hear soft music, move in candlelight, laugh
at small things, lift a fallen autumn leaf and crush it into
yellow-gold particles. How he longed to have the tips of
his fingers touch the insides of his palms.

He made all sorts of promises, took oaths, concocted
prayers. Nothing worked. The frustration continued to
build inside him. He could feel it like a monstrous
pocket of gas turning and bouncing as it grew. It was
pressing everywhere. He tried opening his mouth as
wide as possible in the hope that it would simply seep
out and escape into the atmosphere. It didn't. Instead,
like broken kite cord, he continued his limp fall to the
earth.

And then she came to tell him that she would help
him. She could do what others couldn't because she had
a unique vision. Ever since she was a little girl, she had
been able to see things more clearly than most adults. It
was as though people were born with different frequen-
cies and she was more in tune with the forces of life and
death. Unable to do anything but listen to her, he felt
as though he were slipping under her spell. She was
convincing because she herself was so convinced.

Medicated, put through therapy, diagnosed and
prognosed, probed and poked, X-rayed and injected,
plugged into IVs, his blood sipped out in little drinks
and carried off in cork-topped vials, he remained . . . a
prisoner of himself. Nothing they had done or could do
would change it.

She came to his bed in the night, the small lamp on
the table throwing an indistinct yellowish glow over her
face, making her eyes sparkle with catlike movements,
and held his movable fingers. She touched him to force
an intense concentration and maintain a tighter communication. He listened as she spoke about his body,
calling it a disobedient animal. Seeing it now as some-

thing apart from himself, he was ready to accept her characterization.

"Yes, it has rebelled, refused direction; but we can bring it back, condition it and teach it until it is obedient again." He thought she was whispering, but he wasn't sure whether she was or it was just something else about his body that was failing him. Perhaps his body didn't want to listen. What an idea! What thoughts she was putting into his head!

"I know we can do it, Daddy. Everything I've learned and seen tells me we can do it. If you'll only cooperate. I'll have to make you cooperate. It'll be for your own good. In the end, you'll thank me.

"Mother mustn't know all of it; she would never understand. She couldn't understand, but don't worry. Everything will be under control. Mother and Billy will not interfere. Billy will help and Mother will be occupied.

"You must trust me. No matter what, you must always trust me."

He could do little else. When she set up the Skinner box bar, he tried to resist but was quickly defeated. He told himself that although he would do what she wanted, he wouldn't do it for the reasons she wanted. For a while he could live with that difference. Soon, that diminished too.

In the beginning, he had great confidence in Dorothy. After all, wasn't she the one who had continually warned him about Lois? Didn't she see things he had failed to see? Surely that vision wouldn't fail her now. Whenever she came into his room, he tried telling her. He looked at the bar and blinked his no. Each time she left, he felt sure she had gone down to chastise Lois and end the experiments. But that wasn't happening.

And then he began to notice a change in Dorothy. At first it was just a physical degeneration, but he thought that was somewhat understandable. She wasn't going out very much; she wasn't working in the store as much. He was surprised to see her face get softer, rounder. He couldn't believe she was actually putting on weight, getting chunky and permitting her hips to expand. That wasn't like his Dorothy, the woman who paid such religious attention to her figure and her exercises. He tried desperately to communicate his confusion, but she grew farther and farther away from him.

He panicked when he first recognized the empty-eyed look of someone into drugs. One day her face simply turned into a mask. It was as though she had eyes behind those eyes, lips under those lips. She avoided looking at him. Whenever she came into his room—and that was growing more and more infrequent—she looked at the walls and the floor when she spoke. It was obvious that she couldn't face him, either because she couldn't stand looking at him in his condition any longer, or because she didn't want him to see her condition. He wasn't sure which. Perhaps it was a combination of both.

As time passed she did less and less for him and Lois did more and more. Despite his reluctance, he became totally dependent on his daughter, to the extent that he actually looked forward to her visits, even when those visits were filled with what he considered insane ramblings. He didn't believe it was possible for him to feel fear any longer. What could happen to him that hadn't already?

But when she brought the black box in and threatened him with it, he experienced an all-encompassing chill. It moved over his body like a paper-thin blanket of ice. Although he didn't actually move, he felt himself shudder. When he looked at Lois's face, he believed he had reason to know fear again.

One night Billy came to him. He had little hope that his small son could do anything to change things. He didn't make any real effort to communicate a serious thought. Once he had cried in Billy's presence, but all that had done was frighten the child. Now he saw him only as a pawn of Lois's, carrying out her orders, performing whatever duties she assigned him.

Still, he looked innocent and gentle. His round cherub face had tanned under the summer sun. With his small facial features and tiny fingers, he was doll-like. Gregory longed to hold him again or wrestle with him on the living-room floor.

Now the boy sat at the foot of his bed and bit his lower lip. He traced the lines on Gregory's blanket with his right forefinger. Gregory waited, his stare intent.

"Did you know that Mommy hid Mick and Nick one day?"

Gregory blinked twice.

"Right here in this closet." Billy pointed. "Lois and I came up and we found them behind a carton. Lois told me why she did it," he added, looking down. "I took them back. I got them hid in my room. You want me to tell you where?"

Gregory blinked once.

"Well, Lois said Mommy would probably hide them again, so I—"

"What's wrong?"

Billy jumped off the bed instantly. Lois was standing in the doorway. She was dressed in her nightgown and she was barefoot, which explained why Billy hadn't heard her coming up the stairs.

"Nothing."

"Why are you up here?"

"You know Daddy never knew Mommy took Mick and Nick?"

Lois looked at Gregory for a moment. He tried not to blink. Then she came farther into the room and put her hand on Billy's shoulder.

"Don't believe that," she said. "Mommy never does anything without telling him."

Billy spun around and looked at Gregory. He blinked his no. Without taking his eyes off his father, Billy spoke.

"You mean, Daddy would lie too? Lie now?"

"Of course. He's just being a good adult. Don't mind that."

Billy stared at his father a moment more and then turned around quickly and ran out of the room. She heard him pounding his way down the stairs.

"Don't let that bother you, Dad. Children . . . fantasize."

She shut off the light and left him in darkness. Oh, God, he thought, she's doing something to all of us. The echo of his scream traveled down the corridors of his mind.

15

Professor McShane rehearsed his opening lines as he turned down Turtle Creek Road. Although what he was doing seemed harmless enough on the surface, he felt nervous and insecure. Most ordinary people would be unable to read anything into his behavior. They wouldn't have the insight or the perception that would lead them into suspicions. He had been passing by, on his way to Middletown, and had decided he would drop off the articles and the book because he was sure she would appreciate them. That was his story.

But as he continued on toward Lois's house he was sure she would see through his explanation. Those piercing eyes would penetrate his façade and she would know that he hadn't really come to further her education. He had come to spy on her. In fact, he was so convinced she would realize this that he nearly drove on past the Fleur mansion.

He stopped just beyond the driveway and stared down at the house. It was quiet; there were no signs of life about. No one was outside. The door was shut. The windows all had their curtains and shades drawn, making them into mirrors reflecting light and shadows. He had a short debate with himself and then backed up and turned into the driveway. The Wilsons' car was parked close to the house. He hoped that meant Lois's mother was home.

When he shut off the engine, he waited a moment
to see if someone would come to the door. No one did.
He picked up the books and magazines and got out.
The sound of his car door slamming woke the
sleeping birds. A small flock shot out of the
weeping willow trees, their wings snapping. It was
as though he had brought a painting to life. Small
animals scurried in the nearby forest. He heard a dog
barking in the distance. Patches of small water bugs
rose from the unmowed lawn in maddening circles.
A brisk summer breeze flapped the white sheets
and pillowcases that dangled from a clothesline
toward the rear of the house. That caused the rope
to move and the pulley to scream in high-pitched,
metallic notes.

He pressed the magazines and book against his body
and walked up the steps of the porch. He waited a
moment, looked behind him, opened the screen door,
and pressed the buzzer. He listened intently, but he
heard no sounds from within. After a sufficient pause,
he pressed the buzzer again. This time he accompanied
it with a few gentle knocks.

Little Billy Wilson opened the door slowly and
looked up at Professor McShane. For some reason the
child looked smaller to him now, even more withdrawn
and thinner than he had been the other times he had
seen him. Billy's long, untrimmed hair covered his ears
and half his neck. The cheeks of his face were drawn,
bringing emphasis to his wide-open eyes. The boy
didn't smile. He had the empty look of a refugee child
who had lived through and seen so much tragedy he
could no longer react to anything.

"Hi. Is your sister here?" Kevin looked past the boy,
into the entranceway. Although there were glare and
shadows, he thought the hallway had green stripes
painted down the walls: three- or four-inch bars obviously painted with a free hand.

"No," Billy said. He shook his head. Kevin smiled
and stepped inside, forcing him to back up.

"What about your mother?"

"She's upstairs."

"Oh." The moment he was in, he was assailed by the odors. The place smelled like a dog pound. It nearly turned his stomach. "Well, I'm one of Lois's teachers," he added, moving farther into the house. Billy remained by the door, holding the handle. "And I brought something for her. Maybe I can tell your mother about it."

"She's in her room."

"Uh-huh." He looked through the doorway to his right, into the living room. The furniture obviously had been shoved about haphazardly: the couch moved in such a way that only half of it could be used, the easy chair and end tables clustered. What intrigued him, though, was the long, square wooden box in the center of the room. It looked as though it were filled with dirt and leaves.

"Wow. What's that box?" he asked, trying to act simply curious. He had the feeling that little Billy could easily become frightened. But when he looked back, the boy's face lit up with some excitement and pleasure. He let go of the door and joined Kevin.

"That's my worm farm. Lois helped me make it because I'm helping her. I got over a hundred worms in there."

For a moment Kevin merely stared down at him. Then he looked at the dirt-filled box.

"You built a worm farm in your living room?"

"I wanted it in my bedroom, but Lois said there wasn't enough space, and we got the rabbits and the rats in the study."

McShane looked down the corridor and then up the stairway. There were no signs of Mrs. Wilson.

"Rabbits and rats, huh?"

"And some snakes. I caught a little milk snake yesterday. Ever see one?"

McShane nodded. "Listen. Do you think you could go upstairs and tell your mother I'm here?"

Billy shook his head. "I can't," he said. "Lois told me not to bother her."

"Where is Lois?"

"She went to town on her bike."

"Is your mother sick?"

"Not sick . . . de . . . deeper pressed."

"You mean, depressed?" Billy nodded. "How do you know that?"

"Lois told me."

"Oh." McShane looked up again. "Well," he said, "I'll leave these things with you." Billy took the materials. "Tell Lois Professor McShane was here. I was passing by and dropped this stuff off, OK?" Billy nodded, holding the materials with more concern now. McShane moved back to the doorway. "What are you doing with the snakes?"

"Lois is doing a project," Billy said with obvious respect.

"I see. OK, then." Just as he pushed open the screen door, he heard the gong. "What was that?"

"My father. I gotta go mark it down."

"Mark it down?"

"When he pushes the bar and makes the gong," Billy said and pushed the door with his body to close it. McShane stepped farther out and the door slammed closed.

He closed the screen door and went back to his car. Before he got in, he looked back at the house and thought about the things he had seen and the things Billy had said. Then he looked up the driveway toward the road to see if Lois was back. He wondered if he should wait for her but then decided she might be quite a while and he couldn't justify the time. Instead, he left and went directly to Sherry's apartment. He had to talk to someone.

"A worm farm in the living room? And a gong?"

"Don't forget the weirdly painted walls."

"How did the little boy act?"

"Terrified."

"Oh, Kevin, she is doing something terrible. You'd better tell someone."

"Who? What do I say? I'm not even sure I know what she's doing."

"Why would her mother let her bring all those animals into the house? Ugh. Didn't you get a glimpse of her?" He shook his head. "Maybe she's dead."

"Oh, c'mon." They were both quiet for a few moments. Sherry poured him a glass of red wine.

"Didn't you once tell me about colors and their psychological effects on people?"

"Yeah?"

"Well, maybe she's into that stuff too."

"Could be. I lectured on that once and she was very interested in it. We talked about it afterward also. Sure, that's definitely it," he said, his eyes lighting up. Then he sat back again, a new and heavier realization coming over him. "I wonder what else she's taken from my lectures to use in that house on her family."

"Oh, Kevin, you can't feel responsible. How could you possibly know . . . ?"

"Nevertheless . . . keeping track of the gong." He looked up quickly. "She's running a Skinner box analysis."

"What d'ya mean?"

"Keeping track of responses. Charting her father's reactions to things."

"What things?"

"God only knows."

"When was he here?"

Because Billy didn't answer fast enough, Lois seized him by the shoulders and shook him. He couldn't understand the anger in her face. It confused him. Quickly, he replayed the scene with Professor McShane in his mind, looking for something he might have done wrong. He hadn't disturbed his mother; he had taken the materials and remembered immediately to give them to Lois when she returned. Why were her eyes so wide and her teeth clenched? Why was she digging her fingernails into his skin? He squirmed and tried to turn out of her grip, but she was remarkably strong.

"I told you. A little while after you went to town on the bike. Let go."

"How long was he here?" she asked, still not releasing him.

"Not long."

She eased her grip and stepped back to look at the materials McShane had left. A quick perusal told her that there was nothing terribly earth-shattering about any of it. She had evinced only a slight interest in the book, and she was surprised he had even recalled the references to it. She had made them some time ago.

Billy rubbed each of his shoulders. There were tears in his eyes. When Lois turned back to him, he backed away instinctively, keeping his hands high, as if to protect himself. She saw his anxiety and relaxed her expression.

"So. Did he ask you any questions?"

"He wanted to know where you were."

"What else?"

"He wanted to know about Mommy."

"What about Mommy?"

"He asked if she was sick."

"What did you tell him?"

"She was de . . . . pressed."

"Then he left this with you and walked out?"

"No. He wanted to know about the worm farm."

"You mean he walked into our living room? Where else did he go?"

"Nowhere." Billy thought for a moment. He was afraid to volunteer extra information, but he was also afraid Lois would find out later when she spoke to the teacher. Then he would be in more trouble. "He asked about your snakes."

"Snakes? How did he know about them?"

"I told him."

"Damn. What didn't you tell him? Did you tell him

anything about Daddy?" Billy hesitated. "Did you?" She stepped toward him.

"He heard the gong," he said quickly. Because of the way her eyes burned into him and the way her mouth twisted, he thought she was actually going to hit him. He pressed himself back against the wall.

"What did he do?" Her voice was a whisper, but that frightened him even more.

"Nothing. He just wanted to know what that was. I told him it was Daddy and I had to go mark it down. Then I shut the door and he went away."

"You said that? You said 'mark it down'?" She sounded as though she were talking to someone else. He nodded, and she turned away from him. He breathed relief and looked down the corridor as an avenue of escape. "I can't go back to his classes," she said. She was talking to herself now, the way she often did. He knew that meant she was finished with him and he could go away. "He'd only ask questions that I'm not prepared to answer yet. Why did he come here? Why did he bring this stuff specially?" She looked at the materials again and shook her head. Billy started down the corridor, but she wasn't interested. "He wanted to know about my project. That's why he came here. He wanted to know about it." She looked up the stairs toward her father's bedroom and thought for a few moments.

"He wants to steal it. Sure. He probably realizes the significance of what I'm doing. He'll take the information and use it for his own paper. What chance would I have? I'm just a student, not even a freshman in college yet. Who'd believe me? I won't get the credit. He'll publish the paper; he'll get the recognition. I'd have to be crazy to give him anything. I won't let him read a thing, know a single finding, see a single chart. He's not to be permitted in here," she said, raising her voice. She turned to give Billy the orders, but he was gone.

"Billy!" He came to the doorway of his room. "Don't ever let that teacher in here, ever! Just tell him

no one's home and shut the door! DO YOU UNDER-
STAND?"

"Yes," he said. He had never seen her this mad. Her
fists were clenched and pressed against her body. He
looked at the floor, too frightened to look at her.

"He's a thief," she said, talking more to herself
again, "an intellectual thief. That's very common in
research."

"I don't think he took anything, Lois," Billy said
quickly. He was sure of that and eager to give her the
information in the hope that it would calm her down. It
seemed to, because she smiled.

"Not yet," she said. "But he'll be back to try again.
You can be sure of that."

"Maybe you should tell Patty the cop."

"No," she said. "We'll handle this ourselves." She
looked at the front door. "I'm going to put a chain lock
on here so you can open the door and look out without
permitting anyone to come in. No one comes into our
house unless I say they can, understand?" He nodded
quickly. She looked at the materials McShane had left.
"I'll get this delivered to him so he can't use it as an
excuse to return."

The sound of the gong turned her attention toward
the stairs again.

"That's the fifth time he did it since you've been
gone, Lois."

"That's OK. He wants to see me. He wants things
done for him."

"Will you do them?"

"I will this time, but it can't be this easy anymore.
He's going to have to earn it, and when he earns it, he'll
help himself. He'll cure himself. I'm going to force his
body to behave."

"Won't that hurt?"

"No, not in the long run, and that's what's most
important."

"Lois!" Dorothy Wilson's call was more like a moan
of despair. "Lois!"

"What?"

"I can't stand that gonging. It's driving me crazy. See what he wants."

"I was just about to do that, Mother." She walked up the stairs quickly.

Dorothy Wilson was standing in the doorway. She held on to her doorknob and leaned against the doorjamb. Clad only in a flimsy nightgown, her hair hanging in strands down her cheeks, she looked as though she had just awakened. The gong sounded again. She brought her hands to her ears and moaned.

"Relax, Mother. Why are you so tense today?"

"I can't sleep. I'm trying to get some rest."

Lois took her arm and turned her into the bedroom. The sheets, blanket, and pillow were all crumpled and twisted. It looked like the bed of a person in mental anguish. Clothes were strewn about the room: a pants suit draped over a chair, shoes in every corner and under the bed, undergarments over the dresser and night table. There were empty and partly filled glasses on the chairs and end tables. The curtains and shades were drawn, permitting only a small amount of daylight to seep into the dismal room. Lois saw that a tray with last night's supper practically untouched lay the floor beside the bed. She steered her mother around it and sat her down.

"You've just got to get some sleep, Mother. You look totally exhausted."

"I am. I feel so weak."

"You'll have to take a sleeping pill; you'll just have to do it. Afterward, we'll clean up your room."

"I know," she said, nodding. "Things are just getting out of hand. I wanted to call the doctor today."

"Why?"

"We've got to give up. It's too much; it's just too much. We're all suffering too much."

"Oh, no, Mother. That would be terrible. We can't desert Daddy now, not when he's about to make some improvement."

"I don't see any improvement. All I hear is that damn gong. I know we needed it, but I hear it in my sleep," she added, wringing her hands. She bit her lower lip so hard she nearly split the skin.

"You're too tense. I never saw you this tense. Take a pill. After you've had a good sleep, we'll talk about it again." Lois got her the medication and handed her a glass of stale ginger ale. Dorothy didn't seem to notice. She swallowed the pill and lay back. Lois straightened out the blanket and drew it over her, tucking it in around her. "Just close your eyes and relax," she said. Dorothy turned her face into the pillow. Lois stepped back just as the gong sounded again. "I'll take care of it," she said. "I'll take care of everything. Sleep."

She walked out quickly, closing the door behind her. Then she went to her father's bedroom and closed and locked that door behind her too.

McShane was disappointed when Lois didn't attend his next class. There was only one more class left in the summer session, and he had hoped that they would have another one of their famous afterclass sessions. During that session he wanted to learn more about what was going on at her house.

Later in the afternoon after his class, the college messenger brought his mail. He recognized Lois Wilson's handwriting on the large manila envelope and opened it quickly. The contents surprised him: the articles and the book. There was a letter with the materials.

Dear Professor McShane:

I'm sorry I wasn't home to receive the readings personally. Thank you for thinking of me. There are some interesting points here and information that was of some value to me some time ago.

However, I have since left these topics and gone on to others. Please forgive my returning everything through the mails, but I won't be able to

attend your last classes, as I have too much to do
here yet. There is so little time left. As you know,
my orientation for college will begin in a little less
than three weeks.

Thank you again for your interest. I do hope
you have an intellectually stimulating year.

Sincerely yours,
Lois Wilson

Kevin sat back and read the letter again. Although
the tone was correct and polite, he felt it confirmed his
worst fears. She had decided to cut him off completely
because he had gone to her house and seen some of
what was going on. She didn't want any follow-up
questions asked. She certainly didn't want him coming
around again. How could he go back there? What
would be his pretense this time?

Out of habit, he took Lois Wilson's letter to his file
cabinet to place in her file. Before he slipped it in, he
fingered through some of her old papers from the
college-in-escrow course. He looked at the topics,
mentally reviewing some of their postclass discussions.

He noted that there was a period during which she
had been quite interested in the mental control of the
body, especially control of the so-called involuntary
muscles, such as the heart. She had done a paper on
brainwashing, making references to experiments utilizing techniques during isolation, illustrating that the
subjects so cut off from the outside world would be
more susceptible to behavioral conditioning.

He stopped reading and thought about their relatively recent conversation about Helen Keller and the
way she had related her father in his present condition
to Helen Keller's condition. Then he looked at Lois's
conclusions concerning isolation and behavioral modification.

"It would be possible," she wrote, "under the most
ideal control conditions during isolation to modify an

individual's bodily functions and even command the functioning of involuntary muscles. In effect, behavioral modification might someday be utilized to change man's inherent nature or change it to fit new environmental conditions. It is even possible to consider that total control of bodily behavior could someday be used to force the body to cure itself of any disease or malfunction."

"My God," he muttered, "she's using her invalid father to prove one of her own theories. She's made the entire house into her laboratory and her family into guinea pigs."

16

Dorothy's eyes snapped open. She blinked quickly and looked around the room. The late summer twilight told her it was around seven thirty. The rim of the disappearing sun threw longer shadows over the walls. The breeze had turned cooler, lifting the cotton curtains away from the opened windows. She rubbed her cheeks vigorously and sat up in bed, listening. Thank God there was no sound of the gong. She heard the sound of passing cars, but other than that, the house was remarkably quiet.

Her head felt so heavy and she experienced such a deep weakness throughout her body that she contemplated lying back again. But her mind was clearing and she fought off the urge to close her eyes. It seemed to take all of her concentration to do so. As she focused in on everything, she became more and more disgusted. The room was just a mess. Her reflection in the mirror above the dresser to her left reported even more frightening news. Could that really be she? She ran her hand through her hair to prove her eyes were right. What was she doing? What the hell was she doing?

She stood up abruptly and caught hold of the bedpost to steady herself. The dizziness did not leave quickly, so she held on and kept her eyes closed. Finally she got her breath back. Now she realized how dry her mouth and her throat were. She looked about for something to drink. There were glasses everywhere. Most were filled with a pale yellow liquid that she recognized as flat soda and booze. The odors turned her stomach. It churned in actual pain. Finally, she found a glass of plain water and sipped it, despite its flat taste. Then she looked down at herself. How long had she been wearing this same nightgown? It was stained by spilled drinks and foods. Had she eaten?

When had she eaten last? She couldn't remember. In fact, she couldn't remember when she had come into the room to lie down. It seemed to her she had been in this room for days. Could that be? She looked at the television set on the small end table to the right of the bed. She recalled watching one of her serial programs, but the plot details were confused. It was then that she realized she actually didn't know what day it was. Could it be the weekend?

This was ridiculous. This was really ridiculous. She would shower and get dressed; she would fix her hair as well as she could; she would put on some makeup. What she needed was some fresh air and a substantial meal. She flipped on the room light and immediately brought her hands over her eyes. Why were they aching so? This had to be the worst hangover ever. She experienced nausea and dizziness again and could only wait for it to pass. As soon as it did, she went to the closet and took out one of her nicer skirt and blouse combinations. She rifled through the dresser drawers, looking for a clean bra and panties. Once she found them, she pulled off the nightgown roughly and threw it on the bed. Everything in this room would have to be washed.

What about herself? She should take a shower first, shouldn't she? she thought. There was some reason why she didn't want to, something that prevented her from going into the master bedroom's bathroom and showering. . . . It wasn't that she didn't want to see Greg.

She stood there, naked, holding her undergarments against her body, straining to remember everything. It was as though she had had a series of nightmares and was now trying to distinguish between what was real and what was illusion. Gradually, each thing came back to her.

For the longest time, it seemed (she really didn't know exactly how long), she hadn't wanted to leave this room. Greg's room was painted that disgusting shade of green, and there were those odors. Downstairs, Lois had animals everywhere. There was that thing in the living room—Billy's box of worms. Ugh. How had she permitted it? She couldn't even remember the circumstances leading up to it, but she vaguely recalled there were some promises, something had been exchanged.

And the study . . . all those creatures. The house smelled. And every time she left her room and began to demand that Lois clean out those vermin, something went wrong with something. The last thing she could remember was that business with the fuses. Yes, that was what drove her up here most recently.

She had decided to go downstairs determined to recuperate, to eat a good meal, to straighten herself out and make a serious decision about Greg's continued stay at the house. Lois knew she was coming down for a showdown. She had told her to prepare for it. When she got up and switched on the bed lamp, however, nothing happened. She imagined it had blown a bulb. Moving carefully in the darkness, she found her robe and slippers. She'd never walk out there barefoot since she had seen those mice eating right by her bedroom door.

It was about eight or nine o'clock. She couldn't find her watch, but she estimated the time. When she opened her bedroom door, she was angered because no hall light was on above the stairway and no light was on in Greg's room. She moved along the wall and stopped at the top of the stairs to call down.

"Lois? Lois, is there any reason for no lights? I turned on the switch, but the light doesn't work up here. Lois? Lois?"

The glow of a single candle cast an enormous distorted shadow over the walls before her. She stepped back in surprise. Billy's little face, illuminated by the tiny flickering flame just beneath his chin, appeared. His eyes seemed to absorb the light. Dorothy gasped and brought her hands to her neck.

"Lois is outside, Mommy." The excitement in his face made him appear even more grotesque and devilish.

"Outside? What is she doing outside? Why are you holding a candle?"

"She's looking for a fuse box. Nothing works down here. All the lights are off and the refrigerator and—"

"Oh, God, no. What makes her think the fuse box is outside? I don't think it's outside." She descended the stairs carefully. Just as she got to the bottom, Lois appeared, flashlight in hand. "What happened?"

"I don't know. All our electricity went off. I thought the box was outside, but it's not. Do you know where it is?"

"I don't know anything about fuse boxes," Dorothy said. She rubbed her forehead. There was this continual aching behind her eyes.

"Maybe we should ask Daddy," Billy said.

"You know, that's an idea. I don't know why I didn't think of it myself. Here, Mom," Lois said, handing her the new fuses. "I'll go up and try to get the correct information from him. Go with Billy and light another candle."

Dorothy took the fuses reluctantly as Lois went up the stairs. She followed Billy into the kitchen and lit another candle. She started to look about the kitchen for something to eat and then realized she couldn't cook anything because the stove was electric.

"Mom."

"Yes." She looked toward the stairway.

"I've got it through the process of elimination. It's in the cellar right behind the staircase. Just be careful."

"I never did this before."

"All you do is screw out the old one and screw in the new one. It's easy."

"Why can't you do it, Lois?"

"Daddy needs bathroom. You want to do his bathroom or do the fuses?"

"Damn this house," Dorothy said.

"Should I help you?" Billy asked.

"Just stand at the top of the stairs so your candle will throw down some more light," she said, going to the cellar door. She opened it to pitch darkness. Her candle threw barely enough light to show her the way down. She held on to the banister with her left hand and moved sidewise down the steps, inching on and off each one like an old woman. The odor of dank wood and stone rose to greet her as she approached the bottom.

"Want me to come down now?" Billy asked.

"No, just keep your light where it is."

She felt for the fuses in her bathrobe pocket and turned to go behind the stairs. When she reached the wall, she moved the candle in small circles to wash the darkness away and find the fuse box. She had just discovered it when she heard the first flapping of wings. They sounded soft and close. She turned with a small smile of surprise and the bat flew right past her head, its wings nearly grazing her cheek.

Screaming, she dropped the fuses and backed against the side of the stairway. Suddenly the basement seemed to be filled with bats. There were wings flapping everywhere. She raised her arms to protect herself, and the abrupt movement blew out the candle. The darkness closed in instantly, bringing with it horrifying images of bat faces with vampire teeth. She flared out wildly, and the sound of flapping wings became louder and more frequent. She flung the candle into the blackness and turned to grope her way back along the staircase to the steps. Now she was sorry she hadn't had Billy come down farther.

Just before she reached the first step, however, his candle went out and the upstairs door closed. She stood like one confronting her own sentence of death.

"Billy? Billy! *Billy, open the cellar door!*" She heard nothing but the flapping of bats' wings.

Totally terrified, she went forward, tripping over the first step and catching herself just before her face smashed down into the second. On her hands and knees, she began to claw her way back up the staircase, whimpering and screaming as she slipped and scraped her knees. She felt a splinter pierce her right palm, but she didn't stop to pull it out. Just as she reached the next-to-top step, the cellar door opened wide and Lois directed her flashlight into her face.

"What happened? What's going on?"

"Bats, *bats, BATS!*" she screamed, frozen on all fours. Lois reached down and took her by the upper right arm, guiding her into a standing position and through the doorway. Billy stood cowering in the hallway, his face full of fear. "Why'd you put out your candle and shut the door?" she screamed. He started to cry.

"He got frightened by your screaming, Mother. Don't yell at him; he's terrified enough as it is."

"He's terrified? He's terrified? What do you think I am? I thought we got rid of those bats. I thought we got rid of them."

"Apparently others found their way in here. They're harmless, believe me."

"Oh, God, I feel like I'm going to faint. I'm all banged up. I think my hand is bleeding." Lois directed the flashlight to it and they found a big splinter still embedded. Lois pulled it out quickly.

"Where are the fuses, Mother?"

"I don't know. When that bat flew into me, I dropped them. Somewhere near the box. Oh, my God, my God, what are we going to do? What are we going to do?"

"Just come into the kitchen and sit down. Billy, you stay with her. I'm going down to get the fuses and change them. The lights will come on instantly." Lois spoke with her usual matter-of-fact, calm tone, and, as usual, the contrast made Dorothy aware of her own hysteria even more. She pressed her hands against her temples and shook her head.

"I can't live like this. I can't live like this."

"Calm down, Mother. As soon as I get the electricity back on, I'll get you a tranquilizer. Come into the kitchen now, come," Lois commanded, pulling her forcefully toward the kitchen door.

Billy followed reluctantly. "I wanna go down with you," he said.

"Just stay with her. It'll only take me a few seconds."

She left them both in the darkness—Dorothy sobbing and Billy, still terrified, hugging himself and pressing his body against the kitchen wall. In moments the lights came back on. When Billy saw his mother's condition, he began to cry even more. The sides of her face were streaked with soot. Her hands were black and her robe was torn at the left pocket. There was a long scrape down the side of her left calf.

"Well, that was easy enough," Lois said, coming up from the cellar. "I'm afraid you imagined that stuff about bats, Mother."

"Imagined? What do you mean, 'imagined'? I heard them. I saw one come right near my face and nearly strike me."

"That's highly unlikely. They have a sonar that makes collision impossible. I see no signs of any bats. They would have been revealed instantly when the lights came back on."

"Don't tell me there are no bats down there!" she screamed. Her body shook with the effort. Billy moved away, his eyes wide with terror. "I saw them; I saw them!" She pounded the kitchen table with her fist.

Lois remained calm, staring at her. She was inscrutable. Dorothy began to gag and cough.

"You're just working yourself up for nothing. Everything's under control now."

"Under control?" She gave a maddening laugh and turned to Billy, who inched away. "Under control? My husband's a vegetable upstairs; the house is filled with animals; everything's falling apart; and you say, 'under control'?" She laughed again and then broke into sobbing.

Lois walked to the cabinet above the sink. Opening it, she revealed an entire bottom shelf covered with various bottles of pills. She took out a bottle on the right and shook a pill into her right hand. Then she filled a glass with water and brought it to her mother. Dorothy looked up hesitantly for a few moments. Lois did not move. Her hand was frozen in front of Dorothy's face. Her mother took the pill quickly and gulped it down.

"There, now you'll feel better and get over this."

Dorothy only shook her head. Lois put the glass into the sink, closed the cabinet door, and helped Dorothy to her feet.

"I wanted to come down and get myself back together again," she said.

"You will. You will. Take a rest now and you'll feel better later."

"What else can go wrong? What else?"

"These things are all minor, Mother. We can handle them."

"We can't, we can't. That's why I wanted to discuss sending your father back to the hospital. It's too much, too much."

Lois continued to move her to the stairs and up to her room again.

"We'll discuss it as soon as you get back on your feet. In the meantime, I'll take care of everything."

"I don't want to send him back. It's not something I like doing."

"Of course not."

They paused at Greg's doorway. Dorothy looked in, her face crumpling again.

"Such a nightmare, such a terrible life."

"For all of us, Mother. For all of us." She guided her away from Greg's doorway and into her own bedroom. After she had her covered and in the bed again, she went out and got a washrag and a towel. Then, cleaning her the way she would a small child, she wiped away the soot and dirt. She disinfected her scraped leg but decided it didn't require any bandaging. All the while, Dorothy lay there with her eyes closed, permitting herself to be turned and twisted like a helpless invalid. Afterward, Lois stepped back.

"Just sleep now, Mother. Rest."

"We've got to do something. It can't go on," Dorothy mumbled, her eyes closed.

"We will. We will," Lois said. She put out the lights and closed the door, leaving her to a drugged sleep.

Now that she recalled the most recent reason for her retreat to the bedroom, Dorothy hesitated at her door. Her hand actually shook when she touched the knob. She envisioned every part of the house closing in on her. It became a surrealistic hallucination. The stairway buckled and twisted like a big snake; it was just waiting for her to step onto it. The living room was covered with worms. The furniture was eaten away by maggots. Billy stood submerged in a pool of them, dipping his hands into the rubbery, flesh-colored creatures as though he were splashing in a pool. There were rats everywhere, nibbling on the carpet, burrowing into the walls—little white rats with pink watery eyes, their bodies twitching from the periodic electric shocks Lois sent through their brains. And the bats were at the cellar door, gnawing away at the lock, working their way up and out into the house.

She drew her hand away from the doorknob quickly. Had she felt an electric shock? Did Lois have the entire house wired? The building had become a giant maze. She imagined her daughter peering in at her through some newly drilled hole in the wall or ceiling. She was studying her reactions, waiting to see her decisions and choices. She felt under glass.

Spinning around wildly, she searched the walls, studied the crevices. She felt the floor throbbing under her feet. When she closed her eyes, colors began flashing with lightning jolts behind the lids. All of the hues quickly merged into that sickly green she hated so much, the shade that Lois had painted on the walls of Greg's bedroom and on the hallway walls.

She seized her own throat; it felt as though it were closing in on itself, choking her. She couldn't swallow. Maybe there was something in the air, something Lois had released through the door-lock keyhole. If she listened hard, she could hear a slight fizzing—or was that her own brain burning? Her head felt so hot. She needed air, fresh air. She had to get out, escape.

With paranoia gripping her from every direction, she wrapped a soiled towel around her right hand and went to the doorknob again. She turned it slowly and opened the door inch by inch. It was as though she thought the house would come rushing in on her, as though she had opened the door of a packed closet and was about to be covered by little animals, electric wires, vials of chemicals. She actually stepped away from the opened entrance and paused. Satisfied her first step had gone well, she threw the towel to the floor and peered out at the hallway.

The corridor was dimly lit now. Lois had changed the bulb to a lower wattage. She hesitated. Something to the left caught her eye. It was a small field mouse nibbling on a piece of cheese. She couldn't move because the mouse seemed to grow larger and larger right before her eyes. It took all her control to repress a scream. Finally, an abrupt jerk of her foot away from the door frightened the creature and it scurried over the floor and under the doorway of the unused bedroom.

Once again she started out of her room, and once again she stopped in the doorway. There were all kinds of sounds coming from everywhere in the house. It was a symphony of animal noises: the hissing of snakes, the squealing of mice, the flapping of wings, the gnawing of rats . . . all of it growing louder and louder until . . .

Lois stepped out of Greg's bedroom. She had her back to Dorothy. Her appearance instantly ended the cacophony of the invading creatures. Instinctively, however, Dorothy backed into the bedroom again and closed her door softly. She waited and listened. Lois's footsteps died away as she descended the stairs. One more time Dorothy opened the door and peered out.

The house was empty and quiet, but the walls dipped in and out like molds of Jell-O. She was afraid to touch them, afraid she might be sucked in somehow and consumed. She would be digested into the walls and become part of this insane house. It was imperative that she not even graze the sides of the corridor as she walked through it and down the steps.

She inched forward, hugging herself, drawing her body together as tightly as she could. She kept an intense concentration on the path before her, afraid that if she looked to the right or to the left, she'd lose her balance and fall against the walls. When she reached Greg's doorway, she debated whether or not she should look into it and decided quickly that she had better not take the chance. After she came to the top of the stairway, she paused. Would it become the snake she had foreseen? It had to be chanced. She had to get into the fresh air. Everything that was holy told her that had to be done.

She started down, her body shivering so much she thought she might topple forward and roll into a heap at the bottom. If that happened, the animals would be upon her. They would tear at her skin and hair, claw out her eyes, burrow into her stomach. She had to be careful, extra, extra careful. It seemed to take her hours to get to the bottom, but it was worth the effort. When she got there, she paused and listened. She could hear no one and figured Billy and Lois were in their rooms.

It wasn't necessary to call them; they didn't have to know she was going out. In fact, it was better that they didn't. She took her time opening the front door so they wouldn't hear, but when she went to tug it completely, she was surprised by the chain lock. It made so much noise she was positive they heard. She waited, but they obviously hadn't. She unchained the door, opened it completely, and moved into the night, closing the door softly behind her.

Professor McShane turned his car lights off just moments before Dorothy Wilson appeared at the front of her house. His thoughts had been frantic as he drove down the driveway. He had come to investigate, but he had no idea how he was going to conduct an investigation. How would he begin? What would he say? What demands could he make? He was afraid Lois Wilson would make a fool of him and he'd come away the cause of more grief for this family, a family that certainly had enough on its own.

But the moment he looked at Dorothy Wilson, he knew he was on the right track. She appeared like a fugitive from a mental asylum: barefoot, her robe buttoned wrong and hanging lopsidedly, her hair puffed and wild, her hands up shoulder height and in front of her. She backed off the porch carefully, slowly, obviously afraid someone would see or hear her leaving. She nearly tripped on the top step and caught herself on the column. Then she turned around and came down the porch steps quickly. He got out of his car.

"Mrs. Wilson?"

She stopped her flight and gaped at him. He knew he should move slowly and speak softly. Even so, she backed up fearfully, her hands clutching her throat. He looked back at the house. The small porch light threw barely enough illumination to outline him against the darkness.

Because he stood about Greg's height and had come from a car parked in their driveway, Dorothy Wilson's confused mind revived images of her husband. She tilted her head to the side, trying to focus in on the reality. Was the bad dream over? Had the nightmare ended? Oh, Greg, she thought, Greg, when I tell you what horrible thoughts I've had . . .

"Greg?" she called. McShane stopped his approach. "Oh, Greg, you don't know how happy I am you've come home."

"I'm afraid you're making a mistake, Mrs. Wilson. My name's Kevin McShane. I'm one of Lois's teachers from the community college."

"No," she said, putting her hands together and pushing the air before her.

"I've come to help you. I've got to know what's happening in your house, the things Lois is doing."

"No, no," she said, backing farther away. "I don't want to go back in there."

"You don't have to go back in there. Just tell me about it." She continued to retreat from him. "Where are you going, Mrs. Wilson?"

"I don't want to go back there."

"OK. Why don't you go into my car? I'll drive you to town or anywhere you want. Is there someone you want to go to see?"

She paused to consider his offer. He gestured toward the car. Now that he was farther into the light, she could see he was smiling, and she could certainly see he wasn't Greg. Greg was upstairs; he was still upstairs.

She looked at the second-story windows, her face becoming sorrowful. The nightmare hadn't ended. It was still here; she was still in it. The man came closer. He was one of Lois's friends, one of her teachers. He wanted to bring her back into the house. That's why he had come; that's why he was here.

She turned and ran into the darkness. The man shouted after her, but that only made her run faster. She fell once, fortunately falling on a soft part of the lawn. When she looked back, he was still standing in front of the house and looking in her direction. She got up quickly and ran again. She didn't stop running until she had reached the road. Then she wiped her hands on her robe and looked back. That was when she heard them.

All of the animals were coming out of the house. Lois had sent them after her—rats and mice and snakes. The bats were in the air. She had to get away and find someone to help her. She vaguely recalled the tourist home some distance down the highway. Get to it, the voices told her. Quickly.

In a jog, her robe bouncing against her naked body, her bare feet slapping the pavement, the soles of her feet continually stung by pebbles and debris, her arms swinging widely as she pumped the air around her, she went on. The headlights of an oncoming car caught her coming out of the darkness. With her mouth agape, her eyes wide and maddening, she continued as though she hadn't even seen the automobile.

The driver put on his brakes and looked into his rearview mirror, but she was already swallowed in the darkness. "What the hell was that?" the man wondered. He shrugged and drove on.

After the car was gone, the only sound was the echo of Dorothy's feet rising and falling on a sheet of darkness. She was a winged Mercury gone berserk, carrying a message of insanity into the night.

Back at the house, McShane studied the darkness. The woman was gone. He could go back into town for help, or he could go inside to discover what had driven Dorothy Wilson from her own home. After a moment's hesitation, he walked toward the front porch.

17

McShane opened the door slowly and peered in. There was no one in the hallway and all was quiet. He wondered if Lois knew that her mother had run from the house. Softly closing the door behind him, he moved to the stairway and paused at the bottom. There were still no signs of anyone. Perhaps neither Lois nor her little brother was at home. They would return to discover that Mrs. Wilson was gone. More determined than ever now, McShane started up the steps.

Barely making a sound as he ascended, McShane felt his heartbeat quicken. Unconscious of the fact that he was holding his breath, he had to stop to inhale. He heard the sound of footsteps below, but they died out quickly and it was totally silent again. He continued up the stairway, but the moment he saw the chart on the wall, he stopped.

A quick perusal told him what it was. He shuddered to see something else confirming his wildest fears. From what he understood of the chart, Lois's experiments had been going on most of the summer. He couldn't tell what had been done specifically, but he knew it had something to do with obedience control. She had apparently developed a satisfactory level. For a moment he thought about the charts he had constructed and demonstrated in class. Even though there was nothing unique about this chart's style, it was as though he could recognize his own imprint. He moved quickly to the doorway of what he assumed had become Gregory Wilson's controlled environment.

He was confronted immediately by the bright green walls and ceiling, realizing that they were the same shade as those streaks painted on the hallway walls. Standing in the doorway, he studied everything in the room. Mr. Wilson was supine and unable to see him there.

McShane traced the path of the cable that ran back from the gong to a pulley and down to a small bar dangling a little higher than Gregory Wilson's left hand. He remembered little Billy's eagerness to mark down the sound of it. Its purpose was obvious.

As he studied the bed he realized that Gregory Wilson's right leg wasn't under the blanket. McShane stepped to the left and saw that the leg had been placed on a stool beside the bed. Mr. Wilson apparently had no control of it. But the thing that stunned Kevin and sent shivers down his spine was the wiring around each of Gregory Wilson's toes. The wire was connected to a small terminal that was presently unplugged from the wall socket. She could control the intensity of the voltage.

McShane swallowed and took out his handkerchief to wipe the perspiration from his face. He was almost afraid to walk any farther into the room.

Lying there with his head back, his mouth open, Gregory Wilson looked as though he had already passed away. But the short rise and fall of his chest and the wheezing sound coming from his nostrils proved otherwise. McShane moved closer. Mr. Wilson's eyes were closed, but the eyelids flickered with a nervous twitch every few moments. McShane thought the man had a dreadful pallor and was probably anemic.

He wondered if he should wake the man up. He didn't want to frighten him, and with his limited means of communication there wasn't much he could get out of him now anyway. Later, he would have a lot to

relate. That was for sure. Also, he didn't like leaving
him with his toes entwined in that wire. Gruesome,
gruesome, Kevin thought. All in the name of science.
What hath the New World wrought?

He was about to leave him and seek out Lois when he
saw Mr. Wilson's eyelids flutter. In a moment they were
open, but Greg blinked rapidly as he focused in on a
new face. Kevin could see something of panic in his
expression. He realized that for some time now, everything new that was brought into this room brought with
it new terror for Gregory Wilson. It was only natural
for him to assume that Kevin had something to do with
Lois's work.

"Relax, Mr. Wilson. I'm here to help you."

Even those words brought no comfort; they were
words Lois had used often. Greg began to gag on his
guttural sound, a sound that had diminished in intensity
since Lois had begun her experiments. Kevin moved
closer and put his hand on Mr. Wilson's shoulder.

"Easy," he said. "Just listen. I'm one of Lois's
teachers at college." Greg's eyes widened even more.
He has been driven into a deep paranoia, Kevin
thought. "I became suspicious about what she was
doing here and I decided to investigate on my own. I
just saw your wife running from the house in a panic,
and I can see from all this paraphernalia that my
suspicions were correct. I'm going to put a stop to it.
Please trust me."

Greg's eyes softened. He blinked once, then blinked
once again.

"That's your way of communicating?" Greg blinked
once. "Yes is once. Good, good."

Kevin found the bed controls and brought Greg to a
sitting position. Then he carefully undid the wire from
his toes.

"I have some idea what all this is for, but I have no
idea what she was trying to accomplish, Mr. Wilson.
We'll find out about that later. Right now, I'd better
call the police so we can find your wife and get you to a

hospital." Greg blinked once. Kevin went to the phone
on the night table to the right, but when he lifted the
receiver, he didn't get a dial tone. "This phone's
dead?" He traced the path of the wire under the bed
and saw that it had been ripped from the wall. "What
was the point of this? You couldn't use it." He stood up
and brushed off his pants. "Yeah, but your wife could, I
suppose. Where's your other phone, in the living
room?" Greg blinked twice. "In the kitchen?" He
blinked once. "OK, I'll be right back up," Kevin said.
He patted Greg on the hand. "This is all going to end.
Believe me."

He started out quickly, his mind made up now. If he
confronted Lois, he would call the police first and then
talk to her. This man needed immediate attention, and
who knew where her mother had gone? As he left the
bedroom he looked to his left and then headed for the
stairway. There was no chance he could have seen the
wire in time. Drawn over the top step, it caught his
right foot and sent him headlong. He was barely able to
break his fall with his right hand. The edge of a step
punched into his left side, knocking the breath out of
him as he tumbled over and over until he landed on the
bottom, stomach down. He groaned as the various
messages of pain were telegraphed from different parts
of his body. He felt sure his wrist was broken.

For a moment he could barely move. Then, using his
left hand, he pressed himself into a sitting position. The
moment he did so, the pillowcase was dropped over his
head. The darkness came so suddenly and smoothly
that it confused him. He almost believed he had passed
out. His reaction was slow, mainly because he had
trouble lifting his right arm.

Instantly a cord was tied snugly around his neck,
pulling the bottom of the pillowcase against his skin and
locking out any seepage of light. He felt the knot being
tied, but instead of struggling against it, he started to
stand. Blindfolded and in pain, he reached a crouching
position. The moment he did so, he received a sharp,

hard blow to his groin and crumpled to the floor again. He squeezed his upper body to hold down the aching. Too late he realized that a rope had been dropped over his upper arms. It was wound around him expertly and then tied.

"Open the basement door," Lois commanded. He felt her grab his ankles and begin to drag him across the carpet. He pulled and struggled to resist, managing occasionally to free himself of her grip. But he was helpless in the darkness, and she simply seized his feet again and again, pulling him farther along the way. His head bounced on the floor. He shouted, but his muffled screams did nothing to stop her.

Finally he felt himself being turned. She lifted his legs. He kicked and pulled, but she had his ankles gripped tightly against her body. She was pushing his legs up higher and higher until he was braced on his shoulders, and then his legs went over his head and she was pressing at his buttocks. In a moment he lost contact with the floor. His legs slapped down on the first rung of the basement steps. When his feet caught on the step, his body rose and she pushed him at the shoulders until he went over backward, smashing against the sides of the stairway and spinning over until he crashed against the basement floor, his body twisted. He unscrewed his torso and lay back, trying to fight off unconsciousness. He heard the basement door slam shut. He didn't pass out, but all was dark.

"What did I tell you?" Lois said. Billy was in awe. His sister had always appeared powerful to him, but he couldn't believe the way she had twisted and lifted that man. She had moved with catlike efficiency, blindfolding him with the pillowcase and subduing him with the rope. Not a motion had been wasted. She appeared to know exactly where to put the pressure and how to pivot and lift. Later, she would tell him it was all a matter of physics.

"He came to steal my research. I knew it; I knew it."

"How'd he get in?"

Lois looked to the front door.

"Mother let him in."

"Why?"

"I don't know. Maybe she did it by accident."

"Where is she?"

"Somewhere outside, I suppose. We can't be concerned with her now. We've got to go upstairs and see what he might have done to Daddy. Maybe he took my chart. Thank goodness you heard him," Lois said, patting Billy on the top of his head. "You did a smart thing by coming right to me."

"I remembered him from before."

"Good. I'm proud of you," she said and headed for the stairway upstairs.

Billy hesitated a moment, looked at the closed basement door, and then quickly followed behind.

"I did all I could to keep her on that lounge out there," Sidney Rosenfield said. Patty looked back at Sam Cohen, who had remained in the patrol car. When the call came, he had been playing gin rummy in Miller's Bar and Grill. Sam Cohen, the stout sixty-year-old who owned one of Sandburg's small construction firms, often accompanied Patty when he had an evening call. Local people called him the unofficial chief of police. He had been elected fire department chief twice.

"Turn off the roof light, Sam," Patty called and made a circle with his hand to illustrate what he meant. Then he turned back to Rosenfield and moved with him in the direction he had indicated.

"My wife's been with her, trying to calm her down."

"Yeah, well, she's had quite a scare, quite a scare. We've got to get back to her house right away."

"Thought it was somethin'. Can't get much sense out of her, though. She's too upset. Just babbles."

"Came upon a burglar," Patty said.

Rosenfield stopped. He was a tall, lean man with Abe Lincoln features. "You're kiddin'."

"Nope. Got the call from her daughter just moments before I got here. They piped it over my car radio. Apparently the girl's got him trapped and tied up in the basement. 'Least that's what she told the dispatcher. Said her mother ran off in a panic."

"Don't blame her. You'll have to take her to a hospital. She's in some kind of shock. You'll see. Think they'd leave people alone, seein' the trouble they already have."

"I know it. Like to string the bastard up."

They stopped at the lounge chair. Bernice Rosenfield was wiping Dorothy's face with a damp washrag. She looked up at the two men and shook her head.

"How's she doin'?" Sidney asked.

"Just got her quiet."

Patty looked down at Dorothy Wilson, who lay on her side in the fetal position. Her eyes were closed. He couldn't believe it was Dorothy Wilson—her hair so disheveled, her face so bloated. She looked as though she had gained thirty pounds.

"I think the best thing is going to be the ambulance. Like Sid says, we'd better get her to the hospital."

"Frightened the guests into the house," Bernice said in a loud whisper. "She came out of the darkness screaming like a lunatic. Claims something or someone is after her, right behind her."

"Patty says she surprised a burglar."

"No! No wonder. And she ran all the way. Look how cut up her feet are. I haven't seen her in a while. Looks terrible, terrible."

"Sid, you go back inside and call the station. Melissa's on duty. Tell her I said to dispatch an ambulance."

Rosenfield nodded. They looked to the porch of the tourist house. A number of guests had gathered there and stood watching.

"You'll be all right, Bernice, until they get here?"

"Sure, sure."

"I'm anxious to get this guy," Patty said.

"Don't blame you." Rosenfield headed toward the

house to call for the ambulance as Patty walked back to the patrol car.

"How is she?" Sam asked.

"More or less out of it. Created quite a scene when she first appeared. Let's go make an arrest," he added and turned on his roof light.

Kevin McShane attempted to get to his feet a number of times before he found the wall and used it to guide himself and support himself into a standing position. When he finally did so, he couldn't believe the pain in his left knee. He struggled and squirmed beneath the binding ropes, hoping to loosen them and free himself, but such movement amplified other aches and bruises. He cried out, whimpering like a beaten dog. He couldn't believe how fast it had all happened. Now all he could do was stand there in the darkness, too terrified and too much in pain to move in any direction.

He had no idea how much time had passed before he heard the cellar door open and saw the inside of the pillowcase illuminate with light. When he heard the sound of other men's voices, he felt great relief. In fact, he thought he might cry and wasn't sure tears had not already formed and run down his face.

"I'll be damned," Sam Cohen said. "She was tellin' the truth."

"Of course I was telling the truth. Do you think I could make up such a story?"

Kevin began to shout.

"Relax, buddy," Patty said. Kevin felt the policeman's hand on his shoulder. "You really tied this thing tight. It's a wonder you didn't strangle him."

"I'd like to know how she did it," Cohen said. Kevin felt the cord loosen around his neck. Then the pillowcase was lifted off and he confronted the hamlet's policeman and another man. They both stared at him wide-eyed.

"You're a helluva mess," Patty said.

"Thank God you're here."

"Who the hell are you? What'd ya hope to get from these people?"

"Please untie me. I think my right wrist's broken and I'm afraid of what might be wrong with my left knee."

"Don't try anything," Patty said.

"I don't think he's in condition to do any more than listen hard," Sam said.

As Patty untied him Kevin looked for Lois and saw her standing at the top of the stairs. Her arms were folded across her chest. She looked more formidable than ever.

"What, did her mother call you?" Kevin asked.

"No, but you sure frightened the hell out of that woman."

"I didn't mean to frighten her any more than she was, but when I first saw her, I didn't think there was much I was going to be able to do to calm her down."

"Not under these circumstances," Sam Cohen said. "You should've thought of that before you came here."

"I didn't want to come here," Kevin said. He rubbed his body with his left hand and then felt along his wrist bone. "It's cracked at least."

"We'll have it looked at. You get just as many rights as anyone else."

"More," Sam said. "That's the pity of it."

"Huh?" Kevin looked from the man to the cop. "What did Mrs. Wilson tell you anyway?"

"She didn't tell us anything. She isn't in any condition to talk."

"Probably in shock," Sam said.

Kevin looked up at Lois again. She was unmoving, like a statue.

"But . . . how did you know I was down here?"

"How do you think?" Patty said. "Lois told us. Let's go. Upstairs."

"Wait a minute," Kevin said, pulling back. He grimaced in pain. "I don't think I can walk on this leg."

"Put your arm on my shoulders and lean on me."

"Listen to me," Kevin said again, but the policeman concentrated on moving him up the stairs. "You've got something wrong here."

"That's for sure."

"No. You're telling me Lois called you?"

"Of course."

When they got to the top of the steps, Kevin leaned against the hallway wall.

"You sure do a good job on burglars, Lois," Sam Cohen said.

"Burglar? Is that what she told you?" Kevin looked at Lois, who stood a little way farther down the hall. Billy was right beside her, holding her hand. "Lois, why'd you do this? Why'd you do it?"

"This is the man who came here before?" Patty asked Billy.

Billy nodded and then took a step forward. "Lois said he would come back to steal her 'search."

"Her what?"

"My research. It's valuable," she said.

"My God!" Kevin said. "Is that why you think I came here?"

"Wait a minute," Patty said. "You know each other?"

The radiating pain and the confusion made Kevin belligerent. He clenched his teeth and straightened up as best he could.

"Of course, you idiots. I teach at the college. My name's McShane, Professor Kevin McShane. She was one of my students."

"That doesn't justify anything," Lois said. "He read my material; he knew what I was working on. He came here spying one day and then decided to return and steal what he could. I've made some remarkable progress in behavioral modification. My findings will be published everywhere. He realized it and came to steal what he could."

Both Patty and Sam looked from Lois to Kevin and then back at Lois again.

"I don't understand any of this," Patty said. He came to attention. "Did you break into this house?"

"I didn't break into it. I walked right through the door after Mrs. Wilson ran from it."

"Ran from it?"

"When I drove up, she was already in some kind of shock. God knows what's been done to her."

"You'd like to know," Lois said.

"This is a helluva situation," Sam Cohen said. He squeezed his jaw with his right forefinger and thumb.

"If you think this is something," Kevin said, "just walk upstairs and look in on Mr. Wilson."

"He's just wasting your time," Lois said. "Trying to distract you from the main point. He's guilty of trespassing, unlawful entry, attempted robbery . . ."

"Just go upstairs," Kevin said. "You'll see a wire and a terminal box on the floor. I took it off Mr. Wilson's toes. She was giving him shocks. She had him dependent on a gong and kept track of how many times he used it. I don't even understand half of what she was doing, but . . ." He lowered his eyes as though he shared in the guilt. "It has to do with behavioral modification, conditioning responses, that sort of thing. Do you understand?" Kevin said.

"This is crazy," Sam said.

"Just go up, go up. You'll see the chart on the wall outside his bedroom."

"We were already upstairs," Patty said. "That's the first thing we did when we came in here, just to make sure he was all right. We didn't see any wires or charts. There's a gong device hooked up, but Lois said they did that so he could call them when he needed them."

"Come on," Sam said. "Let's settle this down at the station." Patty seized Kevin's left arm and Sam scooped in under his right arm so he could lean on him. They both began moving him toward the door.

"No, listen to me," Kevin said. Lois opened the front door for them. He could see the patrol car outside, its roof light turning. He felt a great dizziness coming over him and imagined he had something of a concussion. "You can't leave that man alone with her now. There's no telling what she'll do because of this."

He tried holding back, but with his knee damaged and the two of them carrying him forward, he could offer little resistance. In fact, he found himself weakening rapidly. It took everything he had to battle the nausea and unconsciousness creeping over him.

"We're gonna have to get him directly to the hospital too," Sam said.

"The animals," Kevin mumbled, "she has animals all over the house. There's a worm farm in the living room."

"That's my brother's," Lois said, bringing Billy forward. "My mother let him do it. He's been so disturbed because of my father."

"I can imagine," Patty said.

Kevin's good leg gave out on him. They lifted him in the air and moved him quickly down the steps. He lost consciousness for a moment on the way to the car. Patty held him up as Sam opened the back door. Kevin felt himself being stuffed onto the back seat.

"Just . . . go up and . . . ask him if he's all right," he said. "He'll blink twice."

"We asked him that and he did blink twice. Lois explained that means yes."

"It means no. She's lying to you. She's too clever. She's a brilliant mind gone wild." He spoke with his eyes closed, feeling himself continue to drift. "Call his doctor and confirm . . ."

"We gotta get you to a doctor," Patty said. Kevin reached forward and grabbed his jacket sleeve.

"I'll go to a doctor. I'll live," McShane said, his face becoming bloated and red with emotion. "But if we drive off now . . . he might very well be . . . be dead by the time you return. I know his life isn't much as it is, but it's a life and he's suffering. Believe me . . . I know . . . I bear some blame."

"All right, relax, buddy, relax," Patty said, trying to

work Kevin's fingers loose from his jacket sleeve. "I'll investigate; I'll investigate."

Kevin fought to hold his grip.

"Go back . . . you'll see . . ."

"Uh-huh." Patty broke free and began to close the door. Kevin reached forward.

"Listen to me," he said, but the door slammed him into silence. He fell back against the seat, unable to resist the urge to sleep.

Patty walked back to the porch steps and looked up at Lois, who still watched from the doorway.

"We sent for an ambulance to take your mother to the hospital, Lois. If you want me to run you up there after I'm finished . . ."

"I'll call," she said. "I can't leave my father."

"Right."

"Thank you." She smiled and closed the door, little Billy just visible behind her.

18

There was a long moment of silence after the door was closed. Then Lois heard Billy's sobs. She pushed him away roughly.

"What's wrong with you?"

"I'm scared, Lois."

"Everything's all right. Don't you see? Everything's perfect. They won't bother us now; no one will bother us."

"But Mommy. Mommy's sick bad."

"She'll be all right. If you behave yourself, we'll go to see her in a day or two."

He controlled his sniffling and wiped his eyes. Then he waited for orders. Lois was just standing there, looking up the stairway.

"Actually, we're better off with her out of the house for a while. Too much to worry about between the both of them," she said, but he could tell she said it mostly to herself. She took a deep breath and then looked at him again. "You'd better go wash your face." He nodded. "I've got to go upstairs and fix things again. You did very well, though, Billy, very well." She patted him on the head. "I'm proud of you, and when Daddy gets better and hears about all this, he'll be proud of you, too." Billy smiled and ran to the bathroom. "Get your hands good and clean, even under the fingernails."

"Uh-huh."

She heard him go in and then she started up the

stairs. All this confusing activity was certainly detrimental to the subject, she thought. Why, an interruption like this could have the traumatic effect of throwing things back a week. Her father might have already begun to build up renewed opposition to her techniques. She'd have to show him that nothing had changed; she have to show him she was still in complete control.

When she opened his bedroom door and stepped in, the look of disappointment on his face was so great it nearly made her laugh. It was obvious he had been expecting the others.

"I'd think you'd be more happy to see me, Daddy, after all that commotion. Are you OK?" He blinked his no. "I didn't think so, but I'll fix that."

She went to the bureau on the right and opened the top drawer to take out the electric wires and the terminal. Gregory blinked his no's continually, but she wasn't looking at him.

"Now," she said, unraveling the wire, "I know that teacher was in here talking to you, but you've got to disregard anything he might have said. You see," she said, pausing in her work and looking up at him, "Professor McShane had only one real reason for coming here—he wanted to steal my research. He has come to realize how important my work is and what it could mean to the whole field of behavioral science. I'm sure he wanted to do a paper using my data and build himself a reputation.

"You might not realize how important that can be to a teacher in college, Daddy," she continued, working on the wire again, "but publications and significant findings can up their value to other colleges, better colleges. McShane probably wants a good seat at one of the better universities. Well, he's not going to get it at our expense, is he, Daddy?"

She began winding the wire through his feet again, tying the bare copper against his naked toes. He willed with all his might to move his foot, and there was a

barely perceptible movement. She caught the sligh
twinge and looked up quickly. "You moved a little tiny
bit, didn't you? I saw you do it. Do it again. Go on
try." He didn't. "You just don't want to for me righ
now, is that it? I think I understand. You still see m
from a negative viewpoint. But I did see you move tha
foot, Daddy. There has been some progress, and
there's going to be a lot more. I knew it; I knew it." She
worked faster and completed the electric-shock mecha
nism. "And to think those fools almost ruined things."
She stared at him. Tears were running out from the
corners of his eyes, down the temples of his head and
onto the pillow. "Crying is part of your condition
Daddy. Don't worry about it. Well," she said, slapping
her hands together, "I'm going down to prepare you
drink. Just relax, and later on we'll work on the therapy
I've designed."

He didn't open his eyes until after she left. Then he
stared up at the ceiling. If he could only will his own
death, he thought, simply will himself into it . . .

Lois was in the midst of what she called a session with
her father when she heard Billy's scream. She went to
the top of the stairs.

"Who is it?"

"He says he's Patty. There's someone else too."

"Don't open the door." She looked back toward her
father's bedroom. The knocking below became more
intense. They were shouting now. She was halfway
down the stairs when their shoulders hit the heavy
wood and their pressure plus the weight of the door
tore out the chain lock from the doorway molding.
Patty and a state policeman stepped into the house.
Lois turned on the stairway.

"Don't move!" Patty shouted, but Lois continued up
the steps. "Damn, let's go!" The two law officers
lunged up the stairway, but Lois got to the bedroom
and slammed the door shut, locking it quickly.

"Go away!" she shouted. "Leave us alone!"

"Open this door, Lois. We know what you're doing in there now. Open up."

"You don't know. None of you know. You're going to ruin my work. I've made progress. My father's going to be cured. If you'll just leave us alone."

"If you don't open up, we're going to have to knock this door in also."

She looked back at her father. He seemed more alert than ever.

"You're happy, aren't you? You're so stupid. Don't you know they're ruining your best chance for a recovery? Isn't that the most important thing?"

"Lois!"

Slowly she turned the lock on the doorknob and stepped back. Patty and the state policeman stepped in.

"Just wait outside, Lois," Patty said. He saw the electric wires on Gregory Wilson's foot. Both he and the state policeman continued in slowly.

"Holy shit," the state policeman said. "What the hell is going on here?"

"Pull the plug quickly," Patty said. As soon as the state policeman did so, he carefully took the wires off Gregory Wilson's foot.

"I'll go down and call for the ambulance."

"Right. Put the boy in my car and the girl in yours."

"Gotcha," the state policeman said.

Patty stood up and then went to Gregory Wilson's side to take his right hand.

"Greg, Greg. What can I say? I don't know how we missed it before, but your wife was so incoherent, and that teacher looked like he had broken into the house without reason. . . . Lois always seemed so competent, I just . . ."

The tears were streaming from Gregory Wilson's eyes now, and there was a perceptible vibration through his body. Patty could feel it in his hand.

"Easy, buddy. We've sent for an ambulance. We're goin' to get you back to the hospital where they'll check you out and get you on the right road again. And

Dorothy's goin' to be all right, too. Jesus," the tow
cop said, turning away from the crying man. He looke
down at the wires he had dropped to the floor and the
reached up to jerk the gong cable out of the ceiling. H
tore it out, pulley and all, causing the gong to soun
one last time.

"You're not going to need that anymore, buddy." H
patted Gregory's hand. A smile had formed in th
invalid man's eyes. Patty bit his lower lip to contain hi
own emotion. "I'm just going to go downstairs an
check on things. Be right back, buddy."

"Ambulance is on its way," the state policeman said
"and both kids are in the cars."

"Kids. I'd hardly call her a kid."

"What went on here?"

"I don't know all the details. Some sort of science
experiment. Couldn't understand what that teacher wa
babbling about in the car, but when we got to town,
called Mr. Wilson's doctor and the teacher spoke t
him. He told me to get right back up here, Lois wa
performing some cruel experiments on her father. Yo
saw some of it."

"What the hell are we goin' to run into next?"

Patty sent the state policeman ahead, but he waite
in the car while the ambulance came and the attendant
loaded Gregory Wilson back into it for his ride to the
hospital. Billy waited with Patty. The little boy wa
crying continually now.

"Easy, Billy," Patty said softly. "We're going t
follow the ambulance to the hospital, where the doc
tor's going to look you over too. All the while you ca
tell me about those things your sister tried to do wit
your father, OK?"

Billy shook his head. "Lois doesn't like me to talk t
people about it."

"Oh, I'm not people, now, am I, Billy? I'm
policeman. She didn't mean policemen too, did she
son?" Billy wondered. "And you want to do anything
you can to help your father, right?"

"Yes."

"So. That was quite an idea, that gong. I bet that helped a lot, huh?" Billy nodded. "Did you have to do something special with it?"

Billy started to talk about the chart, and as the police car traveled through the night, following the blinking lights of the ambulance, the little boy continued to narrate the tale, the words pouring forth as though language itself had been stifled within him for years.

Epilogue

Professor McShane did not want to go to this session. He wanted no more of it. He wanted the nightmare to end, the images to come apart and dissipate, for he carried all of it like a moral burden, unable to detach himself from feelings of guilt and responsibility, despite all the rationalization he could muster.

Physically, he looked like a war veteran: his wrist in a cast, his knee heavily bandaged, walking with the aid of a crutch, his face still bruised. When asked about the battle, he invariably depicted the enemy as something of himself. Sherry chastised him for that.

"If anything, what you did was heroic, not evil. What should we have done," she asked him, "tried Hitler's history teacher as a war criminal?"

"Not the point, not the point," he replied. "I think we've all got to realize that an idea can be just as dangerous as a weapon, maybe more so. We can't teach in isolation."

"I agree, of course, but the kind of responsibility you're talking about could put an end to original thinking, to creative ideas."

"Maybe that's not such a bad idea."

"Doesn't sound like my scientific idealist. Weren't you the one who said, 'By the close of the twentieth century, man will be on the verge of replacing God'?"

"I said it, and it might just happen if we're not

256

careful. If we're not careful," he muttered. The phrase began to haunt him.

He stopped in the lobby and inquired for directions. He was told to go to room thirty-three. He was nearly late and hobbled as quickly as he could down the immaculate corridor. He opened the door and peered in. They waved him to a seat just as Lois entered the other room.

She paused and considered the chair and the three inquisitors. It was as she had imagined it would be: a very neat and sparse room—one long table for the professors, well lit, no audience, a chair for her with no desk. She was happy to see that one of them was a woman. She had been afraid of narrow-minded males. There was no time nor any place for silly prejudices. They had no nameplates, but that didn't matter. She thought she recognized the man on the right. No one smiled. She didn't mind that either. She liked people who wanted to get right down to business. There wasn't time for frivolity in this sort of situation anyway. The woman, who sat between the two men, indicated that Lois should take her seat. She did so.

"I brought some notes," she said. "I hope that's permitted."

"Of course," the woman said. "I'm Dr. Elwood. This is Dr. Butler," she said, indicating the man to her left; "and this is Dr. Durrel." Lois nodded at the two men. "We're happy you've decided to speak to us."

"Well . . . under the circumstances."

"Yes, we know. You'll be moved to a private room immediately after this session."

"And the books I requested?"

"If this is a satisfactory session," Dr. Durrel said, "you'll get those books."

"I'm ready to answer anything I can," Lois said.

"Good," Dr. Butler said. "I wanted to ask you about your thesis."

"I thought you would."

"When did you first think of the idea?"

"I was reading Lewis Thomas's *Lives of a Cell* and I thought if a beehive could be thought of as though it were one animal with each segment contributing toward the single goal, every bee like a single cell in a large animal, why not apply the concept to Homo sapiens in a similar way: every part of our body contributes to a single goal—the health and welfare of the body."

"Did you put down each and every thing you did to your father, as we requested?" Dr. Elwood asked.

"I didn't do anything *to* him. I did things *for* him."

"However you put it." Lois didn't reply. Dr. Elwood looked at Dr. Butler.

"You asked if it were possible for you to have some laboratory rats, did you not?" Butler said. Lois nodded. "Well, we can't do that for you if you don't do what we ask first."

"I did it," she mumbled.

"What's that?"

"I did it."

"Well, that's good. Do you have it with you?" Lois was obviously hesitant. "You were requesting two rats?"

"Yes. Yes, I have it with me." She took a small packet of papers from her notebook.

"Good. You'll give it to us at the end of the session."

"Go on about your thesis," Dr. Butler said.

"As I said, I was impressed with Thomas's thesis. For me the logical extension of that was: if we could modify the behavior of the whole animal, why not modify the behavior of each of its parts?"

"And you thought you could do that with your father—make each part of his body behave according to the way you directed it to behave, using proven techniques of behavioral science?"

"Precisely. As you will see from some of my findings, I was well on the way to doing that."

"In other words," Dr. Elwood said, "you believe you

can cure disease, any physical ailment or problem, through behavioral control?"

"Yes. If we can cause a single cell to behave in a predisposed way, why can't we do it with groups of cells?"

"You look upon people as merely groups of cells?"

"What do you think we are?" she asked disdainfully. For a moment none of the three spoke.

"Do you think your father liked what you were doing to him?"

"I was helping him," she said. "I was creating new nerve endings. I would have brought him completely back to life."

"Did that make you feel like God? Do you feel like God?"

"I don't know what God feels like."

"I'm sure you can imagine . . ."

"I don't accept the concept," she said quickly. "It's too simple; it makes it easy for us to accept mysteries and not work for solutions."

"Then you don't believe in right or wrong?"

"I didn't say that. I think it's wrong to prevent progress." There was another silence. She looked at each of them. "I need a typewriter, you know. I've been asking for a typewriter since I've been here."

"Yet you haven't asked once about your brother. Are you worried about your brother?" She looked away. "Don't you think about him at all?"

"All right. I'll think about him. I'll write him a letter; I'll type it if you can get me a typewriter."

"And your mother?"

"I'll write her a letter too. I've got to begin working again soon," she added in a more desperate tone of voice. "I never liked wasting time, and those group discussion sessions are a complete waste of time."

"If you don't go to them, we can't let you have a private room, nor the lab animals, nor the typewriter."

"I didn't say I wouldn't go to them. I just said they're a waste of time."

"All right," Dr. Elwood said. "That'll be all for today. Leave those notes with us."

"When do I move into my room?"

"You'll be notified later today. We'll call you to the general office, using your assigned code: two gongs."

"Thank you," she said, standing. She brought the notes to their desk and walked out quickly. The light went off immediately, turning the see-through mirror back into a wall for the people sitting with McShane. He took out his handkerchief and wiped his face. After a moment Dr. Elwood, Dr. Butler, and Dr. Durrel came in.

"If you'll excuse us, we'd like to talk to Professor McShane alone for a few moments," Dr. Elwood said. The other observers got up and left the room.

"Do you see any changes at all? Even the slightest, most subtle thing might help us."

"I don't."

"Well, she is being cooperative," Dr. Elwood said. "Of course, for a price. I hate to resort to the most basic of behavioral techniques, but . . ."

"Well," McShane said, a wry smile forming on his face, "I would wonder whether or not you're really working any techniques on Lois Wilson."

"What do you mean?"

"You're manipulating a great manipulator. She's got to be totally aware of what you're doing. It's ironic and poetically just. I enjoy seeing that, but I wonder if she isn't humoring all of you."

"She's doing things she doesn't want to do," Dr. Butler said.

"And regardless of what she said in there, she participates in the group therapy," Dr. Durrel added.

"Beware of her," McShane warned. "She might not be participating as much as you think."

"I don't follow," Dr. Elwood said.

"She might be subtly taking it over. She's a great subversive."

"I should think our trained personnel would be able

to recognize her methods, Professor," Dr. Elwood said.

"Yeah," McShane said, standing. "I should think so, too."

"We respect the fact that she's a very intelligent girl," Dr. Durrel said, "and we understand why you have these fears."

"Do you? That's good, because I don't."

"Well, we'd like you to stop by from time to time, if you could, Professor, just to observe her progress."

"Sure, sure," he said.

"I suppose we should say, our progress with her," Dr. Elwood corrected.

"Actually, Dr. Elwood, I'm hoping you fail."

"I don't understand. Hoping we fail?"

"I'm thinking ahead to the time when you release her back into the world. Frankly, despite my input and your expertise, I have the gut feeling that none of us will really know for sure whether or not you've made any significant changes in her. She's too clever. She might fool us all. And when she gets back out there . . ." McShane opened the door. "Well, thank you anyway," he said. Then he smiled.

"You see, despite everything, the scientist in me is still intrigued and wants to be part of this. And you know what, fellow scientists. . . ? That's what makes it possible for Lois Wilson to exist."

He left, closing the door softly behind him.